The Human Farm

A Novel

The Human Farm

Abortion on Trial

LOIS AMARI

SIG Communication

Please send all inquiries to:
SIG
P.O. Box 7032
Prospect Heights, IL 60070-7032

ISBN-10: 0-9779336-0-1 (Soft cover)
ISBN-10: 0-9779336-1-X (E-Book)

ISBN-13: 978-0-9779336-0-0 (Soft cover)
ISBN-13: 978-0-9779336-1-7 (E-Book)

Cover design by Fadi Sawaqedy

Printed in the USA

Special thanks...

To the Author and Giver of life for His help.

To those who have done thorough research on the topic of abortion and shared their research with us through writing nonfiction books, articles, and website postings. These resources were helpful to me in writing this novel, especially *Abortion* by Lloyd Steffen and *Why Can't We Love Them Both* by John and Barbara Willke.

To my parents, my sister Sharon, Danny AlKhoury and Martha Mercado-Rios for their encouragements.

To Bruce Bortz for editing the book.

To you, the reader, for picking up a book by a first time author. I hope you will enjoy it.

Lois

Contents

Chapter 1
Welcome to the Human Farm

"Welcome to the Human Farm and Body Parts Factory," said our guide. She was the most beautiful woman I'd ever seen. Even the word "beautiful" failed to describe her adequately. She was perfect—so perfect; I couldn't stop staring at her. I looked at the other men in the group, but they seemed to have control of their emotions. I, on the other hand, was in total shock that such a woman existed.

"My name is Lisa, and I'll be your guide today, gentlemen," she continued. "We'll start our tour in the café, where I'll give you a brief presentation on our great farm and factory."

The café was unique. A flat computer screen on every table allowed people to order food electronically. When an order was complete, the screen changed to the color of the tablecloth, and we were not able to distinguish between the real cloth and the computer-simulated one. A very handsome man next to me took some wires from under the table and wrapped them around his wrist.

"What's the wire for?" I asked.

The man gave me a strange look, then looked around the table at the others. They all exchanged a smile, leaving me feeling as if I was on the wrong side of an inside joke.

"This is to monitor the number of calories I'm taking in," he said. "You can also get real-time information about your cholesterol, blood sugar—just about anything."

"Interesting," I replied. The Farm was certainly a high-tech place.

"Please enjoy some coffee and biscuits while watching the short presentation," the guide said.

I helped myself to one of the biscuits from a tin on the table. It had to be one of the best biscuits I'd ever tasted. I took a second, then a third, fourth, and fifth one before I realized the men at the table were staring at me.

"These are the best biscuits I've ever tasted," I said, my mouth still full.

"Really?" the man next to me murmured, almost to himself, "Very strange." Louder, he said, "BONGO biscuits is a common brand."

"Of course, of course," I said. "I must be awfully hungry." I decided right then to stop asking questions or making comments, and instead to quietly observe what was going on.

"The Body Parts Factory was established in 2015," said Lisa, the guide. "The Farm did not exist then but was added in 2030. With the addition of the Farm, our production rate increased enormously. We are now the world's number one supplier of body parts. Today, in 2060, our stock sells at 250 dollars a share. We use the best technology in both the Farm and the Factory, and our products are guaranteed against any defect. We can ship any part to any place in the world in six hours via our own supersonic planes. We'll tour the Farm first, and the fertilization center and Factory later."

Much to my surprise, the Farm was actually indoors. It

operated out of what looked like a big hall, twice the size of a standard gymnasium. It was windowless, and video cameras were everywhere—mounted on the walls and dangling from the ceiling. About 100 children were scattered around the room.

"This is one of our senior classes," said Lisa. "Everyone here was born at the same time—about eight years ago. The growth of this batch was accelerated, because our technology allows us to control such factors from the time of conception."

Lisa turned briefly and whispered something to a man who had approached her. His uniform indicated that he was an employee. His expression was firm and unfriendly, and I was scared just looking at him. When Lisa finished whispering, the man shouted at the children in the room.

"*Call* All . . . *Begin* . . . Line up . . . *End.*"

Immediately, the children lined up. I noticed then that they were all the same height and shape. When I looked closer, I saw that, in fact, they all looked exactly the same. The extraordinary beauty of our guide, the monitor in the café table, and the best tasting biscuits in the world were nothing compared to seeing 100 identical kids. I looked at each one closely, trying to find something that could distinguish one from the other.

I couldn't help myself. I tentatively put a hand on the shoulder of the child closest to me.

"Hey, you guys are all twins. I mean—" I searched for the right term—"centuplets."

The boy screamed. "8644-67 calling *Begin* alarm *End.*"

"This is amazing," I muttered, unconcerned about the boy's shout.

Suddenly, someone grabbed my hands. It was the mean-looking guy.

"Follow me," he ordered.

"I hope I didn't do anything wrong," I said. "I was just astonished at how all these children look alike."

"Yes, you did do something wrong," he replied.

Fortunately, Lisa came over and intervened on my behalf.

"I'll take care of him," she said. "Please file an incident report." As the man sulked away, Lisa turned to me. "Mister . . .?"

"Livingston," I replied.

"Mr. Livingston, your behavior was totally unacceptable. You are *not* allowed to talk to any RM."

"I apologize. I promise to refrain from talking to your . . . your children."

"Good. And they're called RMs."

As we walked back to the lineup, I wondered why the children were called RMs, but I felt now was not the time to ask. I looked around and noticed that, while all the children were identical, their features were all ugly and strange—inhuman, even. They looked more like monkeys than people. Their bodies were very strong. I couldn't believe they were eight-year-olds.

"Gentlemen," Lisa said, "this is batch 8644. All these RMs were cloned to the same type—"

"Cloned!" I interrupted. "Of course! That explains everything."

"We have the world's greatest cloning technology," Lisa continued, ignoring my outburst. "Our technology is far more advanced than our competitors'. These RMs have perfect genes."

"Those 'perfect genes' produced some ugly children," I murmured. Unfortunately, Lisa heard me.

"Mr. Livingston," she said, "this is done purposely to control environmental interference. And, speaking of interference, we also have a special language for the RMs. Any time you address one of them in English, they will automatically sound an alarm."

"So, how would you ask one his name?" I asked, abandoning my resolution to stay quiet.

The guide went up to one of the children and said, "Call . . . Begin request number *End*."

The boy answered, "*Call . . . Begin* 8644-98 *End*."

"As you just heard, gentlemen, this is RM number 8644-98."

"Doesn't he have a real name?" I asked.

"No, we only give them numbers. Again, this is to control environmental interferences, or *EI*. These RMs are manufactured and grown for a noble reason. We need to eliminate all EIs that would hinder their true mission. For example, they are not allowed to go outside, and they're not allowed to meet strangers until they're much older." She paused. "The younger batches you can see behind glass—they can't see you. This security is quite imperative in order to control EIs.

"No one in the world can beat our RMs," Lisa continued with pride. "Now, gentlemen, please follow me to the fertilization room. On our way, we'll pass by a younger batch."

We followed Lisa through a long corridor, stopping by some windows where we could see the inside of a room. On the other side of the glass was another large hall in which hundreds of children were running around. Again, they all looked exactly the same. We passed many similar halls on our way to our next stop, and each contained children of different ages.

"As you can see," Lisa explained, "we keep the batches

separate. Gentlemen, I'll need you all to wear certain personnel protective equipment before entering the fertilization room."

We were each handed thin, spacesuit-like coveralls to slip over our clothes. Once everyone was dressed, we were ushered into the fertilization room.

Just like the child-filled halls, the fertilization room was huge, but it was furnished with shelves and computers. Thousands of tubes rested on the shelves. Each shelf, we learned, contained a human fetus. Wires sprouting from the tops of the tubes were connected to the heads of the fetuses, and then to a computer center.

"Our latest technology allows us to use magnetic and electric signals to communicate to the brain," Lisa explained. "We have the capacity to produce a hundred thousand RMs annually, all, as I mentioned, with the perfect genetic makeup. There are absolutely no undesired defects in our product.

"Every batch of RMs is connected to one central computer," she said, gesturing around the room. "Since our RMs are young, they are only allowed to hear Farm Basic Language, the one you heard them using earlier."

"Who donates the eggs?" I asked.

"We buy them from EGGSO," Lisa replied.

"EGGSO?"

"The world's largest wholesale egg supplier. We buy two million eggs every month, most of which are used in our experiments. The remaining ones are used for production of the RMs.

"We perform extensive testing on each egg when it arrives, and then clone it to a perfect genetic code. All information prior to cloning is part of that egg's file. We enter a microchip in each RM to help us trace it. This, of course, is necessary for identification," she added with a smile, "since they all look the same."

The group laughed.

"Now, gentlemen, I need you to take your suits off in the changing room. You'll need to wear other PPEs when we get to the Factory."

We went back to the changing room and I took off my suit. *Who are these kids?* I wondered. *Why do they fertilize so many per year? What do they do with them?* But I tried to control my curiosity. I knew the other men were keeping an eye on me.

En route to the Factory, we walked through many passages. Lisa talked nonstop about how great the Human Farm and Body Parts Factory was, and how friendly she found the work environment. She told us of the generous stock options the company offered employees, and even mentioned employees' *special benefits*, including the right to any body part free of charge.

When we reached the Factory, I wasn't surprised to find another large hall filled with automated equipment.

"You're lucky, gentlemen," Lisa said, peering at an illuminated computer screen. "We've just received an order for a particular body part. You'll be given the opportunity to see how we process it."

The mean-looking man entered the room, followed by an RM.

"*Call* 8644-07 *Begin* scan *End*," the man said to the RM. The RM climbed up on something that looked like a scale.

The screen on the machine read, "This is RM 8644-07. Confirmed."

The mean-looking man spoke again to the RM. "*Call* 8644-07 *Begin* mission accomplished *End*."

The boy responded, "*Begin* mission accomplished *End*."

The boy was laid on a moving belt that took him below a machine. A computer screen on the wall showed live video of him. We could see the machine putting belts around his neck, arms, and ankles.

"This is the most interesting part of the production process," Lisa said. "Thankfully, a screen allows us to watch what's going on inside the machine."

Quickly, a blade sliced across the RM's neck, killing him. I gasped. *They killed the boy.* I turned in shock to one of the gentlemen in my group, only to hear him whisper, "Cool."

I turned to another man, who said to me with great excitement, "Isn't that fascinating?"

I lost the ability to speak. I could only stare in disbelief.

"This machine is called HeadSeg," Lisa said, seemingly unaffected by what we'd just witnessed. "It will segregate all components of a head in less than five minutes. Our excellent technology minimizes batch cycle time. Other parts of its body will be put on other machines. Gentlemen, come and see the results of the HeadSeg machine."

At the bottom of the HeadSeg machine, through a glass, we could see the brain, the eyes, the tongue, the skull, and other parts.

After twenty minutes, Lisa, who by now had lost all her attractiveness to me, instructed us to move to the end of the line to observe the packaging area.

"We have now packaged all the RM's body parts. Altogether, they're worth approximately three million dollars."

"Wow," whispered one man, clearly impressed.

"Of course, what's important is that these parts will save many lives. The mission of our company is to save as many lives as possible. We are here to serve our brothers and sisters. Thanks to our great technology, we are now able to do so.

"Gentlemen," Lisa said, turning to us and smiling, "do you have any questions before we end our tour?"

"What does RM stand for?" I heard myself asking.

"Raw materials," she said. With the most beautiful smile I'd ever seen, she added, "Thank you all for taking the time to spend your day at the Human Farm and Body Parts Factory."

Chapter 2
The Lawsuit

The street was crowded with picketers, all holding protest signs and pointing them at each other and the slow moving cars. Most were young activists with graphic pictures of living and aborted babies, as well as posters with clever slogans.

"Let them eat cake—birthday cake."

"No mandatory motherhood."

"Abortion doesn't make you unpregnant. It makes you the mother of a dead baby."

"Pro-life? Then get one and stay out of mine."

"Keep your laws off my body."

"Pro-family, pro-child, pro-choice."

"It is a child . . . there is no choice!"

"The right to choose should mean choose what's right."

I'd gotten used to the scene. I was giving my roommate, Erick, a ride. He was doing a summer internship at an abortion clinic. I, on the other hand, was doing an internship at a law firm a few blocks away from the clinic.

As my friend got out of the car, people gathered around him, giving him pamphlets and pointing their signs toward him.

"Safe and legal abortion is every woman's right."

"Every crime is a choice."

"Some babies die by chance . . . No baby should die by choice."

"Keep your rosaries off my ovaries."

"Equal rights for unborn women."

"Freedom of choice—a basic American right."

"Life—the choice of the next generation."

"Thanks for the ride, Randy," Erick shouted to me. "See you later."

"Wait, wait!" I shouted. "Is there a parking lot near here?"

"Yeah. What for?" Erick asked.

"I'm coming with you," I replied.

"Why?" Erick asked. "Do you want to watch an abortion?" he added with a chuckle.

At that moment, a sign-waving, pro-lifer grabbed Erick and started screaming at him. "Murderer! Hitler! Killer of helpless babies!"

"Erick! Get back in here!" I shouted. He jumped back into the car and we drove away from the scene.

"What a crazy guy," I said.

"There's a back door. Let's use it," Erick said.

We drove for a few minutes in silence.

"Hey, you missed the turn," Erick said.

"We're not going back there."

"What? Where are you taking me, man?"

"Are you sure abortion isn't murder?" I asked.

"What?"

"How do you know that abortion is not the same as murder?" I repeated.

"Randy, stop the car, and tell me what's gotten into you," Erick demanded.

"I don't know," I said.

"Yesterday, you were making fun of the pro-lifers, how backward they are, and today you're questioning all your beliefs. Who have you been talking to?"

"No one," I replied. "It was just a dream I had last night."

Erick burst out laughing, then said, "Listen pal, I'm doing this because I truly believe that women have the right to control their own bodies . . . "

"Yes."

"Think about a society that controls people's bodies. Would you like someone to control your body?" he continued.

A society that controls my body? That would be like the Human Farm and Body Parts Factory, I thought. His argument made sense, and I found myself regretting my sudden confrontation of him.

"Besides, you don't want to bring unwanted children into the world," Erick said.

"I don't know what got into me," I apologized. "It was just a weird dream. I'm sorry if I made you late for work."

I turned the car around and drove back to the clinic. As we passed the crowd of protestors, I noticed that Erick's attacker looked familiar. I must have seen him somewhere before, I decided, turning around at the rear of the building. Erick got out of the car and hurried to the back door. Once he was safely inside, I headed to the law firm.

At work, I couldn't concentrate on my tasks—I was still severely shaken by my dream. My supervisor, Mr. Johnson—a sixty-something, well-respected lawyer in the Chicago area—approached me at my desk.

"Do you have a minute?" he asked.

I nodded.

"Randy, you don't seem to be yourself today. I want you to

feel comfortable about sharing anything with me."

"It's nothing, Mr. Johnson," I assured him. "It was only a dream I had last night. I can't get it out of my head."

"Dreams are very important," Mr. Johnson said. "Sometimes we can only express our feelings in dreams, but sometimes dreams are visions from God. Why don't you tell me about it?"

I didn't believe in God, but I decided not to bother pointing this out to my boss. I spent a few minutes describing to Mr. Johnson what had happened in the dream. When I finished, he sat quietly for a while.

"Randy, that dream is definitely unusual, but I think it may be more so for me than for you."

"What do you mean?" I asked.

"Last week, we were asked by Christ Hospital to represent them in court. They want us to protect them from the law that makes it mandatory for all hospitals in the state to provide abortion services. I was reluctant to take the case—I didn't want to get involved in a trial that's bound to generate so much publicity."

"But isn't having lots of publicity good for business?" I asked.

"Sometimes, but being associated with such a case may bring resentment from our more liberal clients. However, there's something else I fear."

"What's that?" I asked.

"Losing."

"Losing?"

"Yes. But this morning, for some reason, I felt I should take the case, regardless of the consequences. I guess it's worth it to try to save the RMs," he added with a smile. "Randy, thank you for sharing your dream with me. It's certainly helped me affirm my decision."

I was elated. My dream had helped Mr. Johnson!

He stood up, and, with a less serious tone, said, "What do you say to working on this case this summer?"

For the first time since I'd started at the firm, I felt at peace. I'd finally be able to work on a big case and learn what I'd come to the firm to learn. I guess the dream was a call to me too. *Call Randy Begin Start Mission End*, I thought to myself.

"I'd be glad to," I told Mr. Johnson. "I'd much rather work on this case than Calvin vs. Martin—the one I'm currently on," I said honestly.

"Good. I want you to start right away doing research about abortion. Why don't you spend your next few days in the library researching the subject?"

Finally, I felt free of the dream. The idea of doing research made me feel comfortable. I really didn't want to base my beliefs on dreams but on facts, and Mr. Johnson had given me the chance to do just that.

Chapter 3
The Camp

The streets were void of cars or pedestrians. The buildings, however, seemed to stand nearly on top of one another. It must have been a very crowded city, yet no one was outside. I felt like I was the last person left on earth. I entered a building and, to my relief, a very beautiful woman greeted me.

"Welcome to FamilyFirst. My name is Jean. How may I help you today?"

"It's good to talk to someone," I remarked. "It's so quiet outside."

"Today's Saturday—everyone's busy shopping," she replied with a smile.

"The market must be far from here."

"Actually, the market is just a click away. The only way to shop is by using the Internet."

"Oh, that's right," I said.

"So how may I help you, sir?" Jean asked.

"I'm new to this area, and I'd like to learn more about FamilyFirst." I wasn't sure why I was so curious, but something compelled me to ask.

"FamilyFirst is the number one family planning center in the USA. We have fifteen hundred branches across the country," she replied. "We're here to help you plan your family."

"Plan my family?" *Probably an abortion clinic*, I thought. *These days the expression "family planning" is always associated with abortion.*

"Yes, we help you plan for your family through cloning."

"Cloning?"

"We do more than the basic cloning required by the U.S. government," she said. "We do all types, using the best technology available. Our customer satisfaction rating is much higher than our rivals'."

"Rivals?"

"Such as CloneOne, which specializes in business-related cloning. So, if you're interested in cloning prostitutes, or a specific type of worker, you need to go see them. We specialize in designing children." She paused, then added, "Sir, do you want to design your own child?"

"Yes," I replied, again instinctively.

"Daughter or son?"

"A daughter."

"Let me start a work order for you." She began punching keys on a keyboard.

"I'd like to discuss the cost prior to ordering anything."

"Of course. First, we need to perform gene modification number G2174, which, as you may know, is a requirement of the U.S. government."

"Modification number G2174?"

"To ensure that your child is Caucasian. You also need clone number G578 to ensure that the child will have perfect genes. Both clones are available in one package for one thousand dollars."

"That's required by the government?"

"Yes. There are other clones available, including the beauty clones, which we highly recommend you consider. We have pictures of about one million beautiful women you can choose from when customizing the appearance of your daughter. Of course, if you pay a little more—say, about fifteen thousand—our computer will create a completely unique look, which we guarantee cannot be duplicated anytime in the next twenty years."

"That's an awful lot of money!" I remarked.

"You could also choose, sir, to pay just five thousand dollars and clone your child to preexisting pictures, or ten thousand to genetically modify her appearance as she grows. That way, you can get both decent looks and unique ones too."

"I think I'll pass on the beauty clone," I said.

"Sir, this is a good investment for your future child. With the increasing number of Americans being designed to be extraordinarily beautiful, it's very hard to find a job or spouse if you suffer from defective looks. After all, we only get one first impression."

"That's a good point. I'll consider it. What other types of cloning do you do?"

"We can modify the level of intelligence, the physical shape, the social capabilities, the amount of sleep required to sustain your child's body . . . We can clone almost any quality."

"Hmm," I said. "You've given me a lot to think about. I'll need to take some more time to consider . . ."

"One more thing before you go. We can supply the egg with our inventory from EGGSO. But, if you prefer, you can supply your own egg, and we'll extract and fertilize it for free, compliments of FamilyFirst."

"Interesting. May I have your card, please?"

"Certainly," she said, punching a key in the keyboard. A card printed out from her disk. I grabbed it and slipped it inside my pocket. I stood up and extended my hand to shake hers, but instead, my fingers collided with something solid. A 3-D animation screen. I had been talking to a computer. Jean was nothing but a simulation. I left FamilyFirst as quickly as I could.

Outside, the streets were still empty, and the emptiness felt greater after learning I had been talking to a computer. Where were the rest of the human beings? I felt lost.

As I walked, deep in thought, I suddenly noticed an object passing by. I looked up and saw a young boy. *At last,* I thought, *another person on this planet!* I decided to follow him—I needed to get myself out of this maze of lifeless streets. I started shouting at the boy.

"Hey, kid, wait for me!"

Rather than turn around to see what I wanted, the boy began to run. I followed and found myself chasing him. He was running through streets I had never seen before. The longer I pursued him, the more the scenery changed, the more it looked like the America I knew. Finally, the boy reached a street where all the buildings looked very old. He ran toward one of the houses, went inside, and quickly closed the door.

I stopped running and walked toward the house, catching my breath. I could sense that someone was watching me, but there was no one around. I knocked at the door. No one answered. I knocked again, but still no one answered. I knew the boy was inside, and I wondered why he was running away from me. Finally, I tried the doorknob. It turned easily, and I slipped inside. Everything was dark. Suddenly, someone grabbed my hand.

"Who are you?" I screamed.

"Who are *you?*" replied a cold voice as I felt handcuffs close around my wrists.

"What are you doing to me? Please, don't hurt me!" I pleaded.

To my horror, my mouth was then taped shut and a mask pulled over my head. The silhouettes I had begun to make out in the dark house disappeared, and I couldn't see a thing.

"Take him to the camp police," said the voice.

The camp police? What camp? Where am I? I thought frantically.

I was taken a short distance, then left in another room. I heard men's voices murmuring to one another near me, then large hands grabbed me while someone tore off my clothes. *Oh, my god, I hope it's not another Body Parts Factory.*

"He doesn't seem to be wired," one man said.

"Bring the scanner," a second man demanded.

After about two minutes, I could feel cold, rod-shaped metal passing over every inch of my body.

"He doesn't have it," the first man remarked.

"Scan again more carefully," the second voice demanded.

My whole body was scanned for what must have been about ten minutes.

"I'm telling you, he doesn't have the chip," the first man said.

"To be sure, we'd better do a blood test," said the second man. "Go get a needle."

They put a needle in my arm and withdrew blood.

"Dress him," the second man ordered. "Keep him masked until we get the results."

They dressed me and then left the room, shutting the door.

I was alone for what seemed like several hours, and they

seemed the longest hours of my life. *Who were these people? What were they going to do with me? What did they want from me?* I had so many questions, but not a single answer.

Finally, the door opened and I heard footsteps coming toward me. The mask was lifted from my face, and the tape removed. I opened my eyes to see two black men staring at me.

"What's your name?" one of the men asked bluntly. I recognized his as the second voice.

"Randy," I replied.

"Randy what?"

"Randy Livingston."

"Your social security number?"

"929-36-6989," I answered.

"Look him up in the GlobeDir," he said. The man ordered to do this research promptly left the room.

He returned after a minute with a sheet of paper, which he promptly handed to his partner who, I'd surmised, was the one in charge. The leader studied the paper, then looked up at me distrustfully.

"Randy Livingston," he read aloud. "Mother's Maiden name: Jodi Smith. Social security number: 929-36-6989. Date of Birth: June 1980. Date of Death: July 2035." He put the paper in his pocket. "Randy Livingston died twenty-five years ago."

That's a mistake. I'm still alive. I'm studying law, and it's only 2005.

The other man came close to me and said, "Do you want to tell us the truth on your own, or would you rather we make you?"

Shocked, I was unable to answer him.

"We'll be back soon, and you'd better be ready to put the truth on the table."

They left the room and I could hear their voices behind the closed door.

"I don't understand it," the leader was saying.

"His blood tests show he was never cloned, and he doesn't have the chip."

"But he gave us the name of a guy who died twenty-five years ago. I wonder what he's up to . . ."

The last question struck me hard: *What was I up to?* I wanted the answer to that question too. No, I take that back. The question I wanted answered was *what was the world up to?* Completely helpless, all I could do was sleep and dream of a different world—a world I had always known.

Chapter 4
The Abortion Clinic

"Get up."

I awoke and studied my surroundings. The two men had disappeared and Erick was standing by the door with a towel on his shoulder. I was back in my college dormitory.

"You're late," Erick said.

"I must have been dreaming," I mumbled, still confused.

"What's up with you and your dreams these days?"

"I'm so tired," I moaned, ignoring his question and closing my eyes.

"Hey, pal. It's 7:15, and you're going to make both of us late for work."

"I'm not going to work."

"Then can I borrow your car?"

"No, I need it. Besides, I'm coming with you to work."

"What for? Not that dream of yours again?"

"I want to see you abort a baby."

"You know what, Randy? I have something better than that for you," Erick replied.

"What?" I asked.

"I'm going to help deliver a baby soon."

"Change of job?" I asked.

"Nope. I'm going to assist in delivering my nephew. Want to come and watch?"

"Sure. What time?"

"7:35 p.m., central time." Erick laughed. "You can't schedule a delivery, Randy, but it should be sometime this week."

"Forget it then. I want to come to the abortion clinic with you today," I insisted.

"Today's a training day. I've never aborted a late stage fetus before and I'm learning today. It's probably not an appropriate time for you to visit."

I sat up and swung my legs over the side of my bed. "Excellent. I'll learn with you."

"Randy, I don't mind you coming, but I don't trust you anymore." Erick came over and sat next to me. "What you did yesterday was weird. I'm afraid you'll turn into a crazy pro-lifer and kill some doctor . . ."

"I don't have to go to a clinic to do that. I have the opportunity to do it in my own bedroom," I replied, offended.

Erick laughed. "What about embarrassing me?"

"How would I embarrass you?"

"Asking the doctor questions like, 'Don't you think these are humans?'" Erick said.

"I promise you, I'll do none of that." I extended my hand to his and said, "I give you my word."

"Fine, man." He gave in and shook my hand briefly. "Just hurry up."

I got up and started shaving. Erick stood next to me.

"Why are you all of a sudden so interested in abortion?" he asked.

"It's my new case at work."

"You're kidding me!" Erick lifted an eyebrow.

"No. My law firm is representing Christ Hospital. Some new law will force them to perform abortions, despite their religious beliefs," I explained.

"Those guys are crazy. I wouldn't want my wife to deliver in that hospital. They try to save the baby's life at any cost—even the mother's life."

"We all have the right to our beliefs."

"You need to preach this to conservatives, who try to force their beliefs on others all the time."

I nodded. I considered myself to be quite liberal, and my belief system was based on common sense, science, logic, and fact. After all, I was a lawyer—or at least studying to be one. My dreams, however, had raised some questions. For example, could legalizing abortion eventually lead to something like a Human Farm and Body Parts Factory? And, if it could, there had be something inherently wrong with abortion. But if abortion was wrong, I needed be able to see that immediately, and not have to wait until the future, when it would be too late.

I was a reasonable person, a logical person. It bothered me that a recurring dream was challenging my basic beliefs, and I felt as if something outside of me was causing these nightly visions. I wondered if they would ever stop.

All this swirled around in my head as I drove Erick to the clinic. When we got there, the scene was the same as usual—lots of protestors and signs. I drove slowly, trying to avoid hitting people. I saw the same crazy pro-lifer who had tried to grab Erick the day before.

"Do you know the guy who tried to grab you yesterday?" I asked him.

"What about him?"

"I don't know, but I have a feeling I've seen him

somewhere before."

"Really? Where?" Erick asked.

"I don't know, but he looks familiar." I paused. "For some reason, he scares me."

"He scares me too," Erick admitted. "Don't worry about him, though. We've got good security here."

"Just be careful," I warned.

We maneuvered through the crowd, parked inside the garage, and walked safely through the door into the clinic.

Inside, the place looked just like a typical medical office. The waiting room was modest, with rows of padded chairs and framed prints mounted on the walls. The floors were clean and shiny. That morning, the padded chairs were nearly all occupied by women—most of them teenagers. The majority looked uncomfortable, and were nervously glancing at each other, exchanging occasional smiles. There was a beautiful blonde sitting in a corner reading a book, ignoring everyone else. She was dressed professionally and appeared to be in her late twenties. Near her sat a black girl, who looked like she was around eleven years old, and next to her sat a man in his late teens or early twenties. The two apparently were together.

"Randy, wear this gown," Erick said, interrupting my thoughts.

"You see that man? Is he the father?" I asked Erick.

"He could be. We get cases like that all the time; young girls pregnant, not knowing what to do in life."

"How sad."

"I know. It feels good to help them," Erick said with pride. "OK, follow me."

I trailed Erick down one of the hallways. He stopped at a door and knocked.

"Come in," a voice called out.

"Dr. Sampson," Erick said once we'd passed through the

door. "This is my friend from college, Randy Livingston. He's visiting with me today." I shook Dr. Sampson's outstretched hand. From all the stories he'd told me, I felt I already knew Erick's supervisor.

"Hello, Randy, nice meeting you." Dr. Sampson turned to Erick. "Erick, we need you to assist in room thirty-five."

"Sure, but don't forget—I'm scheduled for the partial birth training today."

"I know, but that won't start until late afternoon, or maybe even tomorrow."

"OK."

I followed Erick to room thirty-five. A young girl, around fourteen, was sitting on the bed when we entered. She looked frightened and my heart went out to her.

"Hi, I'm Dr. Frankston," Erick said with a smile. He looked at her file. "You must be Jessica."

The girl nodded her head.

"Jessica, this is Randy. He's going to be observing the procedure today, but he won't be operating on you."

She nodded her head again, but this time her eyes were tearful.

"Jessica, don't worry. As we've discussed, the procedure is quick and almost painless."

"Will my parents know about it?" she asked.

"Not unless you choose to tell them."

She seemed relieved and managed a slight smile.

"What grade are you in?" Erick asked. It was interesting to see him interacting with the girl—I'd never really seen him around kids.

"Eighth."

"Wow, that's great! What's your favorite subject?"

"I like biology," Jessica replied. She appeared to be relaxing a bit.

"That's my favorite subject too. Are you planning to become a doctor?"

The girl nodded her head.

"Jessica, your decision to have this procedure will help you become whatever you want. Right now, you're too young to care for a baby. By aborting this fetus, you'll be able to pursue higher education and focus on fulfilling your goals."

The girl nodded in agreement.

"Jessica, do you have any questions before we proceed with the abortion?"

"No."

"Then I want you to get ready. Please change into this gown. When you're finished, go ahead and crack the door open, and I'll be right back in."

I left the room behind Erick, convinced that the most logical thing for his patient was not to have a baby at fourteen. She was too young—still a child herself. How would she even know how to care for a baby?

A few minutes later, we were back in Jessica's room. Erick, along with a nurse, operated on Jessica while Dr. Sampson observed. The procedure was messy and bloody; I was disgusted. When it was over, we left Jessica in the care of the nurse.

"Is that what you do all day?" I asked Erick when we were out of earshot.

"Yep."

"What a gross and boring job," I remarked.

"Gross? I'll give you that. But boring? No way."

"It's the same procedure, over and over again. It must be really repetitive."

"You're very mistaken, my friend. First of all, you deal with a new person every time. Sometimes, there are complications and challenges, but, for the most part, the gratitude and job satisfaction come from knowing I'm helping people and making a difference in their lives."

"I could never deal with all the blood and cutting into people's bodies," I confessed.

"Gentlemen, what would you say to having lunch with me?" interrupted Dr. Sampson, coming up behind us.

"We'd love to," replied Erick.

When we reached the cafeteria, I was surprised by both its size and the food selection. I guess I was expecting something like the food lounge at the law firm: vending machines and no hot food. The tables were full of doctors and nurses.

"Do all these doctors specialize in abortion?" I asked.

"Yes, we have twenty-five doctors on staff," replied Dr. Sampson.

"Is there a high demand for abortion?"

"Well, we perform about eleven thousand annually . . ."

"Wow."

"About 1 percent of those are late-term abortions," Dr. Sampson added. "Today or tomorrow, Erick will have his chance to help out with that procedure."

"I look forward to watching," I replied.

"What do you do for a living?" asked Dr. Sampson.

"I'm a law student."

"Excellent. Are you attending summer school?"

"Actually, I'm interning at Johnson & Johnson Law Firm for the summer," I told him. Dr. Sampson's face tensed.

"I've heard your firm will be representing Christ Hospital in some upcoming litigation."

"Randy's already on the case," Erick said.

"So what, exactly, is the nature of your visit today?" asked Dr. Sampson. "Did Johnson send you to spy on us?"

"No, not at all," I replied.

Erick came to my defense. "Don't worry about Randy. He

supports abortion."

"Then why did you accept the case?" Dr. Sampson asked.

"Well, as you know, Doctor," I began with a smile, trying to lighten the mood, "interns don't always get to choose their assignments. But I don't think I would've objected, anyway. I'm all about women having the right to choose, but I don't have a good understanding of why I believe what I believe. I want to learn more about abortion so I can better defend my own beliefs."

"Did you learn anything new today?"

"Today, with Jessica, I actually got to put a face to abortion. And it still seemed nothing less than logical to abort her fetus."

"Most of the women who come here are in the same situation as Jessica," Dr. Sampson said, his face relaxing. "I'd think you might want to try to get off this case if you find support for your beliefs before the trial."

"I'll work on the case regardless of my beliefs," I told him.

"I don't quite understand why that is . . ."

"You see, it doesn't matter if I'm pro-choice or pro-life. What matters is that Christ Hospital has the right to decline abortion services if doing so violates the beliefs on which the hospital was founded," I explained.

"Let me tell you something, Randy," Dr. Sampson said. "You believe it was logical for Jessica to have an abortion, right?"

"Yes." I nodded.

"There are many girls in Jessica's shoes who can't get abortions because Christ Hospital won't provide the service. In fact, Christ Hospital is one of several hospitals around the state causing problems for women seeking abortion. What's decided in this case will likely affect the availability of services to women statewide."

"They can go somewhere else," I replied, shrugging.

"In many cities, there's no other place to go to. Abortion clinics, like this one, aren't found in every city in the U.S.," Dr. Sampson replied. "Think about a hospital that doesn't believe in chemotherapy and refuses to provide cancer patients with treatment. Why should the standards be different for abortion?"

"But the important thing is that Christ Hospital is located in a city where there are many abortion clinics," I argued. "Therefore, it shouldn't be forced to provide the service."

"As I said, though, this case will be used as an example for other hospitals that don't want to offer abortion and family planning services." He paused. "Don't think this case is an isolated one. It'll have a big impact. I suggest you try your best to convince your employer to abandon it."

"Frankly, I don't see why hospitals should be required to perform abortions at all," I said, trying to ignore the implications of his last comment. "I mean, why not just offer the service at clinics? Then we wouldn't even have to deal with this issue."

Dr. Sampson took a deep breath and sipped from a water bottle he had placed on the table. "You know why we should move the procedure from clinics to hospitals?"

"No . . ."

"It'd be much safer for both the women and the doctors. You see, every woman who enters this building is most likely here for an abortion, and every doctor is an abortion doctor, and those people outside know that. When you enter a hospital, though, the protestors have no idea why you're there, and you're much less likely to fall victim to some fanatic's violence."

I considered that. "That *is* a valid safety concern . . . But, if

Johnson & Johnson abandons this case, someone else will pick it up."

"That's true, but the key phrase there is *someone else*," he said, lowering his voice. "Johnson is good. I fear he may win."

I laughed inside, knowing Mr. Johnson feared losing. What Dr. Sampson was saying was logical, but doubt still weighed on me. *If abortion is a patient's right as much as chemotherapy, then no hospital should prevent its patients from having it.* I guess the heart of my case was not whether everyone had the right to his or her own beliefs but whether abortion was right or wrong, in an absolute sense.

Chapter 5
The Underground

"Mr. Livingston, you'd better tell the truth, or you'll end up like Mr. Livingston, the dead man."

"I don't know anything. I must have been in some sort of a coma. I got up not remembering anything. I found this information in my pocket, so I assumed I was Randy Livingston." I told them to look inside the pocket of my pants. During the many hours they'd left me alone, I had come up with an answer to their question.

One of the men took the ID and a small notebook from my pocket. They studied the picture on the card carefully.

"You really look like him. You must be related."

"Maybe it's a fake, and he changed the picture."

"We can easily check that in the computer." One of them left the room. The other opened the notebook.

"A business card from the Human Farm and Body Parts Factory," he murmured. "And a business card from FamilyFirst." He looked at me suspiciously. "When did you wake up from this . . . 'coma'?"

"Two days ago," I replied. "On the first day, I visited the

Human Farm and Body Parts Factory, and on the second, I visited FamilyFirst."

"I see." The man didn't seem to believe me.

"The picture on the ID card agrees with the picture of Randy Livingston," his partner said, re-entering the room.

"Victor, he's been to the Farm," said the leader.

"The Farm?" Victor asked, astonished. "How did he get in?"

"He doesn't have the chip, so the alarm didn't catch him."

"What chip?" I asked.

"You don't know about the chip?" asked the leader, who, I learned later, was named Markus.

"But there are other types of alarms," replied Victor. "I don't understand how he got inside."

"Are you saying I can't get back in there?" I asked in a low voice.

The men looked at each other, then answered no in unison.

"You would be imprisoned. Or possibly killed," Victor said.

"Why?" I asked.

"You're not cloned," replied Markus.

"Cloned?"

"Everyone born after 2020 must be cloned."

"I've heard about the two mandatory clones."

"So you know about this?"

"I just learned about it from FamilyFirst," I said.

"By the way," Markus said, passing a card to Victor, "he has their business card with him."

"I see," Victor said. "So, you're trying to create a white child with perfect genes?"

"No, I—what about you?" I asked. "I mean, both of you are black."

"Yes, that's why we live and work in the camp."

"The camp?" I asked.

"Basically, it's an underground world that the government's not aware of. We exchange our labor for food and services. In fact, we have a rather efficient social system here."

"Since I'm white and not handicapped, no one would know whether or not I have perfect genes. So couldn't I work outside the camp?" I asked.

"No, you don't have the chip," replied Markus.

"What's the chip?" I asked for the second time.

"The chip is a computer device installed below the skin at the time of your birth," Markus replied. "It contains all your information: your social security number, your DNA number, all your gene codes, all your genetic modifications, even your assigned bank account number. You can't buy or sell anything without the chip. You definitely can't work without one."

"Do all the people in the camp have the chip?"

"No."

"I need to get this chip," I remarked. "I want to work outside."

"Mr. Livingston, we'll find you a job in the camp."

"But I don't want to work in the camp," I said.

"Mr. Livingston, I'm afraid you have no choice."

"I must return to the Farm to save the lives of the RMs," I blurted out.

"What?"

"I'll give you all the money I make," I said. "I'll give my service to the camp. I'll do anything for you, if you help me out in this." I begged like a little boy.

Markus motioned to Victor to leave the room with him. I could hear them mumbling behind the door.

"Maybe we can do something about it," Markus said.

"Markus, have you lost your mind?" Victor shouted. "He'll get all of us killed."

"Listen to me, Victor—"

"You listen to me!"

"It's a risk we have to take," said Markus. "The Tracko device is real, and it'll be up and functioning very soon. As a matter of fact, it might be running right now. We need contact with the outside world from someone other than the Boss. The Boss won't feel comfortable visiting us anymore if they're tracking his whereabouts."

"We need to speak with the Boss before we do anything," insisted Victor.

The two men reentered the room.

"Mr. Livingston, you'll be given a job in the camp."

The men removed my handcuffs and led me to another room that had a stairway to a basement. Downstairs, I found myself in a very large yard—a neighborhood, even. We walked around for about five minutes, then entered another house. Inside was a huge hall filled with hundreds of machines, all being operated by black children.

"Just like slavery," I murmured.

"Mr. Livingston, you are mistaken," replied Victor. "These days, the only way to be enslaved is to become a citizen of the United States of America."

I was led to one of the machines and given a workstation, where an average-looking woman approached me.

"Welcome to the camp," she said. She nodded to Markus and Victor, and they walked away. I nodded my greeting.

"There's a lot of hard work to be done," she continued. "The game is survival."

"It seems an unnecessary game," I replied. "Why don't you get a chip and work outside? I don't understand why you people settle for this way of life."

"Sir, the outside world isn't much better than this," she said, gesturing around the workhouse. "Yes, we have to work harder, but we get to keep our identities—our natural identities.

"Hundreds of years ago, whites used to say that all blacks looked the same. That's even less true now. We're more diverse than the rest of the world, where everyone is cloned to look alike."

"What do you do after work?" I asked.

"We live a normal life. We have our own social gatherings, parties, families, and problems."

"What kinds of problems?" I asked

"All sorts: political, raising our kids. It's tough to peek at the outside world and see the most extraordinarily beautiful women, and then want to come back and live in the camp."

"Not really," I replied.

"You haven't seen anything yet," she commented.

"I've seen the most beautiful woman in the world, but in the blink of an eye, she turned into a witch," I said. "You, on the other hand, are a very beautiful woman."

The woman brushed the comment off with a wave of her hand.

"I mean it," I insisted. There *was* something very attractive about her. "Are there white people in the camp?"

"There are. About 25 percent of the residents here are white."

"I don't see any working in the factory," I remarked.

"This is the underground factory. We give the underground factories and houses to black and other non-Caucasian families," she replied, "since we're easier to spot than the whites aboveground.

"The white folks who don't have the chips and aren't cloned have to be very careful too, but they work in the upper-ground factories to cover up the noise of the underground ones."

"You have lots of children working here," I said.

"During the summer, we give jobs to our children. We try our best to keep them inside."

"What a tough life it must be for these kids."

"Yes, but we're doing this for their benefit. We've built underground recreation centers for them."

"I still don't understand the mission of the camp. Why don't you just clone your kids to be white and have perfect genes, and then have a normal life and not worry about the camp and the underground?" I asked.

"Sir, we're happy people. Life is tough, but we're free." She added, "You can't trust the government anymore."

"How do you get your electricity, water, and food?" I asked.

"The Boss is our contact to the outside world, and he sets all that up for us."

"The Boss?"

"He's cloned and has the chip. We all work for him. In exchange for our labor, we get this land and everything else we need. If you don't have a chip, you can't own any land aboveground. Everything here is registered in the Boss's name."

"Who is the Boss?"

"No one knows except a few folks at the camp police."

"What if the Boss dies? What will happen to the camp?" I asked.

"That's the question on everyone's mind," she replied. "But we try not to worry about it. The Boss is working to find and train a replacement in case something happens to him."

"What does the Boss get out of the camp?"

"He believes in the camp—and he profits from it. We work hard to make his business succeed, so he can continue to afford to own everything. We don't know what kind of replacement we'll get, but we hope we can make him rich, so he'll continue to work with us."

"So, is that the mission of the camp?" I asked. "People working underground and under the mercy of a boss whom they've never met?"

"No. Our dream is freedom to live aboveground."

"How are you going to gain that?"

"I don't know, but one thing we do is raise large families. Our camp started with a thousand people fifty years ago. Now we have five times that many."

"Fifty thousand!"

"We're raising an underground nation," she said, nodding. "Most of the population is kids, but everyone works. We can't afford not to be productive. We need to make money for the Boss—money so he can buy more land for us."

"More land for an underground world?" I was astonished.

"Yes, but, of course, we build cover-up houses and factories aboveground too," she explained.

"Does anybody ever come from the outside world to the camp?" I asked.

"Sometimes. We now have thirty-five people in the camp prison."

"You imprison them?"

"Yes, the penalty for trespassing is life imprisonment."

"That doesn't seem like a fair punishment," I objected.

"We have no choice. Those people are a threat to our safety."

"The law of the camp is harsh," I observed.

"Those people are prisoners of war. The government has declared a war against anyone who doesn't follow their cloning regulations, and to survive, we have no choice but to fight back."

"What do you do with the prisoners?"

"We lock them up. In the camp prison, there's a factory, and we allow them to work and live a normal life, but they can't leave," she explained. She lowered her voice. "Rumor has it that one of the prisoners was an eight-year-old kid. Residents took him in and raised him. He later became the Boss.

"But, like I said," she continued, her voice returning to its normal volume, "no one knows who the Boss is, for his security and ours."

I wanted to meet the Boss, the man who ran this underground world. The people of the camp were prisoners, but so, it seemed, were the people on the outside. I was moved to help these people, but I knew I was called to a different mission—to save the lives of the RMs.

Chapter 6
The Birth of Mark

"Hurry up, Randy," Erick shouted at me. "Drive faster."

"I'm doing my best. What do you want me to do, break traffic laws?" I replied, my mind still stuck on the continuation of the dream I'd had the night before. I couldn't believe such dreams were still going strong.

"I'll never forgive myself if I miss my nephew's delivery. I promised Nancy that I'd be there."

We finally arrived at Christ Hospital. "You came at just the right time," the nurse said to Erick, ushering us down a sterile corridor.

I felt a little awkward and a bit out of place, and told Erick so.

"Just act like you're an intern," Erick advised. "I'll get you a gown. Keep following me, and, of course, don't touch anything."

We entered the delivery room to find Nancy, Erick's stepsister, looking tired and afraid. The labor started a few minutes after our arrival and, for the next few hours, Nancy did nothing but push, cry, and scream. It was a difficult labor, it seemed—way more difficult than the abortion I'd witnessed. Nancy's husband, Eddy, was by her side, holding her hand and supporting her through the whole thing. It would have been a tough experience for a young woman to go through without the husband there beside her. *Jessica had done the right thing aborting her baby. It must be very lonely to give birth with no one there to hold your hand.*

After several tense hours, the baby was finally born. The joy on Nancy's face was indescribable. I was tired and wanted to go home and rest, but Erick wanted to stay with Nancy and his newborn nephew a little while longer. He asked me to stay with him a few hours more, and I agreed. Half an hour later, the nurse brought the baby back to the room, and Erick and I stepped into the hallway to give the new parents some privacy. *What if she were a single mother?* I wondered, closing the door to the room. *Would she experience the same joy?* I saw a doctor strolling down the hall toward us, so I asked him if there was a single woman giving birth in the hospital.

He looked at me suspiciously and asked for my ID, which I didn't have with me. I told him I had come with Erick.

"Don't worry about him, Doctor," Erick said. "He's one of your lawyers."

"My lawyers?" repeated the doctor.

"Not your personal lawyer, though he's not a bad one to have," Erick replied.

"I'm working on the abortion case," I explained.

"Oh, I see." He looked me over. "You don't look like Johnson to me."

"I work with the firm," I said. "Mr. Johnson has put me on the case."

"Well, we're glad the firm decided to represent us." He

extended his hand. "I'm Dr. Forman."

"Randy Livingston," I replied, grasping his hand in a firm shake.

"So, you want to see a single woman giving birth?" Dr. Forman asked.

"I . . ."

"Randy's doing some soul searching," Erick interrupted in his usual, blunt manner.

Dr. Forman looked at me and raised his eyebrows. "Soul searching?"

"More like research," I answered, smiling politely.

"He's already visited an abortion clinic, and Dr. Sampson of Family Planning is working on him," Erick added. "He's all yours for the next two hours. I warn you, though: he's stubborn as stone."

"I'd be happy to give you a tour of the hospital, Mr. Livingston," Dr. Forman suggested.

"Thank you," I said. "I'd really appreciate that."

We left Erick with his family.

"I need to talk to my supervisor about this, so he'll know where I am," Dr. Forman told me.

"Sure," I said. "I hope I'm not taking up too much of your time."

"Not at all. We have enough doctors on the floor today."

We went to the first floor. At the end of a long corridor was an office with a nameplate attached to the door. "Dr. James, Hospital Manager."

"Do you mind waiting here for one minute while I talk to Dr. James?" asked Dr. Forman.

"Not at all."

A minute later, Dr. Forman and another man came out of the office.

"Hello, I'm Dr. James, the hospital manager," said the

man who appeared with Dr. Forman. "I'm pleased to meet you, Mr. Livingston."

"Likewise."

"Would you like to have a cup of coffee with me before we give you the hospital tour?" he asked.

"I'd be glad to."

We entered his spacious office and sat down.

"You should know," I began, accepting a mug of steaming coffee, "I'm not here on a business visit. As a matter of fact, Mr. Johnson isn't aware that I'm here. I just tagged along with my roommate, who helped deliver his new nephew."

"I understand," Dr. James assured me. "However, I'm very happy that Mr. Johnson accepted our case."

"Mr. Livingston is doing some soul searching on abortion," Dr. Forman interjected.

"Research," I emphasized.

Dr. James seemed suddenly uncomfortable.

"Dr. James, I'd like to assure you of my strong belief that you have the right not to perform abortions if it violates the religious convictions of this hospital," I said firmly. "My personal beliefs about abortion have nothing to do with this case. I simply want to learn more about the procedure."

There was silence for a moment while the two men seemed to consider what I'd said.

"How was your visit with Dr. Sampson?" Dr. Forman asked finally.

"You've been to the abortion clinic?" said Dr. James, looking surprised.

"It was informative," I answered, ignoring Dr. James's question. "He brought up a good argument."

"Do you mind sharing it with us?" Dr. James asked with curiosity.

I told them the argument about a hospital refusing to offer

chemotherapy—a very convincing line of reasoning, in my opinion.

"Aaah, but there's a big flaw in his argument," insisted Dr. James.

"Sampson is known for twisting logic," added Dr. Forman.

"You see, chemotherapy is not the same as abortion. Chemotherapy saves lives, whereas abortion ends them. We can't compare apples with oranges," Dr. James said passionately.

I understood why Dr. James was trying to persuade me in his direction, but I wasn't quite sold. I tried to reassure him that my personal beliefs wouldn't interfere with my work on the hospital's behalf.

"Mr. Johnson will represent you, sir. I'm just an intern at the firm. I don't have a law license yet," I explained. "So please understand that my personal opinion will not prevent you from getting the best defense possible."

"I don't mean to be rude," Dr. James said apologetically. "This case is complicated and requires an experienced lawyer. I have total faith in Mr. Johnson. You seem to be a sharp young man, and I'm sure you'll be of assistance to him."

I thanked Dr. James.

"What other arguments did Sampson give you?" Dr. Forman asked.

"There's not much to his arguments," I said. "It was seeing the young women in the waiting room that moved my heart. Their choices seemed very logical, especially after viewing the birth of a child today. No teenager should have to go through such an ordeal alone."

"Is that why you asked to see a single mother giving birth?" asked Dr. Forman.

"Yes," I replied.

"Well, you're in luck," Dr. James said, looking at a chart

on his desk. "We have three teenagers in the hospital giving birth today." He stood. "Let's go and meet them."

Chapter 7
The Aging Pyramid

The young woman was lying on a bed, a newborn infant asleep on her chest. Her bed was surrounded by flowers, gifts, and balloons, along with a few friends and family members who had come to congratulate her in person.

"Is she famous?" I asked Martha, the woman I'd met at the underground factory.

"No. Birthdays are great celebrations here at the camp," Martha explained. "Our children are our future." She paused, looking at the child, and then added, "This is the only way to win the war—not with weapons but by raising families. We want to outnumber the clones."

She was silent for a moment, then looked at me. "This evening, in Freedom Square, we will celebrate Hope's birth." She looked at her watch. "You have two hours of free time until then."

"Do you have a library here in the camp?" I asked.

"Yes, the Boss built us a big one in Reflection Square," she replied. "Freedom Square is under the largest and noisiest upper-ground factories, so all our noisy events are held there. Reflection Square is under a residential area, so that's where we built the library. You must be careful not to make much noise while you're in Reflection Square."

The library in Reflection Square was enormous. As a matter of fact, it was the largest library I'd ever seen. For the first time that day, I felt at ease. I sat down at one of the many computer terminals and began my search for people, starting with myself. I typed in *Randy Livingston, SS# 929-36-6989.*

"Born in 1980," the computer responded.

That's me all right, I thought.

"Died 2035."

I had lived for only fifty-five years. I wondered about the cause of my death, and as I kept reading, there it was: "Euthanasia." My stomach flip-flopped. *What kind of deadly disease caused me to kill myself?* I continued reading through the funeral records, but there was no mention of any disease. I searched for hospital records during the same year and for prior years, but found no hint of why I would elect to die.

"This doesn't make sense," I murmured to myself, becoming suspicious. "Why would I have myself killed?"

I carefully reexamined the funeral records, and found the name of the clinic where I'd died: E Clinic #235. I quickly called up the clinic's records, then searched for my name in their database.

"Randy Livingston, broken hand."

Broken hand! I wouldn't have killed myself over a broken hand.

I started a new search for the general term "E Clinic," and I learned that the "E" stood for *euthanasia*. The clinics had apparently been created by the government to offer free euthanasia services.

Why would the government encourage people to end their lives?

In a link offered on the E Clinic page, I found an interesting article from a *Chicago Tribune* of July 2030.

"With the flip of the pyramid, the government will establish free E clinics," it said. *The flip of the pyramids?* "Officials say the aging pyramid has officially flipped. The number of aging people, sixty and above, is officially exceeding the number of working people. The Social Security fund has been depleted, and 401-K retirement plans have been taxed more than 80 percent. We are now in crisis. Medical expenses have skyrocketed due to the increase in demand for health services, and a decrease in the number of health professionals available. The overtaxed generation needs relief. Revolutions are erupting all over the U.S. Today, Congress will vote on the Required Euthanasia Bill."

As I read on through the archived articles of that year, I learned that the Required Euthanasia Bill passed easily. The law stated that states were required to have programs in place to provide "the pill" to senior citizens who couldn't afford medical treatment. *Still, breaking my hand wasn't a deadly disease, and I wasn't a senior citizen. Surely I could've afforded the related health costs.*

I looked up hospital records once again for 2035, and found that the cost for a hand cast that year was nearly a million dollars. *That's outrageous,* I thought. I must have had no choice but to die at fifty-five.

How had the aging pyramid flipped? There were many editorials about the topic during the latter part of the year. One of the articles read, "Since *Roe v. Wade*, we have aborted five hundred million children." Abortion seemed to have greatly contributed to the flipping of the pyramid, and, indirectly, to my own death.

A few hours later, I walked down Action Boulevard,

thinking about what I had read in the library. I arrived at Freedom Square to find it full of people. Children were laughing, dancing, and having fun. Everyone seemed to be enjoying themselves. A microphone was placed at a podium, and a speaker approached it.

"Welcome to the camp celebration," he said. "We are here to celebrate all our children born in the month of May."

Everyone shouted and screamed, some chanting "Our children are our future!" I looked around, and everyone seemed happy, but I couldn't enjoy their celebration. I was mourning my own death.

Chapter 8
The Death of John

"The flipping of the pyramid?" exclaimed Erick while I was driving him to work the next day.

"Yes, don't you think that abortion will lead to economic disaster?" I asked.

"No—it's just the opposite," Erick replied. "Most of the women getting abortions are poor and single, and the majority, if they gave birth to their children, would be forced to go on welfare. We save everyone money by aborting these fetuses."

"But we're reducing the population of young people. We're shifting the equilibrium."

"No, my friend, we're reducing the population of children who would be born into families that don't want them, and who can't afford to raise them." He added, "You know, most of these children would turn into criminals or losers. We're helping our society and economy by eliminating them."

"I don't know about that," I said.

"It's common sense," he said.

"I need more facts," I replied. "I can't take anybody's word for it anymore. I need to approach the subject in a more scientific way."

My dreams had convinced me that I couldn't trust anyone. I had to find the truth myself.

When we arrived at the clinic, it was the same scene as always: crowded streets, protestors, and the man who looked familiar. I wondered if the guy had nothing else to do in life but protest abortion. We parked inside the garage and entered the clinic, where I waited in the lobby until Erick called me. The waiting room was full of new faces. One woman looked very far along in her pregnancy. There was an air of depression hanging over the room.

"Mr. Livingston, Dr. Sampson would like to see you," said the receptionist.

Surprised, I followed her to room forty-one.

Dr. Sampson's office was smaller than I'd expected. Pictures of what I assumed were family members hung on the walls.

"Good morning, Randy."

"Good morning."

"Please, have a seat." I sat down on a fancy leather couch. "Randy, I don't think it's appropriate for you to see the partial birth abortion with—"

"But Dr. Sampson—" I interrupted.

"Without me first taking the time to explain the procedure to you," he finished.

"Of course, of course." I sighed with relief. I thought he was going to prevent me from viewing the procedure.

"Two days ago, you saw an abortion performed on Jessica in the first trimester of her pregnancy. Almost all abortions occur at an early stage. Abortions at later stages are rare, and usually take place because the mother's life is in danger. The woman who will have a partial birth abortion today is very sick. She has a heart problem, and if she continues to carry her baby, she will likely lose her life. She has no choice but to abort."

Dr. Sampson went on, telling me how partial birth abortion was very rare, and how it was a necessary procedure. I agreed with whatever he said because I didn't want him to prevent me from observing. When he had finished, I thanked him for his time and for the great opportunity he was providing me.

When I entered the operating room, I saw the lady from the waiting room who had looked so far along. She was reclined on the small bed in the center of the room, her feet in stirrups, and Erick and another doctor were at the foot of the bed. Erick informed me quietly that she was eight months pregnant. The doctor put his hand inside the woman's body and explained to Erick, "I'm now rotating the head, so the body will come out first."

When the body was delivered, the doctor kept its head inside the mother.

"Give me the scissors," he instructed Erick, who was sweating excessively. Erick handed him the scissors, and the doctor used them to cut through the baby's neck.

The doctor put the remains of the baby in a bag, then placed the bag in a refrigerator.

"Why don't you throw it out in the biological waste container?" I asked.

"We use the remains for other purposes," replied the doctor.

"Just like the RMs," I murmured.

"Excuse me?"

"Nothing," I replied. *How did this procedure save this woman's life? Couldn't she have waited one more month to deliver the baby?*

"The nurse will come and clean you up now," the doctor said to the woman.

I seized the opportunity and went to the head of the bed.

"I hope your heart will be OK," I said.

"Why? What's wrong with my heart?" she asked in panic. "I wasn't told of any side effects—"

"I thought you had some sort of a heart problem, and that's why you aborted your child."

"No. Who told you that? I ain't gonna have the baby of my ex-boyfriend," she said, adding, "I broke up with him a month ago. I don't want to bring a lot of baggage with me to the next relationship."

Taken aback, I managed a sympathetic smile for the woman and quickly left the room. Dr. Sampson had lied to me; there had been nothing wrong with that woman's health.

I drove home with Erick that afternoon. We were silent most of the way.

"What if the baby were delivered prematurely. Would he live?" I asked finally.

"Yes. My nephew was premature," Erick replied.

"Would the process of delivering him prematurely be more dangerous to the woman than if she aborted it?"

"I don't see why, especially for this woman," replied Erick.

"So, why didn't you just deliver him?" I asked.

"What's the point, man? He'd live," explained Erick.

"You don't want the child to live?"

"That's the whole point of abortion. It has nothing to do with whether or not *I* want the kid to live. The mother made her choice."

"So, abortion is about killing babies?"

"No, it's about a woman's right to control her own body."

"Well, if she has the right to control her own body, and

doesn't want the child to live inside, she has the option to deliver him prematurely, doesn't she?"

"Yes, but the point is, she didn't want a live baby."

"So it's *not* about a woman controlling her own body," I argued.

"It's about her body and her life in general," Erick said. "Maybe she's not ready to have a child. Maybe a child would bring burden and stress to her life. Maybe he'd be an obstacle to her career advancement . . . You can't force people to become mothers if they don't want to."

"Why would she wait eight months to decide?" I asked.

"I don't know. Maybe she thought she could handle it, then decided she couldn't."

"What if she delivered the baby, and then, after a month, realized she didn't want to be a mother? Would she have the right to kill him then?" I asked.

"No. That would be murder," Erick replied.

"What if she decided to kill him on the day of his birth?" I asked. "What's the cutoff age for when she has the right to end her child's life?"

"I would say . . . anytime before he's born."

"Why?" I asked.

"Because he's still inside her body, and she has the right to control anything inside her body."

"What if he's like John—"

"Who's John?" Erick interrupted me.

"The boy you aborted today. I named him John," I replied.

"You are pathetic."

"Look who's talking! I don't want to argue that with you. Just answer my question. What if the fetus, like John, was outside his mother's womb, except for his head. Would he still be considered part of her body?"

"Yes, and please don't call him John."

"But what if it's possible to deliver John completely. Or what if John's head wants to get out but the doctor forces him to stay inside so he can cut his throat with a pair of scissors, and then vacuum his brain out, would John be considered part of his mother's body, although he's kept inside her against his will?"

"I don't want to discuss this right now. I just got off work and I'm tired," Erick replied.

As we sat in silence, I realized I'd become convinced that partial birth abortion was wrong, but I was still unsure about early stage abortion. I needed to decide on an age when abortion should become illegal. It made sense that beheading an eight-month-old fetus was wrong, but what about aborting one at two months, one month, or a few days after the moment of conception? Where did we draw the line?

Chapter 9
Marcello Research Center

"Of course they feel pain," Dr. Gus Marcello, a former abortion doctor, told me in response to my question. During his career, he said, he had aborted thousands of fetuses. Now in his sixties, he operated his own research center. "I remember many times that I aborted fetuses and could hear them crying from the pain."

"But those were probably late-stage abortions, right?" I asked.

"Actually, by five months, a fetus has fully developed vocal chords, and he does cry inside his mother's womb. Of course, he can't be heard because there's no air to carry the vocal waves."

"So, before five months, the fetus doesn't experience pain?" I asked.

"That's not what I said. By five months, he's able to express pain, but he feels it much earlier. I would say a fetus can feel pain as early as eight weeks," Dr. Marcello replied.

"Eight weeks," I repeated.

"At eight weeks, the fetus's heart is beating steadily and, of course, you can hear this in an ultrasound," Dr. Marcello added.

"So, eight weeks would probably be a good cutoff point," I thought aloud.

"Cutoff point for what?" Dr. Marcello asked.

"For legalized abortion," I said.

Dr. Marcello took a deep breath and asked, "So, you're trying to decide when human life begins?"

"Yes," I replied, a bit surprised he'd guessed my intentions.

"You think you should define a human in terms of when the baby starts experiencing pain?"

"Correct."

"You're using a philosophical—rather than scientific—approach to define what it is to be human," he said. "That can be dangerous."

"What do you mean?" I asked.

"There have been many philosophical theories about when human life begins. Most usually use biological milestones to define a specific beginning, like when there's first consciousness, movement, brain function, heartbeat . . . Some even claim it doesn't begin until there's been an exchange of love. Do you see the problem with philosophical definitions?"[1]

"They are many," I admitted.

"Exactly, and who should determine which one is right? After all, each individual has a right to hold his own philosophic beliefs. People of goodwill can—and do—differ completely on the correctness of these philosophic beliefs and theories, right?"

"Yes, I see," I replied.

"The main problem with philosophical definitions is that none can be proven factually by science. It's easy to find out when a fetus starts feeling pain, but can you prove to me that pain should be the criterion for deciding when human life begins?"[2]

I didn't reply—the answer was obvious. I quietly considered what he'd said. I didn't know what to think or to believe. What I wanted was a grace period for young mothers to be able to abort their babies, and then, after that period, to make all abortions illegal.

"You need to use the scientific approach to define when human life begins," Dr. Marcello continued.

"What is the scientific approach?" I asked with enthusiasm. I was delighted by the word "scientific." I didn't want my beliefs based on emotions or certain philosophies but on facts.

"It comes down to relying on biological facts," he explained.

"And what do the facts say?" I asked.

"They say that each human life begins at fertilization, and that human life is a continuum from that time until death," he answered.

"But isn't that a philosophical belief?" I asked.

"Not really. It's a belief based on scientific facts and logical deductions." He paused. "Let me ask you this: At conception, would you say the fetus is alive?"

"That's what we're trying to figure out, isn't it?"

"I'm not asking if it's human but whether it has *life*. For instance, a cat has life but is not human," he explained.

"Then yes, I would say the fetus is alive."

"Good. So, we've agreed that it has the characteristics of life. That is, it can reproduce its own cells and develop them into a specific pattern of maturity and function. Or simply, it's not dead. And that's a scientific fact. Right?"[3]

"Yes, we agree it's alive, but we still don't know if it's a human being," I replied.

"So, the next question would be: Is this living being a human?"

"That's right," I said. "And I don't know the answer to that."

"Is the being in question a cat or a dog?" Dr. Marcello asked.

"No."

"How do you know that?"

I shrugged my shoulders. "Well, it'll never become a cat or a dog."

"Could it become anything other than a human being?" Dr. Marcello asked.

"I don't think so."

"So, that living being, at conception, can only develop into a human being. Agreed?"

"Yes, he can develop into a human being, but the question is whether he is human *right at conception*," I emphasized.

"Is he a unique being?"

"What do you mean?" I asked.

"When you were conceived, do you think you could have become someone else? Could you, for example, have become a woman? Could you have had a different skin color or eye color?"

"No, I think I could only have developed into what I am right now," I replied.

"So, what would you say about a living being that is unique, totally distinguishable from any other living organism, completely human in all of his or her characteristics, including the forty-six human chromosomes, and can only develop into a fully mature human? Don't you think it's obvious that that living being is human?"[4] Dr. Marcello asked.

"Yes, but—"

"Is he complete?" Dr. Marcello interrupted.

"Complete?"

"Does he need anything else in order to develop into a fully mature human being?"

I was unsure how to answer his question. "He needs food," I suggested.

"Yes, we all do, don't we?" Dr. Marcello said. "The fetus is a complete human at the time of conception. Nothing will be added from the time of the union of the sperm and egg until the death of the old man or woman, except growth and development of what is there at the beginning. All he needs is time to develop and mature."[5]

What Dr. Marcello was talking about was logical, but doubts lingered. It was easy to believe that human life started at conception–I could accept that–but I was struggling with the implications of that belief. I had sympathy for girls like Jessica, and felt they had to be given a choice whether or not they wanted a child.

"Randy, how old are you?" Dr. Marcello suddenly asked, interrupting my thoughts.

"Twenty-three."

"Are you a human being?" he asked.

"I would hope so." I smiled.

"Were you the same being when you were ten years old?" he asked.

"Yes."

"What about at one year old? Were you the same being then? A *human* being?"

"Yes."

"What about on your day of birth–would you say you were the same being then?"

"Yes."

"Now, what about one day before the day of your birth, while you were still in your mother's womb—would you say you were still the same human?"

"Yes."

"I can ask you the same question all the way back to your conception, and you have no choice but to answer yes," Dr. Marcello remarked.

"What about before conception? I was made of an egg and sperm—" I started.

"Before conception, you did not exist. The egg could have united with another sperm and produced a completely different person. At conception, you started to exist. At conception, you were a unique, living human being—the same one I'm talking to right now. You've always been a human."

"That makes sense," I replied. "I think my problem is the way the fetus looks at conception—it's too small to resemble a human being. I mean, it still doesn't think, feel, or even look like a human."

"That objection, of course, is not scientific but philosophical. But suppose we still have doubts about the identity of the unique living being in the uterus. What would be the human way of treating this being?" Dr. Marcello asked.

"You mean whether or not to abort him?" I asked.

"Yes."

"What would it be?"

"Would we not resolve a doubt in favor of life? We do not bury those who aren't dead. We work frantically to help rescue entombed miners, children buried in the rubble of a school destroyed by earthquake, a person lost on a mountain. Does a hunter shoot until he knows it's a deer and not another man? The truly human way of thinking would be to give life the benefit of the doubt."[6]

"That all makes sense," I said, "but I struggle with the

implications . . ."

"What are the implications, in your opinion?" Dr. Marcello asked.

"Well, if what you're saying is true, abortion is always wrong," I answered.

"Have you ever been to an abortion clinic?"

"Yes," I replied. "In fact, my friend works in one."

"Have you seen the signs the protestors carry?"

"Yes."

"Did you ever see a sign that says unborn children are not humans?" he asked.

"I don't think so," I said, searching my memory.

"Exactly my point. You see, abortionists know it's hard for them to fight the scientific evidence that life begins at conception, so they don't bother trying. All they concentrate on is a woman's rights over her body." He paused. "You see, there are only two basic questions to be answered when one considers the abortion controversy. The first question is when does human life begin? That's the simple one because, as we've agreed, we can leave it to science. The second question, which is the one I believe you're struggling with, is should all human life be given equal protection under the law, or can certain human lives be discriminated against? Unfortunately, science cannot answer the second question. The answer to the second question is a function of ethical beliefs, philosophical beliefs, religious beliefs, legal beliefs, etc."[7]

"So, we don't bother to answer the second question because everyone has their own beliefs?" I asked.

"Not really. Murder, rape, and other crimes are similar issues, and we don't ignore them because they're ethically related. The answer to the second question is not that difficult, really. I believe abortion is wrong because it involves the right to life, our most important civil right. I understand that women have their own rights too, but the ethical principle is that, in a hierarchy of rights, the right to life itself is supreme. We all have the right to the pursuit of happiness, but we cannot achieve it by discriminating against, stealing from, injuring, or killing others. And this issue is very important. The freedom of thousands, even millions, of future humans depends on its outcome."[8]

I immediately thought of the RMs. Abortion, it seemed to me, was like killing off the children at the Farm. The RMs, though human, were being killed to satisfy the desires of other people.

I told Dr. Marcello about the lawsuit against Christ Hospital.

"Oh, I've heard about it," he said. He even volunteered himself as a witness, and promised that "we wouldn't be disappointed" with him. I spent the rest of the day touring his center. The visit was very productive, and I had something to show Mr. Johnson when I returned to the office the next day.

Chapter 10
Quality Tissue, Inc.

The alarm woke me up at 6:00 a.m. Erick opened his eyes, glanced at the clock, and fell back into bed. I had decided to stop giving him rides to the clinic, but I had yet to tell him that. I took a shower and returned to the room to dress and get my things together.

"You're up early today," Erick grumbled as I headed toward the door.

"Yeah. I'm leaving for work in two minutes," I replied.

Erick sat up. "Hey, do you have an early appointment or something?"

"No."

"Then, can't you just give me ten or fifteen minutes to get ready?"

"No," I said, feeling awkward. "I've decided to stop giving you rides to the clinic," I explained.

"I see." He was silent for a moment. "Would it help if I told you that I'm not going to perform a partial birth abortion today? I don't think they'll let me do one this summer."

"No, it won't help. I've come to believe that life begins at conception, so no abortion can be right."

"Man, I don't want to argue with you or debate your crazy, fanatic ideas anymore," he said angrily. "Do you know what's worse than abortion?"

"What?" I asked, not really wanting to hear the answer.

"Religious fanatics who try to force their beliefs on others."

"How am I foisting my beliefs on you, if I may ask?"

"You're refusing to give me rides, and . . ."

"And what?"

"And you're questioning my beliefs. You're invading my privacy and trying to influence me. Why don't you keep your beliefs to yourself? I mean, everyone's entitled to their own way of seeing things."

"There are so many loopholes, Erick—logical ones—in what you've just said, but I don't have time to discuss them now. I have to go." With that, I left the room.

Driving toward the firm, I thought about what Erick had said. I honestly couldn't blame him for the way he thought—I used to think exactly the same way. And I still agreed with him on many other issues. For example, I still thought people's religious beliefs should be kept private. I didn't want to be forced to listen to people trying to persuade me about matters involving faith, and I definitely was at a loss on how to respond to them. It was just a messy situation I would rather avoid, even though I'd always considered my opinions to be in accord with the majority of Americans. Now, I was wondering if, as a liberal person, I'd ever been honest in my debates. It seemed my defense had always been to attack conservatives personally, and never bother to listen to their arguments. My research into abortion was forcing me to open my mind to every side of the argument, regardless of its proponents. In just a few days, I found myself willing to listen to others, to try to understand their convictions. The only problem I was having was dealing with Erick, who was still stuck in his close mindedness. I just couldn't be around him—couldn't be there, as I had been so far, helping him achieve ends I now thought to be criminal. Besides, he could always take the bus to work.

Before I realized it, I was driving by the abortion clinic. I wasn't surprised to find myself there—after all, it was on the route I took every day to get to the firm. But this morning, something was different. The streets were empty. It was 6:45—a little more than an hour before the place opened. Few cars were parked in the lot, but I could see a big, white truck that looked like it had a refrigerated trailer. I watched as a man in a brown uniform carried boxes from the back door of the clinic to the truck, and I slowed down on the deserted street. The containers were labeled "biological waste." My curiosity was piqued—I wanted to find out exactly what was going on. I made a U-turn and headed back toward the dorms, driving fast. I made the ten minute drive in five, and as I pulled up to the bus stop outside our building, I saw Erick.

"Get in the car quickly," I shouted.

He looked at me, eyes wide with surprise, but didn't respond.

"Get in. There's no time to waste," I insisted.

"What's all this about?" he asked as he climbed into the car.

"Fasten your seat belt," I ordered and drove as fast as possible back to the clinic.

"So, you didn't find any loopholes in my argument after all, huh?" Erick asked with a cocky smile on his face.

I ignored him. "We're not going to the clinic."

"Where are you taking me?"

"To the biological waste disposal center."

"What's that?"

"It's where they dispose of fetal waste," I explained. Erick's face went from self-assured to irritated.

"Listen pal, I've got to get to work. I have no time for this."

"What time does the clinic close?" I asked.

"Around nine."

"OK, why don't you call Dr. Sampson and tell him you'll work the evening shift today?"

"Randy, I don't want to waste my day at a waste disposal center. I really need to go to work," he said.

"Erick, please," I begged. "Just do me this one favor, and I'll owe you. Please, come with me."

"I guess I don't have any choice," he said, gesturing to the road whizzing by his window. "Give me your phone," he said, promptly calling the clinic.

"Thanks," I said. "You're truly my best friend, though you have some screwed-up beliefs."

"I changed my mind," Erick said. "I won't come if I have to listen to you lecturing me about abortion."

"I won't. I promise."

As we neared the clinic, I saw the truck leaving the parking lot and accelerated to follow it.

"Keep an eye on this truck," I told Erick. "It's carrying biological waste containers from the clinic."

We tailed the truck through the now-heavy rush hour traffic. I stole a glance at Erick, and a slight twinkle in his eyes told me he was enjoying the unscheduled adventure.

After we'd driven for about an hour outside the city, the truck turned onto a side street and parked in front of a new-looking building. The building was surrounded by trees, hiding it from the main street. A sign above the front doors read "Waste Disposal, Inc."

"Now what?" Erick asked.

"Do you have your school and work IDs?" I asked.

"Yes."

"OK, here's the plan. I'm going to introduce myself as an environmental studies student doing research on biological waste. OK?"

"OK," Erick replied uncertainly.

"Then, I'll ask to be let in to tour the facility. We'll go from there."

We got out of the car and walked to the entrance, where a guard was posted.

"Hello, sir," I greeted him.

"How may I help you?"

"We would like to tour the facility."

"We don't give tours," he replied curtly.

"But, sir, we're students doing research on—"

"I told you, we don't give walk-up tours. If you'd like to see the plant, you must make an appointment."

"May I speak with the manager, please?" I asked.

"The manager's not here."

"OK, what about the acting manager?" I insisted.

"He's not here, either."

"I don't believe this," I said, feigning exasperation. "We drove two hours to come here, and we won't leave until we see a manager."

The guard seemed displeased, but after a moment's hesitation, he gave in.

"Follow me."

As we entered the building, I noticed a sign that read "Quality Tissue, Inc."

"There's a change in plan," I whispered to Erick, who frowned and looked as if he wanted to respond, but he was cut short by our arrival at an office door.

The guard knocked and a tall man opened the door. He

looked at us in astonishment.

"These two gentlemen insist on seeing you," explained the guard.

The man looked down his nose at us. "Yes? How may I help you?"

"My name is Randy Livingston and I work for Christ Hospital," I said carefully. "And this is my friend Erick, a medical student currently interning at the Sampson Family Planning Center." At the mention of the clinic, the man's shoulders relaxed. "We're doing research on fetal tissue, and Dr. Sampson recommended we visit your company," I added.

"Dr. Sampson is a great friend of mine," the man replied with a smile. "As a matter of fact, I had lunch with him just yesterday. He didn't tell me you were coming by."

I gave him my most apologetic smile. "We didn't tell him we were planning to visit. In fact, we just had a casual conversation about it."

"We're actually here doing research for the university, not for work," Erick added. "By the way, here's my ID for the clinic, if you'd like to see it." He gave the card, along with his school ID, to the man, who scrutinized both before returning them.

"My name is John Martin," he said. "What exactly are you researching?"

"Basically, we're trying to get general information on what kinds of fetal tissues and organs are in demand, and how their use has helped medical research," I replied.

"I see. Please come in and I'll find someone who can help you out."

We sat in straight-backed chairs in the office while Mr. Martin set off down the hall. I could tell Erick was nervous.

"Why did you bring Dr. Sampson into it?" he whispered. "He knows Martin personally, and I can get into a lot of trouble for this."

"What's been said has been said," I apologized. "Now, let's make the best of this experience."

"Man, I shouldn't have come with you," Erick said, shaking his head.

Mr. Martin reentered the room, followed by a young woman. "This is Julie. She'll be your guide and answer all your questions," he said, smiling.

"Thank you very much. We appreciate your time," I said. Erick and I took turns shaking Mr. Martin's hand.

"Hello," the woman said warmly once we'd stepped into the hall. "Welcome to Quality Tissue."

Erick introduced himself confidently and thrust his hand toward her—a drastic change from the nervous friend who'd been by my side only moments earlier. Once he had released her hand, I put my own forward, less enthusiastically.

"I'm Randy."

"So, what questions do you have for me?" Julie asked as we walked down the corridor.

"Lots of questions," I replied. "To start with, which fetal organs are most in demand?"

"Blood, eyes, livers, brains, and thymuses, among other things," she replied.

"So, your company sells those parts?"

She nodded. "But, we really don't sell for profit so much as to cover the cost of processing," she explained. "We basically work with tissue researchers, pharmaceutical companies, and universities to find out their needs, and then we collect the fetuses from abortion clinics all over the U.S. We dissect the fetuses and deliver the organs to their destinations."

"How much do these parts typically sell for?"

"Not much—just enough to cover the cost of operation," she replied.

"How many fetuses do you guys process each week?" I asked.

"About two hundred."

"Would we be able to watch you dissect one?" Erick asked eagerly.

She looked disappointed. "I'm sorry, no. John advised me against it. I can only answer your general questions."

"Come on. I'm a medical student and I witness abortions every day," Erick pleaded.

"You work at an abortion clinic?" she asked.

"Yes. Yesterday was my first partial birth abortion, but I've helped doctors perform numerous early stage ones," he added.

"You might even dissect the fetus that Erick aborted yesterday," I interjected with false enthusiasm. "I saw them put it in a special container, and today your truck came and picked up the remains from the clinic."

"Oh," she said, her eyes lingering on Erick, who smiled back innocently. "You know what? John won't have to know you were in the lab. Let's go over there."

"Can I help you dissect?" Erick replied.

"I don't think so, but you can watch," she replied, smiling.

The lab was fairly small. Five employees were working there when we arrived, and it didn't look like the place could hold many more people.

"Do you guys dissect all two hundred fetuses each week by yourselves?" Erick asked.

"No. In fact, we usually prefer to do it in the abortion clinic or hospital, but some clinics—like yours—don't have enough space for us," she replied.

"Yeah, our clinic is really busy," Erick conceded. "It's one of the largest in the Chicago area. We have about twenty-five doctors working there."

I glanced around the lab, and saw a truck driver carrying

containers into the room through a back door.

"And the ones you do dissect," I began, "are they all OK to sell?"

"Well, only about 2 percent have abnormalities, but the remaining are healthy, sellable fetuses," she replied.

Julie began opening the containers the truck driver had brought in, helping another employee put the fetuses in a large, stainless steel refrigerator. "Of course, we can't dissect everything today, so we store the others in the fridge. Everything must be dissected by the end of the week."

She opened another container and said quietly, "This one's alive."

Julie filled a large sink and held the fetus's head below the waterline. I was shocked. *She murdered the baby*, I thought.

"It was probably an inexperienced doctor who performed that abortion," said Erick, looking slightly disturbed.

"Maybe not. From time to time, we have live fetuses come in," she explained. "As a matter of fact, we've asked the doctors to alter the abortion procedure so we can get the most intact specimen possible, which sometimes results in nonexterminated fetuses.

"I think I'll start with this one." She pulled the fetus from the sink. "He's dead, all right." She turned her attention to us. "I'll need you two to wear some protective clothing." She gestured with her head to a set of lockers against one wall. We walked over and pulled out gloves, lab coats, goggles, and face shields.

Once we were dressed, Julie started dissecting the fetus. *A minute ago, this fetus was a living baby boy*, I thought, watching her slit his throat deftly and drain his blood, then pull his eyes out.

"We sell the eyes for seventy-five dollars," she said.

Then she set about opening the skull and removing the brain. "As you may notice, this is a rather difficult procedure. That's why we charge a thousand dollars for the brain." She continued to dissect the body, quoting prices as she worked.

"The ears are usually sold for 75 dollars. An intact trunk fetches 500 . . . a whole liver, 150."

She spent an hour and a half dissecting the fetus. "It usually takes longer than that, but thanks to Erick's help, we were able to do it quickly," she said, smiling at Erick. I was silent throughout the procedure. I just couldn't shake the fact that this had very recently been a living child. My thoughts were interrupted by the cry of a baby.

"Oh, another living one," Julie said. The man unloading the truck took a pair of tongs and started beating at something inside one of the containers. "Tony likes to use a pair of tongs and beat the fetus to death," she remarked. "Sam, the guy on the far bench over there, usually breaks their necks. I prefer to drown them."

"And Erick likes to cut their necks with a pair of scissors, then vacuum out their brains," I added. Erick gave me a dirty look.

Julie escorted us to the storage center next. "We used to go around to the universities and different companies and ask what they needed, then dissect the fetuses according to those needs. Now, we operate using the green store concept, which means we'll always have supplies according to demand."

We left Quality Tissue, Inc. after we thanked Julie and Mr. Martin for the time they'd given us. As soon as we got in the car, Erick spoke.

"I'd like to remind you of your promise not to talk about abortion."

I was quiet.

"And of course, the other promise," Erick continued, "lunch, which is actually dinner now." He looked at his watch. "Man, time's passed quickly today."

We went to the nearest restaurant in silence. I ordered a salad, Erick a steak sandwich. I couldn't even think about eating meat.

"Are you going back to the clinic?" I asked, trying not to think about the events of the day.

"I have to, at least for an hour. I said I was going to be there in the evening."

"I'll take you," I offered. "Not that I've changed my mind about giving you rides but because I want to come down with you."

"What for?" Erick asked. "Didn't you see enough already?"

"Yes, but this'll be my last visit to the clinic."

"Good. In that case, we'll leave after about an hour," said Erick, his mouth full of beef.

It was about five o'clock when we reached the clinic. The streets were quiet. The few protestors left looked tired and ready to head home. In the waiting room sat about ten women, all of whom looked older than the last ones I'd seen there. All looked *very* pregnant.

"So, partial birth abortion is usually performed in the evening," I observed aloud.

"Yeah, because it's done by experienced doctors who work other jobs in the morning," Erick explained. "Wait here while I sign in."

I waited in the reception area for about five minutes before Erick came back and said he had to help a doctor perform an abortion, and it might take more than an hour. I said I was willing to wait, as long as I could watch.

I entered the operating room with Erick. A woman in her

seventh month of pregnancy, I'd been told, was lying on the bed. The older doctor performing the procedure frequently asked Erick to help him out as he operated. He pulled the baby slowly out of the womb and, when the head came out, Erick gave him a pair of scissors to sever the neck.

"We won't cut through the neck this time," the doctor told Erick. "Quality Tissue has requested ten fully intact fetuses for next week."

He delivered the whole baby, then put his hands on the infant's mouth and closed its nose. "Here, Erick, come hold the nose. Don't allow it to breathe."

Erick did as the doctor instructed. He was sweating.

"She's bleeding," the doctor said suddenly. "Go get me two units of blood." He turned to me. "You, finish the baby."

"I can't," I replied. "That's murder."

"Erick, leave the baby and get the blood," the doctor ordered again. Looking back to me, he added, "This baby was going to be aborted anyway. Wouldn't it be better for the medical community to benefit from it than to let it go to waste?"

"I still think it's murder," I replied firmly. I had nothing to lose; this was my last visit to the clinic.

Erick returned and the doctor attended to the woman, leaving the baby on the operating table, breathing. Suddenly, the baby started to cry. The doctor looked up quickly—nervously—then grabbed the baby and broke its neck.

At that moment, I realized there was no difference between killing an RM and aborting a baby. As a society, we were well on our way toward the Human Farm and Body Parts Factory.

Chapter 11
The Chip

"Be very careful not to lose the watch," said Markus. "It contains a chip."

I took a watch from him, along with a scrap of paper.

"We kept your name as Randy Livingston to make it easier for you to remember, but you have a new social security number, bank account number, DNA identification number, and cloning code number, all of which you'll find written on this slip of paper. Memorize them, then destroy the slip. You have fifty thousand dollars in your bank account—use it wisely. You're now set to go to the outside world."

"Will I be tracked by the government?" I asked.

"Most likely not. You're not important enough to be followed," Markus replied. "But you still must be careful. When you enter the underground, take the watch off and put it in this special case."

"What if they check the government database and don't find my name there?" I asked.

"The Boss took care of it," he replied.

The Boss, I thought, *must be a very powerful man. No wonder he needs to be careful.*

"We will give you an apartment on the outskirts of the camp. Remember: in everything you do, the most important thing to consider is the safety of the camp." He looked me in the eye and added, "Don't waste your time saving the RMs. You can't do it on your own. Don't do anything crazy and get all our heads chopped off. The best solution is growing this camp. When the underground occupies the city, we will overthrow the government. The Boss wants you to become a contact for him and the camp. He will contact you at the right time. Be careful. Our lives are in your hands."

Promising to be cautious, I set out. It was great to breathe fresh air and see the sky again. I felt like I had been in the underground for so long. The streets above the camp were quiet empty. No one knew that, underneath them, thousands of people were planning a revolution, and that, one day, the streets would erupt like volcanoes. When I reached the end of the camp, I took the watch from its case and put it on.

Not far from the camp, I found my apartment. I entered the outer door of the building and located my quarters. But when I looked for the knob to the door, I found nothing but a surface like a computer screen. I reached out and touched it, and immediately a computerized voice responded.

"Please scan chip."

I brought my watch to the screen.

"Welcome Randy Livingston, status: resident."

The door opened and I stepped through it guardedly, watching in wonder as it closed itself behind me. There were no knobs or locks on the inside either. Reluctant to trust my safety to a computer program, I went straight to the kitchen and grabbed a chair to put behind the door. But as I placed my hands on the chair and began to pull, it spoke.

"Destination requested."

I jumped. On a screen set into the back of the chair, there was a blueprint of the house. I touched the location I wanted to move the chair to and it set off, sliding across the floor to precisely where I had wanted it to go. Suddenly, I was afraid of the whole apartment. I started looking behind all the furniture, trying not to touch anything. All the heavy items had screens implanted into their rears labeled "MovingAid."

The apartment consisted of one bedroom, a living room, a study, and a kitchen. The main door opened into a very short corridor, which led to the kitchen and the living room. The living room had two doors leading to the study room and bedroom.

After acquainting myself with the furnishings, which I was now a little more comfortable with, I went back to the kitchen to check out my food supply. On the refrigerator door was a screen labeled "FoodTracker." I pulled out a jug of milk and the screen immediately showed that the milk had been removed. There was an option on the screen to order food, so I looked up the shopping list. On it, I found the biscuits from the Farm, so I ordered a few tins.

In the study, I found a computer and decided to put in a few hours browsing the Internet. I was amazed at how comfortable the house was. In fact, I had no desire to go outside. *No wonder the streets are empty all the time.* I spent the evening enjoying the house's amenities, and it was quite late before I realized I had go to bed; I needed to get up early for my job interview.

Before bed, I took a shower. The bathtub was amazing—it provided all kind of massages. I went to the bedroom and sank into the mattress. By the side of the bed, there were several buttons that I could use to adjust the mattress firmness and angle in any way I wanted.

As I played with the different buttons, I thought about how we were constantly trying to make life more comfortable. Yes, we'd come a long way in the process, but somehow, in our pursuit of comfort, we'd lost the true meaning of being human. Why did we care so much about making one man's sleep more comfortable, but at the same time, not care about saving the RMs' lives? Why was it so important for us to have the body parts of the RMs to prolong our own lives? Why was it important for some people to live longer, and not important for others to live at all?

As I was thinking, I heard a loud thud, followed by "Destination requested."

The chair behind the door, I thought. *Someone else is here*. I got up and walked slowly toward the living room. A noise came from the direction of the kitchen, so I headed toward it. When I arrived, I found a young man standing in the middle of the room.

"What are you doing here?" I demanded, trying to hide my fear.

"I'm delivering the groceries," the boy replied.

"Why didn't you knock?" I asked.

"Sir, in the account you set up with us, we're allowed direct access to your house. If you wish to change this, please contact us to change your account preferences."

I stood quietly, watching the young man empty his baskets. When he left, I went to the cupboards to see what he'd brought me. *The best biscuits in the world*.

Unfortunately, I'd lost my appetite.

Chapter 12
The Job Interview

His office was plain. Children's drawings peppered its walls, while a wedding photo sat on his desk, but those were the only decorations. I was here so Mr. Dorian, the manager of the Human Farm and Body Parts Factory, could interview me for a job.

I sat as he gathered some pieces of equipment necessary for our talk.

"We'll find everything in a minute, I'm sure," Mr. Dorian said, breaking the uncomfortable silence. Just then, a boxlike machine was wheeled into the room. "Aha!" he said brightly. "You've probably seen this machine before. Who hasn't, right?" He chuckled as he untangled some wires. I smiled.

"Let's scan your chip," he said, and I put my hand inside the machine. It beeped loudly. When the machine had finished printing, Mr. Dorian removed a sheet of paper and began reading.

The interview, I later learned, was not a real interview but a chip-screening session. A person's job history, education, and genetic codes were all stored in the chip.

"Hmm, you only have the basic two required genetic modifications," Mr. Dorian said, looking at me. "Don't you know, Mr. Livingston, that I can find much better workers than you, workers who don't get as tired as you, as hungry as you—workers who are cloned to fit this job?"

"Yes, sir, but I'm a hard worker. I'm sure I'll contribute significantly to your company."

Mr. Dorian smiled sarcastically. "I'll give you a chance," he said after a moment.

I stood and shook his hand. "Thank you very much."

"Don't thank me—thank the person who put in a good word for you with Mr. Smith."

"Mr. Smith?"

"The CEO," Mr. Dorian replied. "He only checks in here about once a year, but he still runs the place."

"Mr. Dorian, I promise you won't regret hiring me."

"I hope not," he said. "You'll be an RM Overseer. Your job will be to maintain the rules. Usually, we try to limit the number of people the RMs see in their lives. We try to keep the same overseer from the birth of the batch to its processing in the factory. When we train a new overseer, we train him on late batches. These batches are fully developed and may be processed within a few months. After the trainee learns the language and meets other requirements, he may be promoted to a lead position.

"So, Mr. Livingston, I offer you my congratulations. I'd like to give you a tour of the Factory."

I walked with Mr. Dorian through corridors that looked familiar. Mr. Dorian was talking about what a great company the Factory was to work for. He had been working there for ten years and was planning to stay until he retired.

When we entered the Factory, Mr. Dorian introduced me

to the workers.

"This is Randy Livingston, the newest addition to the Farm."

Several men in white uniforms greeted me kindly. They all seemed to be nice, normal people, but I couldn't forget that everyone there was my enemy. I had already declared a war against the company, and that included its workers.

Just as the introductions were winding down, an RM entered the processing room, followed by the mean-looking man I'd met during my first visit. The man looked at me, and I could tell he was shocked and unhappy to see me. Mr. Dorian called him over to us.

"Charles, I'd like you to meet Randy Livingston."

"I believe Mr. Livingston and I have met before," Charles replied.

"Oh really? Where?" Mr. Dorian asked.

"At one of our guest tours."

Mr. Dorian turned to me with a look of mild surprise.

"You've been here before?" he asked.

"Yes, and I was impressed with the company then," I lied. "And decided to apply for a job." Charles was staring at me suspiciously.

"Mr. Livingston, it's been a pleasure," Charles said, his tone of voice suggesting that he meant the opposite. "I'm sure we'll meet again soon." His eyes narrowed one last time, then he walked away to meet the RM. *That guy scares me*, I thought as he left. *I can sense he'll be my toughest opponent.*

"Charles is one of our best workers," Mr. Dorian was saying. "He's probably witnessed over twenty thousand processings. He's an excellent employee to learn from."

We watched as Charles called the RM in their strange code.

"Call 8644-77 . . . *Begin* . . . Mission accomplished . . . *End.*"

The RM lay down stiffly on a large conveyor belt, closed his eyes, and answered, "Call . . . *Begin* . . . Mission accomplished . . . *End.*"

A sharp knife dropped from the machine and sliced through his neck. At that moment, I was overcome by a wave of nausea. I wanted to cry, to shout, to punch someone—but I felt the others watching me. Maybe this was part of the job interview.

"Why does the RM say 'mission accomplished'?" I asked, trying to avoid the murderous silence.

"We train them to know that their purpose in life is to die. They know this is the last step in their mission," Mr. Dorian replied. He was clearly unaffected by the scene we'd just witnessed.

"Do you drug them prior to processing?" I asked.

"No, we don't want any drugs in their organs. That's why our product is such high quality."

It must hurt, I thought, then said aloud, "It doesn't seem to hurt them."

"I've watched thousands of processings, and there's never been any crying or expression of pain," Mr. Dorian said. "Of course, there shouldn't be any pain. We're not talking about humans, just RMs, after all."

"RMs don't feel pain," I murmured. I guess pain wasn't a good definition of when human life begins.

I left the Farm later feeling disgusted, depressed, and angry. The killing of the RM had greatly affected me, and I hoped I'd be able to maintain my sanity while working there.

Somehow, I decided, there was a lack of consistency in defining a human being, and that bothered me. Why weren't the RMs considered humans? The line between human and nonhuman was blurred, arbitrary—a function of another man's will, just like abortion, when the identity of a human being was left to the mother's desires and wants.

In this world, family planning was no longer about a woman choosing to have a baby but about anyone buying eggs, cloning them for whatever purpose, then controlling them— even to the point of cutting off their body parts and selling them. *Our humanity must be saved at the egg stage; otherwise, we're on our way to disaster.* I was finally fully convinced that life started at the moment of conception.

Chapter 13
Farm Basic

"Ready for the test?"

"Yes." I took a deep breath.

"Every statement must start with the keyword . . . ?"

"*Call*."

"The keyword is always followed by . . . ?"

"An identifier."

"What are the types of identifiers we have?"

"Specific—such as the RM's number—and general—such as *all*."

"Every statement is enclosed between what key words?"

"*Begin* and *end*."

"List the action verbs."

I listed all the action verbs. Farm Basic Language was limited to words like *sit*, *eat*, *walk*, *sleep*, and so on. The RMs were trained to ignore statements not spoken in Farm Basic Language.

"What other types of statements are there?"

"Alarm statements."

"What conditions trigger an alarm?"

An alarm is one of the limited ways an RM can communicate. I'd heard, however, that there was a secret language, called *Farm Plus Plus*, used to add new vocabulary to Farm Basic. The RMs were taught the commands for learning new words, but the overseers weren't—only a limited number of managers knew the code. It had been about ten years since the last key term had been added to the language, and that was "*mission accomplished.*" Though the language had been frozen since those last words were added, the RMs were still taught the code for learning new language, just in case the need arose. I wished I could get a hold of the code for Farm Plus Plus.

"Mr. Livingston, you have passed the first test," the trainer said. "The second test requires you to talk to an RM. We will record your conversation."

I was led to a small room and was asked to sit on a chair. Through a window in the room, I could see an RM sitting motionless in an adjacent room.

"Here's a speaker and microphone, so you can speak to the RM," the trainer said, handing me the equipment. "Here are the actions we want you to tell the RM to perform."

The woman gave me written instructions in English to translate into Farm Basic, then she left the room. The RM was staring at the wall. I followed the instructions, asking him to sit, walk, stand, etc. I felt as if I was talking to a dog, but even a dog was better than an emotionless RM.

After I'd completed the test, I asked the woman if I could practice some more with the RM while I waited for my results. She consented and I turned my microphone back on.

"Hello," I said to the seated figure, but I realized quickly that he wouldn't acknowledge me if I didn't use the proper language. I tried hard to talk to him; I even tried to get his attention by making all types of noises. But, it was all in vain.

What was I thinking? *Of course I was unable to undo years of brainwashing—unable to reverse the genetic manipulations the RMs had undergone.* I stared quietly at the RM, quickly losing hope, waiting for the results of my test.

"Congratulations, you've earned a perfect score, Mr. Livingston," a voice said, interrupting my thoughts.

"They sure know how to obey the language!" I remarked.

"Yes, we train them, just as in the army, to follow directions."

Just as in the army, I thought. Of course. I needed to come up with a plan that used the limited vocabulary of Farm Basic, or get a hold of the code for Farm Plus Plus very soon.

"Mr. Livingston, Charles will be your trainer for the rest of the day."

I tried not to show my displeasure as Charles entered the training room. He seemed equally unhappy to see me.

"The RM meal is due at 9:30," Charles said brusquely. "We have fifteen minutes. Follow me to the kitchen."

As I trailed Charles, he cast several skeptical glances back in my direction.

"You seem to want to work here very badly, Mr. Livingston."

"Yes, I really need a job," I replied.

"Where do you live?"

"Not that far from, uh, from here." I was going to say *not very far from the outskirts of the camp,* but I caught myself just in time. I wasn't sure why, but I just didn't feel comfortable with Charles.

"The meal is at 9:30?" I said, trying to change the subject.

"Yes. You have to bring it to their room. They're not allowed to leave their room, and haven't since they were born."

"I suppose the room contains facilities to make that

possible," I said.

"They don't use the bathroom."

"They don't?" I was astonished.

"They're engineered not to. The amount of food we give them is calculated for the total amount of activity they perform per day. No extra waste."

Charles took a container full of biscuit bars from a shelf. "Each container contains fifty bars." He opened one container and withdrew a bar. "This is their food for today."

"I don't understand."

"What?"

"How can this biscuit be sufficient to keep the RMs alive and healthy?"

"It has the exact number of calories and food type distribution needed for the activities they perform."

"I see." But really, I didn't. "How can you determine the exact number of calories they need each day?"

"We have sophisticated programs that calculate their dietary needs as a function of the activities performed."

"I see."

"Follow me."

We left the kitchen and walked to a room on the first floor. A group of RMs was sleeping on the floor, which was covered in thick, spongy carpet.

"*Call* All *Begin* . . . Wake up . . . *End*," Charles called.

The RMs stood and formed rows, like army soldiers.

Charles instructed them to perform some exercise for one minute, then gave them their food and asked them to sit and eat. He left the room, saying he'd be right back, and I decided to take the opportunity to talk to the RMs.

"Call All *Begin* . . . Stand . . . *End*," I said.

They stood.

"Call All *Begin* . . . Sit . . . *End.*"

They sat.

"Call All *Begin* . . . Stand up . . . *End,*" I said again, and again, they stood. They all looked the same. I walked over to one and ordered, "*Call Begin* . . . Identify . . . *End.*"

"8645-20."

I took a Post-it note from the training folder Charles had given me and wrote the number on it. I stuck it to the RM's shirt. I moved on to the next RM and asked for his number.

Just then, Charles reentered the room, looked at the RMs, and said, "*Call* All *Begin* . . . Sit . . . *End.*" As they obeyed, Charles turned to me and said, "What do you think you're doing?"

"I'm just practicing the language."

"Listen to me. You have to follow the program exactly. Their food has enough energy only to sustain the activities planned."

"I apologize."

"And besides, routine is important. They've been following this routine all their lives."

"Yes."

Charles scanned the room, his eyes stopping on the Post-it I'd stuck to 8645-20. He ran to the boy and tore the note from his shirt. "What is this?"

"I'm trying to learn their names so I can remember who's who, in case I need—"

"You don't have to know their numbers," he interrupted. He spoke to me calmly and slowly, as if addressing a child. "This batch is well trained. All you have to do is follow this written program."

"I see," I said, feigning understanding.

"I trained them perfectly," Charles said with pride.

"If you don't mind me asking, how do you know who's who when they're young and untrained?"

"I have a special device, called Tracko. Here, let me show you." Charles pulled a small machine from his pocket, about the size of a Palm Pilot. He opened it and placed it next to one of the RMs. The number of the RM showed up on the device.

"You see, it tells you the number of any RM you scan," he explained. "Of course, you can adjust the setting, and it'll tell you everyone who's within a hundred feet of you. It's also connected to the Farm satellite."

"The Farm satellite?"

"The one that tracks the chips of all the employees and RMs. All these doors have scanners," he said, pointing around the room, "and if an RM leaves, an alarm will be triggered." I nodded my understanding.

"Make sure you follow the program carefully," Charles continued. "This batch is scheduled to be processed soon. If you do a good job, you may be promoted to oversee a younger batch, and that means more money for you."

He handed me a sheet of paper and I quickly scanned it. It was a daily activity program for the RMs.

"It doesn't have many activities," I observed. "Do I have to watch over them the whole time they're just sitting?"

"When they're young, yes. At the current stage of your batch, not really. This batch will be processed in two months."

"In two months?"

"Yeah, you're a lucky guy. You'll be able to see a hundred RMs processed in the next two months. You only need to view a thousand before you get promoted."

"Promoted!"

"Don't ask me about the salary. It's too good to be true."

With that, Charles left the room. I stood, staring at the RMs. I had only two months to save their lives. I'd have to come up with a good plan. Everything here seemed to be wired and controlled. How could I save the lives of batch 8645? Kidnapping them wouldn't work. The doors would scan their chips and activate the alarms. My movement was also tracked.

My only option seemed to be to declare war, kidnap all the workers, take control of the whole farm, and save the lives of everyone. And, I had only a very short time in which to do it all. When I'd heard the call "*Call* Randy *Begin* Start Mission *End*," I didn't know that the mission was going to be impossible.

Chapter 14
The Submarine

"Foreten?"

"No, *Fortran*," I repeated.

"Never heard of it," the librarian said.

"What languages *do* you have?"

"French, Italian, Spanish, Portuguese—"

"Computer language," I interrupted, clarifying.

"Hmm . . . let me see." The librarian rubbed his head and entered a new search in the computer. I sighed.

"Do you need help, Mr. Livingston?" said a voice from behind me. I turned and saw Martha, the woman I'd first met when I came to the camp.

"I'm looking for a book on interpreting computer language," I told her.

"What's the application?"

I hesitated, reluctant to share that information with her.

Martha sensed my discomfort and suggested we take a walk together. I accepted her offer, and we strolled quietly to Reflection Square.

"Fortran!" she exclaimed when we were well into the

square. She laughed. "Where have you been?"

I looked at her, surprised, but kept quiet.

"That language hasn't been used since my great-great-grandfather's time," she said. "And you don't look old enough to have been around when he was."

I gazed at the scenery around the square and remained silent. I was growing tense and confused.

"Seriously," she said, her look of amusement fading. "What's the application?"

"Something for work," I said.

"The Human Farm?"

"Yes." Apparently, she knew more than I thought she did.

"Does it have something to do with saving those controlled humans there?"

I nodded.

"In what way?" she asked.

"Well, I plan to kidnap them and burn down the Factory," I told her bluntly.

Martha stopped walking and looked me in the eye. "You're planning to kidnap how many RMs?"

"There are at least twenty batches, and each batch contains approximately a hundred RMs. So, around two thousand, I guess."

"Two thousand!" Martha laughed. "And suppose you're able to succeed with your mission. What are you going to do with them afterward?"

"Bring them here—to the camp."

"Ha! To the camp?"

"Yes," I said, walking on.

"Mr. Livingston—" she called after me.

"Randy."

"Well, Randy Livingston, you need to abandon your plan immediately," she said seriously, walking fast to catch up with me. "You'd be endangering our camp."

"I won't do anything to endanger the camp," I promised.

"How do you plan to bring two thousand people—with chips—to the camp and *not* endanger us? What if you're followed?"

"I won't be followed."

"Oh, really?" she said sarcastically. "This is extremely high risk, Randy. Don't you think the government will notice that two thousand RMs are missing? Don't you think their tracking devices can locate them through the national satellite service?"

"Listen, Martha—"

"OK, suppose you're able to bring them here safely," she said. "Who's going to take care of them here? They can't do anything on their own. They can't even go to the bathroom. We'd need a whole department to calculate the calories they should take in and give them activities to do, minute after minute."

"Martha—"

"They'd be a burden to the camp."

She had a point. Truth was, I'd never thought of the aftermath of my actions. All I'd thought about was saving the RMs from the HeadSeg machine.

"Martha," I shouted in frustration. "What's the alternative?"

"There *is* an alternative—"

"To let them die?"

"The alternative is the camp."

"How can the camp help the RMs?"

Martha stopped walking and turned back to look at me.

"Randy, please listen to me." She took my hands in hers. "The government is evil. Do you think this is the only Human Farm and Body Parts Factory out there? You can't solve the problem by yourself. If you kidnap these RMs, the government will simply raise more. You need a real solution, and the solution is the camp."

"What will the camp do to help?"

"We're creating an underground nation, Randy. We're training the biggest secret army in the world. One day, we'll revolt and take over the government. And then, there'll be no more cloning laws, no more human farms, no more body parts factories. Our plan is working. We are already fifty thousand strong. Give our children ten years, and our army will be big. If you want to help, why don't you work in a place where you can get us important technologies, instead of working in the Human Farm?"

"Ten years is a long time, Martha," I said. "Didn't you tell me that every life is important?"

"Yes, and I believe it is. But saving a hundred RMs could cost the lives of fifty thousand campers."

"What if the camp wasn't involved? Then would you help?"

"I can't see a way to save those drones without involving the camp."

"There is."

"How?"

I resumed walking. "The only thing the RMs can do is follow instructions. And they will be given instructions that will save their lives."

Martha looked puzzled.

"I need microtransmitters and receivers, and I need to create a computer program that sends communication signals to the receivers."

"And the receivers will be given to the RMs?"

"Exactly. I'll insert them in their ears."

"I see."

"The program will give them instructions on how to leave the compound."

"And this is how you'd be able to kidnap them all simultaneously?"

"Exactly." As the plan played out in my mind, I grew more and more excited.

"But I thought the RMs had limited language knowledge. How are you going to communicate with them?"

"The only time an RM is allowed to leave the room he was born in is when he goes to the Factory for processing. Overseers use the command 'Follow,' and the RM will follow them anywhere. Obviously, I can't be everywhere at once for them to follow me."

"There goes your plan of giving verbal instructions via transmitters," Martha said.

"Not so fast. I have a hundred RMs in my care, and I can train them in the next two months to take different paths out of the Farm and Factory."

"How are you going to make them leave their room during your training sessions?"

"They won't leave the room," I replied, thinking fast. "I can draw floor maps on large sheets of paper and practice with them. What do you think?"

Martha looked at me and didn't answer. She seemed uncomfortable. "Let's sit."

"Floor maps," she murmured to herself as we collapsed onto a wooden bench. "What other obstacles are there?"

"Each batch only takes instructions from the assigned trainers. There's a code that introduces the trainer to his batch. I need the RMs of my batch to go to the other rooms, introduce themselves as trainers, then ask the others to follow them. Meanwhile, the computer program will be giving instructions to each RM leader on how to leave the building."

"So you're looking to train brainwashed, biologically modified humans? Big probability of failure there."

"I plan to test the theory before executing it."

"OK, we've identified two great obstacles so far," Martha said skeptically.

"The third," I said, "is calculating the calories needed during the training and the execution of the plan."

"Not to forget," Martha added, "keeping things secret during the training."

"Staying undercover is possible if I have a machine like Charles's Tracko."

"Still risky, and where you are going to get one? They're illegal to own."

"Another obstacle," I conceded, pondering.

"And the fifth obstacle?" she asked.

"The fifth is that the RMs' chips can activate the alarms in every door of the Farm."

"And don't you think they already have an automatic response for that?" Martha asked. "The outside gates could automatically shut once an RM passes a certain point, or the police could be called—the list goes on and on. You don't know what's awaiting you after the alarms ring, do you?"

"No." I looked at my shoes. "Five great obstacles."

"No, no. There are more," Martha said. "Number six: how are you going to transport them? Seven: where are you going to take them? Eight: how are you going to take care of them after that? Nine—"

"Transportation can be taken care of. Large commercial trucks ought to do it." I turned to her with renewed hope. "I have two months to plan it, you know."

"Fine, but where are you going to take them?"

I didn't answer right away. Martha looked at me expectantly.

"We had to go through the whole plan before you'd admit the camp would be involved," she said.

Try as I might, I couldn't see any other way. She was right.

"You don't believe in the camp, do you?" she asked softly.

Do I believe in the camp? I believed they were right in fighting a government that forced them to be cloned and wanted to track the whereabouts of every human. I agreed that the government was evil because it allowed such places as the Human Farm to exist. But I wasn't sure I believed they'd ever be able to win the battle their way.

"Do you?" Martha pressed. "Do you even care about us?"

"I care, but . . ."

"But what?"

"I can't wait," I confessed. "I can't allow the slaughter of innocent humans to continue."

"It won't continue. One day it will stop."

"One day? When?" I asked. "Martha, when?"

"When the Boss sends us the signal."

"The Boss," I murmured.

"We're getting ready," she said. "Follow me. I'll show you."

We left Reflection Square and entered a neighboring quad. There were men standing all around, eyeing us.

"I want you to keep a low profile. I'm breaking the law."

"Martha, breaking the law of the camp?" I joked.

"I have no choice. It's too risky to keep you in the dark." To my surprise, she was quite serious. "I want you to believe in the camp."

"I believe, Martha," I tried to assure her. "I believe."

"Believe in our plan too."

I didn't respond. We continued walking.

"You said that when the camp revolts and takes over the

government, there'll be no more human farms. Is that right?" I asked.

"Yes, no more human farms or body parts factories," she whispered.

"But what are you going to do with the RMs?"

"Free them."

"But who'll take care of them? Wouldn't you create chaos within the newly liberated government? The camp must have a plan on how to deal with the RMs. Otherwise, the outsiders will revolt and take back their government."

Martha didn't respond.

"Don't you think it'd be a good idea to free the RMs? Maybe they could become part of the camp army—they're good at following instructions."

"You see?" she replied. "You don't believe in the camp. I have to make you believe or else . . ."

"Or else what?"

"Do you know what the penalty is for posing a risk to the camp? Life imprisonment."

"Are you threatening me?"

"You're the one who's threatening our safety, Mr. Livingston," she replied.

"Everyone in the camp is a prisoner." I laughed. "There's no freedom anywhere in the world. All I have seen around the camp are people building their own world and getting used to it. All that talk about revolution is a lie."

"Look, we have a plan, and it's a good one. I wish you could be part of it," she said. "You'll have to see it for yourself."

We came to a small house. Martha swiped her hand across a chip reader in the front door, which promptly opened.

"You have a chip in your hand?"

"It's not what you think . . ." she began, turning away from me and entering the house.

The first room we came into was simply furnished. Martha moved a chair to reveal a door beneath it. She scanned her hand again and the door opened.

"Get inside," she said.

"Where are we going?"

"To the submarine."

"The submarine?!" She nodded and gently pushed me toward the stairs. As I descended, I heard her footsteps behind me.

"The submarine is the camp underground," she said. "This is where we keep our defense technology and research labs. We also store weapons—"

"Weapons!"

"For the upcoming revolution."

The stairs were long; it must have taken us five minutes to get down them. When we reached the bottom, I saw what seemed to be a whole other world, more modern than the camp itself. We continued walking for some time and came across a large building, which Martha pointed to.

"In that building, we develop new defense technology," she said. "The Boss used to buy us many weapons."

"Used to?"

"He used to buy them from the black market, but he stopped about ten years ago because he felt that the government was on to him," she explained. "Now, we try to develop our own weapons technology." Martha pointed to another building. "This is where we do research on chips and tracking devices."

That reminded me.

"Why do you have a chip?"

"It's a necessary evil," Martha said, "for the safety of the camp."

"So the campers, like the outsiders, have chips that track

them?"

"Randy, it's not the same," Martha insisted. "First, only a few people have the chips—the people that can enter the submarine—for security. We can't let just anyone enter here who doesn't work here. The majority of the campers don't have the chip."

I didn't respond.

"We are an underground nation at war with the government. When you're at war, there are certain necessary—if unpleasant—precautions that must be taken."

We came to a building that looked just like the White House. I saw what must have been soldiers hiding and creeping around the edifice. We watched as the soldiers shot at different targets for about five minutes.

"Good job! The Capitol team's up next," a man shouted.

The "White House" suddenly disappeared and was replaced by what looked like the U.S. Capitol building. The soldiers regrouped.

"What happened to the White House?" I asked.

"These are just 3-D simulations for army training."

"Simulations?!"

"I'll show you."

Passing hundreds of young men and women in blue army uniform, we entered the chip and tracking device building. A man wearing a white robe came to greet us. The robe looked brilliant against his dark brown skin.

"Hello, Martha," the man said, extending his hand toward her with a welcoming smile.

"This is Randy Livingston," Martha said after warmly shaking the man's hand.

"I'm Jonathan. Nice to meet you, Randy," he said, offering his hand, which I shook firmly. "What can I do for you?"

"I wanted to give him a quick tour of the center," Martha

said.

"Sure, just sign your name in this logbook." Jonathan pointed to a book lying open on a small table behind him.

"Can I borrow your photo scanner for a few minutes?" Martha asked as she signed us in.

"It's in the other room."

She left the room, leaving me with Jonathan.

"I'm looking for a micro cell phone," I explained to Jonathan while we waited. His warm welcome had put me at ease, and I'd decided to see if he could help me.

"Let me see what can I do for you."

Before we got any further, Martha returned and asked me to follow her. We went into the lobby, where she stood and pointed a small device at different spots on the walls.

"OK, let's get inside this hall. I believe it's relatively empty. Oh, one second. I need to get the projector," she said. "Wait here."

After a few minutes, Martha came back, carrying a gadget about the size of her hand.

"This is a laptop and a 3-D laser projector," she explained as she connected the scanner to it. Suddenly, a 3-D image of the outside lobby was projected onto the wall in front of us.

"I don't believe it. It looks as if we're really in the lobby!" I said.

"That's what we use for army training."

"Hey, that could be better than using maps to train the RMs," I said.

Martha's expression suddenly changed. "Let's go give this back to Jonathan."

We headed back to the room where we'd met Jonathan.

"Randy, I have the solution for you," he said when he saw us.

"Solution for what?" Martha asked.

"Here's a micro cell phone. Put it behind your ear." Jonathan gave me a small device roughly one-tenth the size of a watch battery. I placed it behind my ear.

"What are you doing?" Martha demanded.

"I already programmed something in M-D sharp, the language you need," Jonathan continued, ignoring Martha's question.

"Jonathan, thanks for your demonstration, but we have to leave." Martha tried to pull the device from my ear, but I grabbed her hand.

"Mr. Randy Livingston," came a voice came from the earpiece, "leave the room."

I left the room, pulling Martha out with me.

"I knew it was useless to try to put some common sense into you," she said.

"Turn right and walk to the end of the hallway," the voice commanded.

"You are a risk to the camp. Where are we going?"

"Open door number 112 and wait there," the voice said.

I found the room and opened the door.

"This room is top secret, Randy," Martha warned. "You can't go in."

I ignored her, and inside found a room full of electronic devices and computer screens. Jonathan came in shortly after us.

"This is awesome!" I said.

"I thought you'd like it," he said.

"Jonathan, I thought this area was classified," Martha said, objecting.

"I thought you wanted to give Randy a tour," he replied, looking at her meaningfully.

"Oh, of course." Her expression changed suddenly. "Yes,

of course!"

"You want me to continue with the tour then?" Jonathan asked.

"Yes, but briefly, please," Martha replied.

"This is the chip lab," Jonathan began, returning his attention to me. "The government tries to develop chips that can only be tracked by its special devices. This is where we develop our own."

"By the way, as I told you before, it's illegal to own these devices," Martha said sternly. "Only the government has the power to track people."

"Here are some of the tracking devices we've developed," said Jonathan, showing me a shelf that contained different gadgets of various shapes and sizes. "The one on the left is the latest model. It can track any type of chip, even our own.

"Our chips are made of a special material that the government is unaware of, so their tracking devices are not designed to trace it," he continued, "though they are improving their design.

"Over there, we're developing different materials that can hide a chip and prevent it from being scanned by even the best devices." Jonathan picked up a square of cloth from a stack on a table beside him. "This contains a chip that the outsiders wear." He took the tracking device and waved it over the cloth. A screen on the tracker showed that chip number 1245 was within two inches.

"Now, let's put this inside that piece." He pointed to a larger stack of dark-colored cloth, then removed a square of it. He placed the larger piece on top of the smaller one and scanned the pair. The tracker was unable to detect the chip.

The door scanners can be taken care of easily, I realized. I felt Martha's eyes on me, so I looked up.

"Why don't I leave you with Jonathan?" she said quickly. "I'll be right back."

"To block the chip, do you have to wrap this piece of cloth around a person's hand?" I asked, so lost in my thoughts that I'd hardly noticed Martha's comment.

"Not exactly. We've developed this ultra thin, transparent material," Jonathan took out what looked like a roll of tape from a cabinet. "Martha, give me your hand before you leave." Martha turned around just as she was about to walk out the door. She hesitated, then returned, offering Jonathan her hand. He carefully placed a piece of the tape over the center of her palm, then scanned her hand. The tracker didn't respond. He took the tape off and tried again. This time, the screen displayed Martha's name and ID number.

"I'll be back," Martha said again, this time hurrying from the room.

"You need some micro cell phones for your projects?" Jonathan asked, seemingly ignoring Martha.

"Yes. I'm being trained as a spy to the outside world," I said, leaving out my real reason for needing the equipment.

"A spy?"

"Yeah." I took the watch from my pocket that Markus had given me. "The camp police gave me this to use."

"That's one of our models," Jonathan said, walking over to a computer and quickly typing. "Yes, your name is listed there as one of the few who has this device. So, what else can I do to help?"

I asked for everything I could think of.

Jonathan left the room but I hung back, thinking about the RMs. Was it possible to save their lives without compromising the camp's safety? Would they be able to follow directions and leave the buildings? Who was going to put tape on all their hands to hide their chips? When was the best time to kidnap them? Would anyone else be there? How would I transport them? So many questions, but at least I'd gotten a few answers from Jonathan.

"Randy, here's your safe case," Jonathan said, returning. "Nothing can be scanned inside it." He opened the case. "Here's your laptop, complete with 3-D projector and scanner." The laptop, like Martha's, was a little larger than a deck of cards. "Here's another scanner to use in the rooms and hallways." He handed me a ring-shaped scanner that I could wear on my finger. "And here are the earpieces you'll need. Each has a unique number, so you can program them separately. The laptop has a transmission chip built in. Oh! And here are some transparent pads to conceal the chips."

"Thank you so much. I really appreciate this," I said, taking the supplies.

"Now, you just need to fill out these documents . . ." He handed me a few sheets of paper. I filled in all the blanks with Martha's name.

"Thank you so much," I said again. "I'll wait for Martha outside."

Outside the building, I could see Martha at a distance, talking with the camp police. I turned quickly and returned to the building lobby.

"On second thought, I need to leave for an appointment," I told Jonathan, "and I don't see Martha out there. How can I leave the submarine?"

"Here's a loaner card to get you out," he said, handing me a small plastic card. "It will only work once."

"Thank you so much."

I left the building quickly, spotting Martha and two police officers coming toward me. I hid behind a bush.

"Where is he?"

"In that building."

"How could you let him in?"

"I was trying to help . . ."

They entered the building and I started running, but I realized right away that I couldn't remember where to find the exit. As I ran, searching for something familiar, I passed several buildings—including one labeled "Biological Weapons."

After a few minutes of running, I saw a sign that read "To Reflection Square" with an arrow painted on it. I followed the direction the arrow pointed and ran straight into a house, then up the stairs and out of the submarine. When I emerged, I saw the library not far ahead.

"A sharp M.D.?" the librarian asked. "This is a library, not a hospital!"

"No, M-D Sharp programming language," I said.

Finally, I got the book I needed and left the camp. As I walked on the upper streets of the camp in the outside world, I began to think that I might not be able to enter the camp anymore—now that Martha had contacted the police. I was probably wanted for threatening the safety of its inhabitants, a crime whose penalty was life imprisonment. Martha's betrayal had shaken my faith in my mission. Would my mission actually compromise the plan of the camp to overthrow the government? Was I being selfish? Why did I have that nagging feeling in my heart, telling me I should pursue my plan? *Should I follow my heart or my mind?*

I arrived at my apartment exhausted, but there was work to be done. I spent hours reading the M-D Sharp programming manual, then, placing an earpiece behind one of my ears, I programmed some simple code.

"*Call* . . . Randy *Begin* . . . Start Mission . . . *End*," the computer voice transmitted to the microphone.

With that, I remembered my first calling, which was to the mission, and I felt at peace. I went with my heart.

Chapter 15
The Book

"You look tired," one of the Farm's employees said to me while I sat in the cafeteria the following day.

I nodded. I was tired. I had come early to the Farm and spent hours taking digital pictures of the place.

My coworker took wires from the table and wrapped them around his wrists. "I'm trying to maintain my weight," he said to me with a smile. I looked at his tray and saw he had enough food for two people.

"Does it work?" I asked.

"Does what work?"

"The calorie counter." I pointed to the wires.

"Oh those? You bet. They use technology similar to calculating the caloric requirements for RMs."

"Really?" That bit of information certainly piqued my interest.

"Yes, it's very accurate."

"You're kidding!"

"You new here?" he asked, smiling at my curiosity.

"Yeah, I just started work as a trainer."

"I thought so. I haven't seen you before. My name's Ricky. I work in the kitchen."

"In the cafeteria?"

"No, in the RM kitchen. I prepare their meals."

"Oh," I said. "Hey, do you think I could visit you there? Kind of get a feel for how you prepare their food?"

"Anytime." He took a chicken leg and bit into it. "Everybody's nice around here. You're going to like it."

After lunch, I went to my RMs' room carrying my safety case. *Time to test the technology on the RMs.*

"*Call 8645-23 Begin* . . . Stand up . . . *End.*"

One of the RMs stood and I approached him. I carefully attached an earpiece behind his ear, then opened my laptop. I ran the program I had installed the night before—Test 1. The RM started receiving instructions from the computer.

He sat down. He stood up. It was working!

Next, I started the 3-D projector. An image of my apartment hallway was projected. The RMs' expressions changed. They were troubled. I grabbed the tracker Jonathan had given me and went back to 8645-23.

"*Call 8645-26 Begin* . . . Follow . . . *End.*"

The RM followed me as I walked between the simulated hallways. I turned. He turned. I stopped. He stopped. Suddenly, a light appeared on the tracking device. Someone was coming! I ran to the computer. The RM followed.

"Go back!" I shouted, closing the projector. "Go back!" I closed the tracker and put everything in the safe case. The RM remained beside me as the footsteps grew louder. I grabbed his hands and dragged him.

"Call Alarm . . ."

Oh my God! "Don't, please not now."

"*Call 8645-23* . . . *Begin* . . . Stop . . . *End.*"

He immediately stopped.

"Call 8645-23 *Begin* . . . Follow . . . *End*." I went back to where the rest of the RMs were sitting, 23 in tow.

"Call 8645-23 *Begin* . . . Sit down . . . *End*." He sat down.

"Hey, Randy, what're you up to?"

I turned and saw Charles.

"I'm going to send them to their afternoon nap," I said over my pounding heart.

"That's why I came by. I was wondering if you want to join me while they're asleep."

"Sure. Just give me a minute." I sent the RMs to sleep and went into the hallway where Charles was waiting.

"I always try to exercise during the noon break," Charles said. "It's a nice day for a swim."

Even in his friendly mood, Charles looked unattractive.

"So, how do you like your job so far?" Charles asked as we were walking toward the recreation center.

"It's OK. It's a bit slow," I replied. "I'd like more action, more responsibility, more challenge." *And more access to other batches.*

"You'll get all that as soon as you move to younger batches," Charles replied. "I tell you, that job is anything *but* boring. It's hard to teach those young RMs to stop thinking and behaving like humans."

"I bet," I replied. I wanted to ask him why it was so tough. *Is it because they're already humans? How does one teach a human to stop thinking as a human?* The sad part was that the overseers were succeeding. I decided to ask him something else.

"What about you, Charles. How do you like this job?"

"I love it," he replied without hesitation.

"Why?" I really wanted to know what kind of satisfaction a man got from chopping up human bodies.

"This job has brought me nothing but happiness. It has fulfilled my dreams. I've got what every man wants."

"And that would be . . .?"

"For one, I've got the most beautiful woman in the world," he replied.

"Oh, there are tons of them," I commented.

"Not like Christina," Charles said.

"More beautiful than Lisa, or Samantha, or Helen, or . . ."

"What are you talking about? Those women are average compared to Christina," Charles insisted. I was quiet.

"You don't seem to believe me," Charles observed.

"I believe that she might be beautiful, and I believe that you consider her the most beautiful woman in the world," I replied. "But what does she have to do with this job?"

"Christina is a special gift from Mr. Smith."

"Mr. Smith?"

"The big boss."

"Huh?"

"He gave her to me because of the excellent work I've done around here." Charles paused. "Her beauty has been patented. Forty-five artists worked on her design."

I couldn't believe what he was saying.

"I've been waiting for her for a long time. She was born ten years ago and has been in the accelerated growth program. She'll turn theoretical age twenty-one next week, and we'll get married soon after that."

"Huh." I still couldn't believe him. Maybe he was exaggerating.

"Have you proposed to her?"

"No, I don't need to. She was created and designed for me."

"What if she doesn't love you?"

"She will. They did intensive studies on my character and

she's designed to be extremely compatible. She was raised to love no other man but me. She's excited to meet me."

"When's the wedding?"

"July 4."

"I can't wait to meet her."

"Speaking of the wedding, I need to ask you for a favor."

I knew he must have had an ulterior motive for inviting me to spend the noon break with him. I braced myself.

"What?"

"The boss is hosting the reception because he gave her to me. The Farm and Factory will be closed down that day."

"Closed down for your wedding?"

"Yeah, but we can't exactly close it down entirely. Someone has to be here to keep an eye on things. I was wondering if you could work that day."

"Will I be here alone?"

"There will probably be about five other employees here."

I pretended to hesitate.

"OK, I guess," I said finally. *I can handle taking down five employees*, I thought.

"Thank you so much." He patted me on the shoulder. He had already changed into his swim gear, so he merely laid his jewelry down by the side of the pool and dove into the water, leaving me to my thoughts. I glanced down at Charles's pile of jewelry and noticed his watch. It looked a lot like the one Markus had given me.

"Hey, Randy. Why don't you get in the water?" Charles shouted.

"I need to get a towel," I said. He shrugged and dove under. As soon as he'd submerged, I bent down and quickly replaced his watch with mine.

"I'll be back soon—don't leave," I called as he surfaced. "I need to hear more about that Christina of yours."

Watch in hand, I left the recreation center. *Let the door scan the watch,* I pleaded silently as I entered the Farm. It did. *So Charles isn't cloned . . .* But I didn't have time to think more about him. I knew that he had access to any room in the Farm. *Where should I go?* I wondered. *The record room.*

I scanned the doors to the language control room. I needed the codes to teach the RMs new language. I looked all over the room before I finally saw the drawer. *Alarm will sound when this drawer is opened,* warned a sign. I didn't know if I should open the drawer or not. *This guy has access to everything. Should I take the risk or wait for another time?* July 4 was only forty days away. I couldn't wait.

I scanned the watch and the drawer opened by itself. I heaved a sigh of relief and then, inside the drawer, I saw it: *The Human Farm Language: Secret Codes.* I took the book out and stared at it. There were bar codes all over it. I tore off the cover, put it inside another book, and took it out of the room, locking the door behind me. I ran to the locker I'd been issued at the recreation center, dropped the book inside, grabbed a towel, and rushed to the pool. By that time, ten minutes had passed, but it felt like hours. My heart was beating and my face was hot. I jumped into the pool. When I surfaced, the sun was in my eyes and Charles was looking at me. I smiled.

"You're right—it *is* a beautiful day."

I flipped onto my back and floated, thinking of Farm Plus Plus. *What new words should I teach them? Turn left . . . Turn right . . . Down the stairs . . . Up the stairs.* I plunged into the icy water and suddenly remembered I hadn't returned Charles's watch. I pulled myself out of the pool, dried the watch, and carefully made the exchange as Charles swam laps.

"There's a processing in half an hour," he said as I dove

back into the pool. "Why don't you come and see it? You'll get credits toward your promotion."

We showered, dressed, and walked to the Farm, where Charles picked up an RM. We continued on to the Factory. The operators there greeted us.

"*Call Begin* . . . Identify . . . *End*."

"8644-83."

"Call *Begin* . . . Mission accomplished . . . *End*."

"Call *Begin* . . . Mission accomplished . . . *End*," repeated the RM.

The RM was placed on the moving belt. A knife cut through his neck. As I looked at him, I heard a voice within me saying, "Call Randy *Begin* . . . Execute plan . . . *End*."

Chapter 16
The Chair

"Excellent job, Randy," Mr. Johnson said to me.

"Thanks," I replied.

"Randy," Mr. Johnson continued while thoroughly studying me, "you seem to be a different man."

"In what way?" I smiled.

"I don't know, but there's something different . . ."

"I feel different." I smiled. "I've changed my position on abortion."

"How so?"

"I always believed my position on abortion was the right one, until something happened."

"You had your dream?" Mr. Johnson asked. I was ashamed of my dream. I didn't want people to think I based my beliefs on dreams and superstitions. After all, I was a lawyer, a scientist, a logical person.

"No, no, not the dream." I flushed. "Well, the dream encouraged me to look into my beliefs . . ."

Mr. Johnson smiled. "Randy, we don't have to be ashamed of dreams."

I didn't respond.

"My decision to take this case was influenced by your dream," Mr. Johnson continued.

What did I have to lose by telling Mr. Johnson the truth? He wouldn't make fun of me like Erick would. I decided to be open with him.

"Well, the dream created doubts about my beliefs." Mr. Johnson's kind eyes encouraged me to continue. "I was extremely confused, and emotionally upset."

Mr. Johnson cocked his head to the side and looked at me quizzically.

"My journey came to an end yesterday. I now know what I believe in and why."

Mr. Johnson smiled.

"If someone had talked to me a few weeks ago about abortion, I would have treated them as a religious fanatic. But now I realize I was wrong."

"Let me ask you a question: How do you know you're not wrong now?" Mr. Johnson asked.

"Well, now it *feels* different," I began.

"It feels different?"

"I mean, how I feel about myself. I used to be confident about what I believed, but now, I'm confident in a different way. I've looked at the data and I've examined the evidence, and now I believe I'm walking the right path. But, I'm still open to change and debate. There's so much to learn."

"Interesting, Randy," Mr. Johnson replied. "You know, I'd like to continue this discussion with you, but I'm very busy with clients today. What do you say to dinner at my house this evening?"

I accepted the invitation.

***

Mr. Johnson lived in a nice neighborhood. He answered my knock with a warm smile.

"Welcome, Randy. I'm glad you were able to make it."

I entered a beautiful living room to find two women sitting on couches. One of them was in her late forties or early fifties. The younger one looked to be in her late teens or early twenties, and she was gorgeous. She had thick blonde hair that fell—straight and shiny—to just below her shoulder blades. Her eyes were deep blue and her smile was brilliant.

Mr. Johnson introduced me to his wife and daughter.

The older woman got up from her seat and extended her hand to me. "Oh, Randy, I'm so glad you were able to make it. John has told me so much about you." She seemed kind, just like her husband.

The young woman didn't move from her seat, so I went to her and offered my hand. "Hello."

But she didn't accept the shake. I let my hand down, awkwardly, after a moment.

"Pleased to meet you. I'm Victoria," she said, flashing me a radiant smile.

"Pleased to meet you too," I said, choosing my words carefully. I was puzzled by her behavior, though I had to admit she seemed nice enough. How could a kind father and mother not teach her to shake a person's hand when it was extended? I decided not to let it bother me—after all, Mr. Johnson *was* my employer, and I was really interested in getting a permanent position with him when I graduated from law school and passed the bar.

I sat next to Victoria.

"John told me you had a dream that caused him to take

the abortion case," Mrs. Johnson said. "What was your dream about?"

"Gloria, I've already told you–" Mr. Johnson interrupted.

"John, please," Mrs. Johnson objected, then turned back to me. "My husband refuses to tell us about your dream."

"I don't think it's a good idea," Mr. Johnson said. "I hate to admit it, but after you told me about it, I couldn't sleep. It disturbed me. I don't want Victoria to hear about it."

"Dad," said Victoria, "you don't need to worry about me. Besides, we can all afford to lose a night of sleep if it's such a good dream." She looked sweetly in my direction. Her dad crossed the room and sat by her side. He hugged her and gave her a kiss on the cheek.

"Maybe later, after dinner." He took a glass of water and lifted it to her mouth. *That's weird*, I thought.

"So what was the dream about?" Victoria asked, undeterred. There was something about the way she asked her question that was odd. She would look at me from the side of her eyes and wouldn't turn her body completely toward me.

"It was about the future."

"The future?" she said stiffly.

"Let's postpone the conversation until after dinner," Mr. Johnson pleaded. "Randy, the bathroom is right down the hall if you'd like to wash your hands."

Grateful for the excuse to end the conversation, I excused myself to go to the bathroom. The family was nice, but I didn't know what to make of Victoria.

When I returned to the living room, the two ladies had already gone in and Mr. Johnson stood alone, waiting for me. He led me to the family's spacious dining room, where Victoria was seated at the head of the table. Her parents sat on either side of her. Mrs. Johnson had prepared a dinner of roast beef, vegetables, and rice. We dished up and began eating.

Mr. Johnson took a piece of beef on his fork and put it in his daughter's mouth. I involuntarily stopped chewing and stared. *Why is he feeding her?* Realizing the awkward silence in the room, I swallowed the food in my mouth and tried to get some answers.

"Do you have any siblings?" I asked.

"Yes, I have a younger brother. His name is Joshua," Victoria replied.

There goes the only child theory! Then why did they spoil her like that?

"How old are you, if I may ask?"

"Eighteen."

"Are you done with high school?" I asked.

"Yes, and now I'm attending the Johnson & Johnson Law School," she replied.

"The Johnson & Johnson Law School?" Her parents laughed.

"My dad is teaching me law," she explained, smiling. "I'm planning to go to college next year, but I'm taking a year off, and my dad is teaching me. He gives me two hours a day of his time."

"Why don't you go directly to college?" I asked.

"I'm waiting for my brother to graduate from high school so we can go to college together."

I wanted to ask why, but I decided not to pursue it.

"I'm sure the Johnson & Johnson Law School is great," I said instead. "You're getting your lessons from one of the best lawyers in Chicago."

"It *is* a great school, especially since my dad promised to take me to court with him when he goes."

"So, will you attend the abortion trial?"

"I hope so. Right, Dad?"

"We'll see," Mr. Johnson replied as he took another chunk of beef and put it in his daughter's mouth.

Victoria smiled at me as she chewed and I smiled back. I really couldn't understand her. She would chew her food, then wait until either her mom or dad put another bite in her mouth. Her parents seemed to shower her with love continuously. I wondered how her younger brother handled all the attention his parents gave her.

"Excuse me, Mom?" Mrs. Johnson leaned close and Victoria whispered something to her.

"Sure, sweetheart," her mother replied. She got up from her seat and walked around Victoria's chair, stopping right behind her daughter and placing her hands on the chair back. She pulled the chair from the table and I finally understood. Victoria was in a wheelchair.

"Oh, I didn't see the wheelchair," I murmured as the two ladies left the room.

"Victoria is quadriplegic," said Mr. Johnson, spooning some more rice onto his plate.

"Oh, that explains it," I said. "I'm sorry to hear that. How did it happen?"

"She was born that way," Mr. Johnson replied.

"Oh!" I was at a loss for words. Suddenly, I felt bad about judging her as spoiled.

"I'm glad both she and her brother are interested in law," Mr. Johnson said absently. "I think she'll make the better lawyer." He smiled.

Mrs. Johnson and Victoria returned, the mother pushing her daughter back to her seat at the head of the table.

"What law school are you planning to attend?" I asked.

"The University of Chicago, if God wills it," she replied.

"If there's a will, there's a way," I found myself saying.

"But I want God's will, not mine, to be done," she answered.

"I don't believe in God," I replied automatically. It had been a habit of mine to avoid any discussion of God by stating that I didn't believe in him. In reality, I didn't know if I believed in him or not. I just didn't think about it much.

"Why not?" Victoria asked.

"If God exists, why is there so much evil in the world?" I gave her another answer I had memorized. I'd accepted the questions I had about God as justifications for why he didn't exist. Admittedly, I was never sincere in finding answers to my questions, but I was satisfied with the question as an end point of my research.

"God is with us in the suffering," Victoria said in refutation. Then she began lecturing, using colorful, cozy, Christian language. I looked at her while she was talking and I couldn't believe her. Why would she want God's will to be done, when God already had willed her to be quadriplegic?

"What about all the innocent children dying from hunger every day?" I asked. "Is God in *their* suffering too?"

"God is still the answer to their problems," she replied. "Funny that the people who ask the question are not the people going through the pain and suffering but the outsiders. Why don't you ask the people who suffer, and they'll answer you. I'm quadriplegic, and I know God is with me. You can't ask the question and then refuse to hear the answer." She was getting emotionally worked up, then added, "I thank him for making me quadriplegic."

"I don't understand why someone would thank God for such a horrible thing," I blurted out.

"It's not horrible. It made me become the person I am right now. I learned to trust in God more, and to experience joy in a different way," she replied. "I'm a happy person. I sense God's presence all around my chair. Do you sense his presence in your life?"

I looked at Mr. Johnson, and he seemed to be OK with our conversation. He was neither offended by my argument nor visibly uncomfortable with Victoria's. It occurred to me then that this family would never put me down because of what I believed—they would never make me feel wrong for having strong feelings, or for being confused about my feelings. They would always encourage me to open up and express myself.

"Are you happy?" Victoria asked again.

I felt like Victoria was able to open my heart and see what was inside. And what was in there were doubts about God. *Was* I a happy person? I was happy with being an atheist. Being an atheist was the way to keep the lid on a can of worms. For the rest of my life, I could keep using questions as answers, or I could try to find some real answers. I chose to open up to her.

"I don't know. After I had this dream, I felt something outside of me was causing it," I replied honestly.

"I always felt God was leading you. I believe your dream is from him," Mr. Johnson remarked. "You know, Randy, you told me this morning that you had altered your position about abortion. You changed your beliefs because you were able to ask the questions and to find answers for them. You need to do the same thing about all your beliefs."

"Especially beliefs about God and eternity," Victoria added. I had never met a woman with such enthusiasm for God. I felt I couldn't argue with her—her words were backed by personal experience. I had nothing to say to her.

"I guess I have to admit I haven't done enough research on God," I said, though I didn't plan to do any research on him. I had enough going on in my life; I had no time for God.

"And whenever you want to start researching, I'm willing to help in any way," Victoria replied.

"Thanks. I'll keep that in mind." I continued eating. I wanted to change the subject. "This food is wonderful, Mrs. Johnson."

"Oh, thank you, dear. I'm glad you like it," Mrs. Johnson replied.

After dinner, Mrs. Johnson played the piano while Victoria sang some religious songs. I was familiar with one song she sang: "He's Got the Whole World in His Hands." I still didn't understand why, if God had the world in his hands, there was evil in it, like Victoria's wheelchair? But that chair—to Victoria—didn't seem to be a burden. Actually, it seemed to be affecting me much more than it was her.

Victoria had a wonderful voice.

"He's got the little tiny babies in his hand."

Does God have the babies in the cell tubes in his hand? Did he have in his hands the baby that was still breathing when that crazy lady at Quality Tissue, Inc. drowned it? Did he have the baby in his hands that Erick aborted? Does God care about the little tiny babies?

Victoria continued singing, "He's got you and me, brother, in his hands."

Me? God's got me? I was disturbed by the idea—the idea of losing control. I had already lost control with my dream. Someone other than Randy Livingston had made me have the dream. Someone else was leading my life, and I was not happy about it.

At the end of the song, I thanked the family and left for the evening. Mr. Johnson walked me to my car.

"Randy, I'm so happy you got to meet my family," Mr. Johnson said. "I wanted to share something with you." I stopped, waiting for him to speak.

"You know, about Victoria . . . I had encouraged my wife to abort her when we found out the chances were good she'd be quadriplegic. But, thank God, he prevented that from happening. She's really a blessing. I can't imagine life without her."

"But, Mr. Johnson . . ." I wanted to say something more, but I stopped.

"What is it, Randy?"

"I don't know if I should ask," I replied hesitantly.

"Please, ask," Mr. Johnson insisted. "I love it when you ask questions. I enjoyed our conversation. I hope we didn't push any of the God talk on you."

"Victoria is a very beautiful young woman. She has a pleasant personality. It's easy to see why you love her. But what if she were mentally handicapped? What if she couldn't talk back to you?"

I could tell Mr. Johnson was listening to me with his whole heart.

"I would love her still."

"Not as much, though," I suggested.

"Before she was born, I asked myself if I would be able to love a girl who couldn't walk and who lived all her life sitting in a chair. I wasn't even thinking of mental handicap but about the chair." He paused. "The chair has taught me much about life. I thank the good Lord for it. You know what? Victoria was right to say that most people who question the pain and suffering of others are not those who suffer themselves but outsiders. You can't understand or accept it unless you are sitting in her chair.

"You know, we need to fight for people like Victoria, Randy. We need to win this case."

We shook hands and I got into my car. On the way back

to my dorm, my mind was whirling. *Who am I to question Victoria's worth?* She seemed to be happy. Her mere presence had made me feel good. Her beautiful voice still echoed in my ears. "He's got the whole world in his hands."

Chapter 17
The Court (Court Day #1)

Erick started dating Julie from Quality Tissue, Inc. I couldn't understand how he could go out with a child killer.

"She's just doing her job," he said.

"But she drowned that baby!"

"That baby was already dead."

"He was alive when she drowned him," I insisted. "I don't know why I'm arguing with you. You're no better than her. As a matter of fact, you're worse."

"She's a good woman. She makes me feel good about myself . . ."

"Of course she wants to do that, because she's in the murdering business too."

Erick rolled his eyes and changed the subject.

"Why are you wearing a suit today?"

"I'm going to court."

"For the Christ Hospital case?"

"Yes."

"I wish I could go."

"You are going. We're calling you as a witness."

"A witness to what?"

"Many things, including Quality Tissue, Inc."

"You'll get into trouble if you do that. Mr. Martin called Mr. Sampson, and he learned that we lied to him about Mr. Sampson sending us there for research. I guess they'll use that against you guys to reduce your credibility," Erick said.

"Thanks for the warning."

"It wasn't a warning; it was a trade-off."

"A trade-off for . . .?"

"Don't put me in the witness chair."

"I'll think about it," I said. "I'm late. I've got to meet Mr. Johnson at the office before we head to the courthouse."

***

"Good morning, Randy," Mr. Johnson greeted me. "Ready for court?"

"Yes, I'm excited, but I'm very nervous too."

"Me too," Mr. Johnson admitted.

"But you're the greatest lawyer in town," I replied. "You couldn't be nervous."

"This is the hardest case I've ever dealt with, partly because it's so highly politicized. By the way, would you like to ride with me? It's hard to find parking near the courthouse."

"Sure, I'd love to."

Mr. Johnson drove a van. Another lawyer sat in the front, so I climbed into the back. When I opened the door, I noticed Victoria already sitting back there. She was wearing a long skirt and a jacket, and looked very professional. Her wheelchair was strapped in.

"Hello," I greeted her. "I wasn't sure you'd be coming today."

"Hi. My dad promised to bring me every day." She smiled.

"I'm excited about the whole case."

"Me too."

Victoria quietly listened to the conversation between her father and the other lawyer up front—a large, dark-skinned man named Mr. Maxwell.

When we got out of the van at the courthouse, Mr. Johnson released Victoria's wheelchair from the special hooks inside. He carefully wheeled her down the ramp he had extended from her side of the van moments before. I marveled at the amount of work it took for her dad to bring her to court with him. He had to feed her and be with her at all times. I thought her presence would almost certainly be a major distraction for him, but I didn't say anything, especially since she was so excited about being there.

After entering the courtroom, we met and greeted members of the Christ Hospital administration. Their spirits were high. Mr. Johnson took his place behind the counsel's table. Mr. Maxwell sat next to him, and I sat next to Victoria in the row behind them.

The judge entered the room and I heard Victoria whisper, "Yes, let's start!"

I hoped she wouldn't continue to play commentator throughout the case.

"Will the plaintiff deliver its opening statement?" the judge asked.

"Yes, Your Honor." A tall man stood up and moved to the center of the room.

"Identify yourself for the record."

"My name is Samuel Nicholas, and I, along with my team, represent the state of Illinois. The state has been receiving numerous complaints by women, all Illinois citizens, that Christ Hospital is refusing to provide them with abortion services in accordance with Illinois Law 1105_ILCS_12.9. We have submitted to the court the affidavits of twenty women, all denied treatment by Christ Hospital. Christ Hospital has been turning these women away with the unsubstantiated excuse that abortion is contrary to its religious beliefs.

"Although some hospitals, like Christ Hospital, are owned by religious institutions, they themselves are *not* religious institutions; they must follow all regulations and laws related to hospitals. Abortion is a medical necessity for both a woman and her fetus, and it's a violation of a woman's constitutional rights for the hospital to refuse to provide a service that is so necessary. Your Honor, it is very important not to give exceptions to hospitals that claim special treatment because of religious beliefs. This will lead to an increase in illegal abortions, an increased mortality rate among women, an increased number of crimes committed by those who oppose a woman's right to choose an abortion, and definitely strip women of their federal and state rights to control their own bodies.

"When it comes to medicine, we must put aside philosophies and beliefs and do what is scientifically and medically right. Therefore, we ask this court to rule that Christ Hospital, within one month, must establish a program to provide abortion at any legal stage during pregnancy. We are simply asking the court to require the hospital to obey existing law."

Samuel Nicholas sat down. His speech was charged. A month ago, I would have applauded him, but now there was something dishonest about his remarks—he had no regard for the humanity of the unborn child.

"Will the defendant's counsel identify himself?" the judge asked.

Mr. Maxwell stood up and moved to the center of the

courtroom.

"Counsel Matthew Maxwell from the Johnson Law Firm, representing Christ Hospital, Your Honor." When Maxwell mentioned the Johnson name, the judge looked at Mr. Johnson and nodded his head.

"Counsel, you may proceed with your opening statement."

"Your Honor, the state passed a law that forces all hospitals to perform abortions. In doing so, the state is forcing Christ Hospital to perform acts that are against its core principles of medicine, science, and humanitarianism. The hospital believes that human life begins at the moment of conception, and that abortion is murdering innocent children. Therefore, the hospital refuses to comply with state statute. In enacting and enforcing the statute, the state has violated the rights of the hospital, which is a private institution, to uphold its core values."

Mr. Maxwell paused for a few seconds. "With this law, the state has also violated the civil rights of the unborn—chiefly the right to life. At the same time, the state is endorsing a procedure that's detrimental to the well-being of the mother. Except for the limited cases where the mother's life is in danger, the abortion procedure is anything but a medical necessity. It is dangerous to the mother's health and emotional well-being. Alternatives, such as adoption, are available to meet the economic, social, and emotional needs of both the mother and her child.

"To force Christ Hospital to perform this barbaric procedure is not only contrary to the interest of the hospital but also to all the doctors involved. Having the same doctors sustain life *and* take it away undermines patients' trust in those doctors. As a matter of fact, Christ Hospital is the number one choice of thousands of Illinois citizens to deliver their babies, chiefly because of the respect the hospital shows for life, regardless of age—whether a seven-month-old fetus or a seventeen-year-old mother—and regardless of residency, whether outside or inside the womb. Christ Hospital will continue to refuse to kill innocent people. Your Honor, the defense will bring in experts who will prove that life begins at the moment of conception."

As Mr. Maxwell was taking his seat, Samuel Nicholas stood up and said, "Your Honor, I object to bringing any of these so-called experts to this court."

"Why so, counselor?" the judge asked.

"For one, this case is not about abortion but about the fact that Christ Hospital is refusing to comply with Illinois Law 1105_ILCS_12.9 due to its religious beliefs. Any discussion about the legality of abortion is outside the scope of this proceeding. This proceeding is to determine whether a private hospital has the right to refuse necessary medical procedures required by the state."

"Your Honor." Mr. Maxwell stood up. "We plan to show how the medical experts of Christ Hospital believe this procedure is far from a medical necessity, and that it kills innocent children. The reason it continues to refuse to comply with this law is because it goes against sound science and medicine. As a medical institution, Christ Hospital has the right to disobey any law that forces it to violate sound medical procedures and beliefs."

"Your Honor," said Mr. Nicholas, "our lawmakers have listened to the medical experts and concluded that abortion is a medical necessity. A law was put in place to protect the women of Illinois from extreme religious groups, like those who own Christ Hospital. Christ Hospital's only motive for disobeying this law is religious and has nothing to do with science."

I was happy with what Mr. Maxwell had said. Liberals—and I still counted myself as one—have the tendency to marginalize conservative ideals because, they say, they're merely religious beliefs. I was going to listen to all the arguments, though, before I made my decision. *I was learning to be an honest liberal*, I thought.

One more thing I was learning about extreme liberals was that they refused to believe that conservatives had motives other than religion. To liberals, conservatism was synonymous with religion, which, in their view, was synonymous with irrational beliefs. By their way of thinking, you simply couldn't be a religious or conservative person and also be scientific and logical. Liberals, on the other hand, saw themselves as liberated from the bondage of religion and wish-washy thinking, and therefore, they alone were capable of clear thinking and rational deliberation.

"Do I understand you to say, Mr. Maxwell," the judge said, "that because Christ Hospital doesn't believe abortion is a medical necessity for a woman, and because it believes that a fetus is a human being, it refuses to perform abortion?"

"Yes, Your Honor."

"And you will bring experts to court to prove that abortion is not a medical necessity?" the judge continued.

"Yes, Your Honor. In addition—"

"Your Honor," Mr. Nicholas interrupted, "those experts were heard by our lawmakers, and the lawmakers concluded that abortion *is* a medical necessity that *must* be provided by every medical institution in the state. This court should not allow Christ Hospital to ignore the legislative process."

"We are not bypassing the system," Mr. Maxwell responded. "We're the ones being sued here."

"Mr. Nicholas," said the judge, "I'm afraid I agree with

Mr. Maxwell. I don't see a problem with the defense approach to the case. I'll allow the experts to testify."

"But, Your Honor, our lawmakers already listened to those experts."

"Counselor, I've reached my decision."

"In addition, Your Honor, I'd like to have experts testify that abortions involve the killing of innocent people—"

"Your Honor, I object. That issue is irrelevant to this proceeding."

"Why is that, counselor?" asked the judge.

"The U.S. Supreme Court has already determined that unborn children are not persons. It is meaningless to talk about killing innocent people when those people are not persons. Mr. Maxwell's experts may insist that the glob of tissue within a mother's womb is a legal person, but they cannot avoid the explicit declaration by the U.S. Supreme Court that an unborn child is not a legal person."

"It is true," argued Mr. Maxwell, "that the Supreme Court did not grant legal personhood to unborn children, but it said nothing about whether or not they are human beings."

"That's ridiculous!" said Mr. Nicholas. "I'm sure if they were human beings, the court would have granted them legal personhood."

"I don't think so," said Mr. Maxwell, smiling. "And we know that the Supreme Court makes mistakes. In 1857, the Supreme Court declared in the *Dred Scott* case that slaves are not legal persons. I'm sure Mr. Nicholas does not accept this interpretation of the Constitution, although that decision was the most explicit statement about the personhood of black people made until more modern times." Mr. Maxwell paused. "I'm sure Mr. Nicholas favors more recent statements of equality, although they may not be as assertive and explicit as those of the *Dred Scott* court."

"Your Honor, we know that the Supreme Court has completely changed its position about slavery," Mr. Nicholas responded, reddening, "but it has never changed its interpretation about the personhood of fetuses."

"We hope the Supreme Court will reverse its position about the legal personhood of unborn children," Mr. Maxwell said, "but Christ Hospital refuses to kill the unborn not because they are legal persons but because they are human beings. The medical experts we will bring to this court will prove that."

"I've heard enough objections to the defense's intentions. I see no problem with them," the judge said. "Counselors Maxwell and Nicholas, I would like you to give me the list of all experts and witnesses you intend to bring to court. Our next session is next Wednesday at 9:00 a.m."

With that, court was adjourned for the day.

Mr. Johnson got up and gave Mr. Maxwell a firm handshake. "You did an excellent job," he said.

"I'm glad we used this strategy instead of religious rights versus state rights," Mr. Maxwell replied.

"They weren't expecting it," Mr. Johnson agreed. "Here, take a look at this preliminary list. Several of their witnesses were experts on religious institutions."

***

On the way back from court, Mr. Johnson and Mr. Maxwell talked nonstop. I sat next to Victoria, silently thinking about the day. I, too, was happy with our strategy. Yes, Christ Hospital was owned by a religious institution, but it strongly and sincerely believed that a fetus was a human being, and that abortion killed an innocent child. It wouldn't be fair for the court to decide the case without listening to our experts.

"Randy, you seem very excited about this case," Victoria said, interrupting my thoughts.

"I am," I replied.

"That puzzles me," she said.

"The fact that I'm excited puzzles you?"

"Precisely."

"Why, if I may ask?"

"Because I can't reconcile the fact that you are against abortion, yet don't believe in God," she explained.

"Oh, I see." I was not expecting that. "So, you agree with Mr. Nicholas that pro-lifers are people motivated by religion and not by science and logic?"

"Yes."

"Yes?"

"We are motivated by our religion," she explained, "but our religious beliefs do not contradict science and logic."

Maybe I wasn't right about conservatives after all. Maybe they *are* motivated by religious beliefs. And when it came to abortion, maybe it was pure luck that their religion didn't contradict science and logic.

"True, in this case," I said. "The religious beliefs of Christians don't conflict with science and logic, but you can still treat them independently. For instance, we can both agree about the conclusion but arrive at it differently—with me using science and logic and you using your own religious beliefs, whatever they happen to be."

"I don't see how science and logic alone will lead you to the conclusion that abortion is wrong," she replied.

"I'm a nonreligious, liberal person, and science and logic were what led me to that conclusion," I said.

"How?" she asked.

"Science and logic say that a fetus is a human," I replied

"OK," she said. "What's wrong with killing humans? What's wrong, say, with killing a ten-year-old boy?"

What a stupid question, I thought. "It's wrong," I said, shrugging my shoulders.

"How do science and logic help you come to the conclusion that it's wrong to kill a ten-year-old boy?" she asked again.

I didn't have an answer to her question because it seemed obvious. I acted as if it was rhetorical, so she continued talking.

"Science and logic are tools," she continued, "but the ultimate moral decisions are not made by using them. I mean, if there is no life after death, if a human is just like any other animal, then why is it wrong to kill another human? We kill animals to eat their meat, to wear their furs, or simply because we don't want them to live in our houses. If it serves our needs, what's wrong with abortion, even if it kills humans?"

"You have a good point," I admitted. "But I still think I'm consistent in my belief about abortion. I believe it's wrong to kill a human. I believe that humanity starts at the moment of conception. And, therefore, I believe abortion is wrong."

"Yes, you are consistent, but you still don't know why you believe what you believe."

"Of course I know why I believe what I believe," I objected.

"You don't know why it's wrong to kill a human," she replied with a smile. "And that puzzles me. I, for one, believe that God is our creator, and that our value as human beings comes from him. He said, 'Thou shalt not kill,' and he urged his commandments into our consciences.' That's why, intuitively, you know that killing a ten-year-old is wrong. You needed some science and logic to let you know that a fetus is as human as a ten-year-old." Her expression changed and she asked me bluntly, "Why don't you just admit you're not actually governed by science and logic?"

"What else is motivating me?" I asked sarcastically.

She looked at me and smiled. "That dream of yours."

Again, I was not expecting her reply.

"The dream may be the ultimate motivation," she added, "but science and logic are the tools."

Victoria was right. The dream of the future was my ultimate motivation to stop abortion.

Was Mr. Nicholas right? I asked myself. No, he was wrong. A man has the right to be motivated by his passion, his dreams, his religious beliefs, and his philosophies. Even Mr. Nicholas was motivated by some sort of passion or nonscientific beliefs. People's sources of motivation should not be used against them. It's the arguments themselves that we must listen to and examine, and the scientific evidence is clear: fetuses are human. As far as why it's wrong to kill a ten-year-old boy, that was something I needed to think more about.

Chapter 18
The Senator (Court Day #2)

"What's wrong with killing a ten-year-old boy?" I asked Erick

"Are you starting another lecture about abortion?" Erick asked.

"No." I sipped the coffee he'd made. He never prepared himself breakfast. He usually ate on the run, but today, he was up early, so I joined him at the table. "It was a question Victoria asked me."

"Victoria?" Erick put his mug down on the table. "A new lady friend?"

"Mr. Johnson's daughter."

"The daughter of a famous lawyer, a good catch. Not bad, not bad . . ."

"She's young and handicapped, and . . ."

"Whoa. Calm down, man." Erick smiled. "And she wants to know why it's wrong to kill a ten-year-old boy?"

"No. Yes. Well, she knows why it's wrong, but she wants to know why I believe it's wrong."

"Man, it's a no-brainer." Erick sipped some coffee.

"Enlighten your atheist friend."

"First and foremost, it's illegal."

"Wow. I'm totally enlightened now," I said sarcastically.

"Seriously, man. What else is there to it?"

I started laughing.

"What's so funny?" Erick said.

I continued laughing.

"I got it, man." Erick jumped from his seat. "I got it. It's cool. Remember Philosophy 112?"

"Sure, with Professor Jackson."

"Yep, Dr. Jackson. Remember about how civil societies start and the thing about the 'veil of ignorance'?"

"Yes, I remember . . ." I was delighted. Now I knew why it was wrong to kill a ten-year-old boy. "Our laws derive from our civil society." I sipped some more coffee. "And if there is no civil society . . ."

"Then it's not wrong to kill a ten-year-old boy." Erick laughed. "That's why we're called civil people. We honor our contracts."

I was happy to have an answer to Victoria's question. I didn't need God to help me respect human life. I left my coffee unfinished and ran out of the apartment to meet Mr. Johnson.

***

Victoria was dressed in a blue skirt and white blouse. Her hair was styled to the side. I was glad to see her. I couldn't wait for the opportunity to tell her why it was wrong to kill a ten-year-old boy.

I didn't have to wait long. Before leaving for court, we waited for another firm lawyer to show up. Mr. Johnson and Mr. Maxwell were standing outside the van. I got inside and sat next to Victoria. We stared at each other and smiled.

"What?" I found myself saying.

"Nothing," she said. With that, we sat quietly for a few more seconds.

"Well, OK. Have you figured out why it's wrong to kill a ten-year-old boy?" she asked, still grinning. She was waiting for my answer as much as I'd been waiting for her question.

"As a matter of fact, I have." I explained to her the argument about the establishment of civil societies, how we all hide ourselves under a veil of ignorance, where we strip ourselves of personal knowledge gained from gender, race, social status, etc. We all enter into a contract to protect each other's lives. We consent to such a law because the veil of ignorance makes unanimous consent possible. "Our laws are derived from our civil society," I explained.

"Oh," she said, dropping her jaw.

"Didn't expect an answer that doesn't include God, did you?" I said.

She didn't answer.

"You know what? Religious people don't have a monopoly on morality." I smiled. I was happy to demonstrate to a fanatic Christian that I could be an atheist and a moral person at the same time. I didn't need God.

"Randy and Victoria, I want you to meet Laura Smith, the newest addition to our defense team," Mr. Johnson said, interrupting our discussion.

Laura was a young and beautiful woman in her early thirties.

"I'm glad to meet you both," said Laura.

"Likewise," I said.

I had to move to the back seat of the van so Laura could sit next to Victoria. I sat quietly throughout the ride, listening to their conversation.

When we arrived at the courthouse, the police were

present everywhere, and security was heightened.

"They're calling the senator to the stand today," commented Mr. Maxwell.

"A state senator is coming to court? Which one?" Victoria asked. She seemed excited about the idea of seeing a state senator testify.

"Senator Maria Anderson."

Senator Maria Anderson, in my opinion, was a successful woman in every sense of the word. She was one of the state's top lawyers. She was—or at least seemed to be— happily married to a similarly successful man. She had a charismatic personality, and she was very attractive. When she first ran for election, she was often talked about in the press on campus. She was young, beautiful, and real. I voted for her. And I was excited to meet her.

The prosecutor called the senator to the stand as soon as the day's proceedings began.

"Senator Anderson," Mr. Nicholas said to her after she took the oath. "You were the senator who authored and sponsored this bill?"

"Yes, but I'd like to point out that this bill was approved by 95 percent of the Senate—a truly bipartisan effort, and an excellent example of how members from both parties can work together in serving our community." She was polite and professional, a good politician.

"Senator Anderson, why did you introduce this bill to the Senate?"

"It was necessary for the protection of women and the advancement of women's health. It's very important to give a woman and her doctor control over her reproductive health by giving her access to all major hospitals."

"We know that, before this bill was introduced, many institutions offered abortion services to women, anyway.

Right?"

"Yes."

"So, why require all hospitals to perform abortions? Aren't our existing abortion clinics sufficient to give women control over their reproductive health?"

"A woman should be able to work with her primary doctor and her doctor's hospital for all of her medical needs, not be forced to go to a clinic with an unfamiliar staff.

"In addition, this law protects women's right to privacy. Most women who enter an abortion clinic are there for one obvious reason, and anyone who sees them there knows it. At a hospital, however, you can't tell why a woman is there—she could be seeing her doctor for any reason. Having an abortion in a hospital protects the patient from the harassment of the pro-life protestors we typically see outside clinics."

"Those are overwhelming reasons for requiring hospitals to provide such an important service to women," Mr. Nicholas said. "But what about the hospitals whose religious beliefs lead them to oppose abortion? Why require them to offer this medical treatment?"

"If they take women as patients, then they should also offer abortion services. Hospitals can't say they want to treat women, then refuse to provide them with one of the basic procedures needed for their reproductive health.

"Mr. Nicholas," she continued, "hospitals are not religious institutions. They cannot accommodate the religious beliefs of every organization. Their goal should be to guarantee that every woman receives the best medical treatment for her total health. Furthermore, this law doesn't put any additional burden on these institutions; big hospitals have the capability to perform abortions, and most of them already offer the service in very limited cases. A woman's right to have control over her body must be respected by every medical institution."

"Senator, when this bill was discussed in the Senate, did you listen to the expert witnesses' testimony?"

"Of course."

"And were there opposing expert witnesses who testified?"

"Yes, and as I recall, one of the experts was from Christ Hospital."

"So, Christ Hospital was given the opportunity to present expert testimony on the Senate floor?"

"Oh yes, and they had the ears of more than a hundred senators, but we still decided in favor of the law."

"Are you saying that Christ Hospital's defense today has already been seen as irrelevant by the Senate?"

"Christ Hospital was given ample opportunity and time to present on the Senate floor, and over ninety senators found that their case had no merit. I don't think they will bring anything new to this court. They're simply trying to bypass the legislative system."

"Thanks, Senator," Mr. Nicholas said and then turned to the judge. "Your Honor, I have no further questions."

Mr. Maxwell got up and moved to the witness stand.

"Senator, did *Roe vs. Wade* bypass the legislative system?"

"Objection, Your Honor. That's irrelevant to this case," Mr. Nicholas objected.

"Sustained," the judge said.

"Senator, you said that you considered women's rights to reproductive health, and you also considered the conflict between your proposed law and hospitals that oppose abortion. But did you consider the rights of the unborn?"

The senator moved closer to the microphone. "Definitely. The best way to protect the needs of the unborn is by giving a woman the right to choose what is best for her and her unborn child. After all, parents know what's best for their children. Do you want to make the choices for your own kids, or do you want the Senate to do it for you?"

Mr. Maxwell went to the defendant's table and got a drink of water, then moved closer to the senator. "Since you asked, no, I don't want the right to life of the unborn to be decided by senators or by any other human, for that matter. How does your law take into account the rights of the unborn?"

"I'm sure you don't believe that a glob of tissue smaller than your fingernail has rights equal to your wife, mother, sister, daughter, or any woman in the world. Do you?" replied the senator.

"Wait a second, Senator. This bill does not limit abortion to when a fetus is the size of a fingernail. Does it?"

"No, but most abortions are done when—"

"It includes the cases where the fetus is fully formed, as in partial birth abortion?"

"Yes. Again, it gives the woman the right to have one if she needs it."

"This bill allows abortion for any reason, doesn't it?"

"We can't limit the reasons why a woman should be allowed to have an abortion. Some need to have it because of health, economic, or psychological reasons. A woman and her doctor will know what's best for her, and we should empower both to do the right thing."

"Senator, you've still failed to specify why abortion is needed for the reproductive health of a woman."

"Well, when the woman's life is in danger—"

"Let me rephrase my question," Mr. Maxwell interrupted. "Other than the case of where the mother's life is in danger, why is abortion, at any stage of pregnancy, a necessity for women's reproductive health?"

"It's necessary for total health, including psychological, economic, social—"

"Are you authoring a new bill forcing hospitals to provide financial advisors too?" Mr. Maxwell interrupted.

"Objection, Your Honor." Mr. Nicholas stood up. "The senator is not an expert on women's health."

"Your Honor, the senator should know enough about women's health. After all, she listened to all the experts and authored the bill. And, let's not forget, she is a woman herself."

"Overruled," the judge said.

"I listened to the experts, and, at that time, I felt strongly supportive of this law. I don't recall everything that was said about women's health, but I would be happy to send you a copy of the transcripts."

"There is no need for that," Mr. Maxwell said. "I have no further questions."

The prosecutor then called Dr. Janet Austin to the stand.

"Dr. Janet Austin, as I understand it, you are the founder of the Voice of Women."

"Yes."

"And what does your group do?"

"The Voice of Women is an organization dedicated to advancing the cause of women."

"And why is abortion a basic right of women?"

"It maintains a woman's rights to social equality, personal fulfillment, control over her body, procreative choice, moral agency, privacy, reproductive health, and last and not least, her right to life."

Mr. Nicholas took a large piece of paper and wrote down the following:

Social equality
Personal fulfillment
Control over body
Procreative choice
Moral agency

Privacy

Reproductive health

Life

"Writing it down will make it easier for us to remember," he said, pinning the sheet to a large easel brought to the courtroom floor. "Let's start with the woman's right to social equality. What is this right, and what does it have to do with abortion?"

"Everything. We all know that someone must care for an infant, providing it both material resources and lots of time and attention. The human infant is very needy and very dependent. For women, social equality depends on being able to participate as freely as men in education and in the economy. If a woman cannot control when and how she will be pregnant or rear children, she is at a distinct disadvantage, especially in our male-dominated world."[9]

"So," said Mr. Nicholas, "if abortion is outlawed, women would be forced to have children when they don't want them, and hence would be put at a distinct disadvantage, from an economic and educational point of view?"

"Exactly."

"Let's move to the woman's right to pursue happiness and personal fulfillment. What is this right?"

"First," answered Dr. Austin, "abortion is necessary for women's sexual fulfillment, and for the growth of their uninhibited self-confidence."[10]

"Sexual fulfillment?"

"Yes. Women, like men, should be allowed to be sexually active without constantly fearing pregnancy."

"You're claiming sexual fulfillment as a basic right for women?"

"Of course! I know it's difficult for people to accept, but women, no less than men, have the right to sexual fulfillment."

"You said there were other reasons why abortion is necessary for a woman's personal fulfillment."

"Yes. The need for an abortion arises when women encounter an unwanted pregnancy. A woman who's permitted to have an abortion is not forced into an unwelcome, intrusive, and unintended relationship with the fetus."[11]

"And how do these relationships with the 'unwelcome, intrusive, and unintended' party affect women?"

"They are detrimental to their mental health. Denying women the right to an abortion is, in effect, psychological rape."

"And what's the basis of a woman's right to control her own body?"

"That right comes from common law. When opting for an abortion, a woman exercises a basic right of bodily integrity."

"Can you describe what you mean by 'the right of bodily integrity'?"

"By that, I mean a couple of things. First, the fetus is a trespasser in the woman's property—her body. If the woman doesn't want the fetus inside her own body, no one can coerce her into pregnancy."

"You mean that the woman has the right to decide who, if anyone, resides in her own body?"

"Yes. Second, the fetus is a parasite taking necessary resources from the woman," Dr. Austin continued. "No one should be forced to provide such resources against her will. An undesired pregnancy compels a woman to do just that."

"So, a fetus is not only a trespasser but a parasite that the woman has the right to abort if she chooses?"

"Exactly. In addition, a woman has the right to decide what she wants to do with her body. If she does not choose to undergo the physical demands of a pregnancy and birth, she shouldn't be required to. No one forces any other human being to submit to surgery against their will, but everyone seems to want to force women to undergo the surgical procedure of giving birth. There is something very wrong with that."

Mr. Nicholas went to the easel. "'The right as a moral agent.' What, exactly, is that right?"

"Simple. Women have the right to decide when and if they want to have children. No one else should be involved in this decision."

"And banning abortion deprives the woman of the decision as the sole moral agent in the matter?"

"Yes, and that would leave the decision making to biology and chance."

"Is the woman's right to privacy the same thing the senator talked about?"

"Having an abortion in the hospital greatly protects women's right to privacy. But here, I mean that abortion, itself, protects a woman's right to privacy."

"Can you elaborate?"

"Certainly. The decision to have a child should be made by a woman in private. The whole community should not be part of this process. Neither should the whole community know about the decision, and hence Illinois Law 1105_ILCS_12.9."

"Moving on, 'the right to reproductive health'? Please explain this one to us."

"Pregnancy and the birth process affect the overall health of a woman, and her right to decide how to seek treatment for her own health is extremely important."

"What about the woman's right to life? Are you talking about instances when the woman's life is in danger?"

"No, I'm talking about every single case of abortion."

"How is the right to life relevant in every case of

abortion?"

"As we all know, the fetus, over a period of nine months, acts as a parasite, depriving a woman of resources and energy."

"True, but what about the right to life?"

"Childbirth involves both physical and psychological risk."

"You mean there's a real risk that a woman can die during the birth process, and this risk is mitigated by abortion?"

"Yes, and because her body bears the burden of the risk, it's only proper that the woman, alone, should be allowed to choose between pregnancy taken to term, on the one hand, and abortion, on the other."

"Almost everyone in both pro-choice and pro-life camps believes that abortion should be legal in the situation where the mother's life is in danger. Is that correct?"

"Yes, this is universally agreed upon," Dr. Austin continued. "I'm here to tell you, though, that *every single* pregnancy is a risk for a woman, and therefore the woman's right to life is always present."

"Thank you, Dr. Austin."

I felt the arguments Dr. Austin provided were good. Abortion definitely touches on so many rights of women. If I were a woman, I would resist any law banning abortion. How, after all, could we force women to become mothers? I was curious about how Mr. Maxwell was going to respond to her.

"Your Honor, I would like my colleague, Ms. Laura Smith, to cross-examine the witness," Mr. Johnson said.

"Very well, counselor," the judge responded.

Laura Smith approached the witness stand.

"Dr. Austin, you stated that abortion is a basic right of women, and you mentioned several rights that I would like to discuss with you, namely, the right to social equality, the right to pursue happiness, the right to control one's own reproductive health, and the right to procreative choice. These are all good things for women, and I agree that all women in the world should have them. But, Dr. Austin, don't you think a woman can achieve these rights by using birth control?"

"Mistakes happen, and they happen all the time."

"Are you saying that these unwanted pregnancies are a result of women's mistakes, or the result of not exercising their rights when they should have done so?"

"Do you want to punish women for making mistakes?" Dr. Austin retorted. "In addition, birth control methods often fail, and many women cannot afford birth control, or lack access to it."

"I'm not 'for' punishing women. In all your dialogue with plaintiff's counsel, you portrayed women as being forced into pregnancy by others, of being robbed of all their rights. But now, we're learning that it isn't a compulsory pregnancy when the woman had full opportunity to exercise all these rights by taking proper precautions."

"When you take these rights away from a woman, you are punishing her for mistakes that happen all the time as a result of human nature or circumstances she has no control over."

"Surely we don't want to punish the innocent, unborn child, who had no choice about being conceived under these circumstances. Do we?"

"This is not an innocent child! He is an intruder, a parasite—unwanted and undesired!" Dr. Austin shouted.

"Dr. Austin, why shouldn't a woman be responsible for her actions? You talked about the woman's right as a moral agent. In my definition of the term, a moral agent must bear the consequences of her choices."

"It's true that some women are irresponsible in their sexual activities. But this irresponsibility doesn't take away their rights—not in the slightest."

"Why is that, Dr. Austin?"

"Because losing those rights is not a fair punishment for making a mistake. After all, we don't send a thief who stole five dollars to the electric chair. Remember, the woman didn't intend to become pregnant; women don't allow themselves to get pregnant, knowing they'll have an abortion later. These pregnancies are unplanned, unexpected, and undesired. If a woman knew in advance that pregnancy would be the result of her sexual act, she would, generally, do something to prevent it."

"So then, Dr. Austin, what *is* a fair punishment for sexually irresponsible women?"

"First, counselor, what about sexually irresponsible men? Why should women have to bear all the responsibility of sexual intercourse? Women, under such circumstances, need compassion and love, not punishment. We need to have mercy in our hearts. Even Christ said that those without sin should throw the first stone."

I looked at Mr. Johnson, who seemed uneasy. I looked up in time to see Laura Smith glance at Mr. Johnson too. He nodded slightly. "Your Honor, I've finished my part of the cross-examination," she said, returning to her seat. "I'd like cocounsel, Mr. Maxwell, to pick up from here."

As Laura sat down, I saw her face was pale.

"I bet you she's proabortion," Victoria whispered to me.

"You think?" I asked.

"She started good, but she tripped at the end, when she asked about a fair punishment for abortion."

But that was a good question, I thought. What was a fair punishment for abortion? Could we have crime without punishment? We surely didn't want to punish women for their mistakes. The topic was not as easy as I had thought.

"I don't know. Maybe Dr. Austin converted her," Victoria continued.

"That Dr. Austin was good," I said. "Wasn't she?"

"Yup." Victoria turned her head toward Mr. Maxwell. "He's good too."

Mr. Maxwell was standing by the easel, reading out the eight rights of women Mr. Nicholas had listed. "Dr. Austin, I am particularly interested in this 'right as a moral agent.' If a woman gets all the other rights but this one, the decision will not be hers alone but society's, which may or may not grant her the right to choose. This is a very important right, wouldn't you agree?"

"It's a basic right of every woman." Dr. Austin nodded her acquiescence.

"Women alone should be making the decision about abortion?"

"Yes, women can be trusted to make decisions that are in the best interests of their families, children, and society, while enhancing their own health and other interests."[12]

"Ma'am, all humans are moral agents. Would you accept the abolition of rape laws, for example, because men are moral agents?"

"Rape is wrong."

"Abortion is wrong too, ma'am."

"No, it's not."

"Why not?"

"Because it violates a woman's right to choose."

"Which is the most important and overriding question: is rape right or wrong, or do men have the right to choose rape?"

"Is rape right or wrong, of course."

"Why can't we apply the same logic to abortion? Why can't we ask, 'Is abortion right or wrong?' Only then would we consider a second question, 'Who has the right to choose to do this?' After all, no one has the right to do what is wrong."[13]

"I completely agree with you on that, but I'm saying that women, alone, should answer the question: 'Is abortion right or wrong?'"

"Why?"

"Almost all other moral decisions we make affect other people. But when it comes to abortion, a woman is making a decision that involves her body and her life. And since it's the woman's risk, burden, and body, she alone should decide whether or not to eliminate the product of her pregnancy," she replied.

"But, with abortion, women are deciding to end the life of an unborn child."

"The child is an intruder, a trespasser, a parasite with no rights."

"Ma'am, you told my cocounsel that women should not be punished for their mistakes. I don't think we should punish the child, even if he or she is guilty of all you say," Mr. Maxwell said. "So, why should the woman be allowed to act as the sole moral agent in the matter?"

"Again, it's her risk, burden, and body."

"That, it seems to me, is the exact reason why she cannot be the sole moral agent."

"Pardon me?"

"I'll concede that the pregnant woman is subject to potential burdens arising from a pregnancy. But it has never been thought right to have an interested party, especially the more powerful party, decide his or her own case when a conflict of interest may be involved. Abortion involves a powerful person, the woman, versus the powerless, silenced claimant. In fairness, can a woman be the sole judge of whether the fetus should live or die?"[14]

"Women don't just have an abortion for the sake of

having an abortion. They have abortions only when the child is unwanted. I fail to see any conflict of interest."

"But isn't the woman already biased, especially when the child is unwanted?" Mr. Maxwell said.

"The mothering instinct present in all women allows them to look past their bias and consider the big picture, Mr. Maxwell. They're not likely to have an abortion simply because they can."

Mr. Maxwell moved back to the poster where the rights were written. He took a few seconds to glance over the poster. "Let's discuss the right to control one's body. This is the second most important right you talked about," he said. "Would you agree, Dr. Austin?"

"All the rights are important, and abortion can be justified by any single reason alone."

"Well, we need to discuss this point before continuing," Mr. Maxwell said. "Suppose you have a one-day-old infant, and you decide you don't want him anymore. You don't want any more children. You realize your child will be an obstacle to your advancement in the workplace. Could you invoke these rights and, at that point, kill the infant?"

"No."

"Why not?"

"Because he is no longer inside the woman's body."

"Exactly. So this right to control one's body is the key right. The other rights cannot stand on their own to justify abortion. Can they?"

"The right to life could."

"OK, but, for now, the right to control one's body is so important that no other right, except for the right to life, can be grasped before the right to control one's body is realized. Isn't that the case?"

Dr. Austin didn't answer.

"Isn't it?"

"The right to control one's body is very important, and it must be realized and respected."

"Let's discuss that," Mr. Maxwell continued. "Dr. Austin, it is true, isn't it, that under the law, a person has the right to control his own body, but the law also recognizes that it's wrong to harm others, especially if they're immature, dependent, or otherwise powerless?"

"Yes, that's true, but when one life is completely reliant on another, the dependent party doesn't have a right to life. Where would we be if the law required us to give blood transfusions or bone marrow to others? And where would we be if refusing would be a criminal offense?"[15]

Mr. Maxwell seemed to consider the questions. "Pregnancy is not like a cancerous growth or infestation by a biological parasite, Doctor. It's the way every human being enters the world. Having a baby is not the same as being hooked up to an artificial life-support system or donating organs for a transplant. Do you agree?"[16]

"A fetus is a biological parasite. Where does it get its food, its oxygen?"

"Fetuses always get their blood from their mothers, but only temporarily—just nine months," Mr. Maxwell continued. "That the reliance is physiologically normal should be heavily considered in the context of abortion and pregnancy. Proabortionists have distorted the relationship between a fetus and its mother, ignoring the fact the mother is responsible for its existence and the fact that this relationship is a natural one."[17]

"But you are ignoring the fact that a woman has the right to do whatever she wants with her body, whether or not you consider the fetus a parasite, and this right must be protected by the law."

"It's not fair to anyone that a fetus's rights are a philosophical question, while abortion rights are determined by the legislature. If it's appropriate to legislate on one subject, it's appropriate to legislate on the other."[18]

"Mr. Maxwell, in plain and simple English, a fetus is a trespasser because it is unwelcome by the woman. The fetus is a parasite because it robs resources from the mother. And, most importantly, it is a foreign object inside her womb. She has the right to kick anything out of her body anytime she chooses."

"Dr. Austin, again in simple English, the fetus didn't choose to enter his or her mother's womb. Rather, he or she is there only as a result of the mother's actions. The mother must have known the consequences of her sexual activity." Mr. Maxwell paused, appearing to organize his thoughts. "OK. Let me ask you another question: do women have abortions because they don't want their children to rob them of their resources for nine months? Is this a woman's main concern in abortion?"

"Well . . . "

"Ma'am, isn't the main concern actually the fact that they don't want to have a child after the nine-month pregnancy? All this talk about parasites is nothing but an excuse to shirk the responsibility of dealing with a child. Isn't it?"

"These are not children, Mr. Maxwell. They are tissues. A woman has the right to do anything she chooses with those tissues because they are inside her body."

"And if these tissues were persons, then would she still have the same rights?"

"Yes, no parasite has full right to life . . ."

"I have no further questions for Dr. Austin at this time." Mr. Maxwell returned to his seat.

"It's a good time to break for lunch," the judge said. "The court is adjourned till 2:00 p.m."

***

The cafeteria at the courthouse was large. We took a table in the corner.

"That was certainly a challenging morning," Mr. Johnson noted.

"I'm sorry I wasn't able to cross-examine Dr. Austin the way you wanted," Laura said.

"You started strong, Laura," Mr. Johnson assured her, "but I would have liked you to continue the same way." He turned to Mr. Maxwell. "We still need to give a more convincing argument about women's rights."

"Yes," Mr. Maxwell sighed. "I think a woman's right to control her body still needs to be addressed. We didn't hit a home run there."

"Our next witness is an expert on women's rights. We may be able to do just what we need to get back on top," Mr. Johnson said.

"More women's rights discussions?" The words slipped out of my mouth before I could censor them.

"Do you have problems with women's rights, Mr. Livingston?" Laura asked.

"No, but I don't think . . ."

"You don't think *what*?"

"I don't think that argument will get us anywhere. After all, we know that pro-life people don't support women's rights. Why can't we just emphasize the personhood of the fetus and play down women's rights?"

"Women's rights are very important, Randy," Mr. Johnson commented. "And you're making a broad generalization by saying pro-lifers don't support those rights. If it were not for women's rights, we would not be here today." Mr. Johnson took a piece of his sandwich and put it in Victoria's mouth, then took another one and put it in his own mouth. "We need to discuss these rights thoroughly. Laura, I'd like you to cross-examine the next witness."

"*What?*" Victoria objected.

"Victoria!" Mr. Johnson gave his daughter a warning sign with his eyes. "Laura will do a good job—I'm sure of that."

"Thank you, Mr. Johnson," Laura replied.

"Laura, I want you to get ready by first eating a good meal, and it's on me," Mr. Johnson said with a smile.

"When I eat a good meal, it usually puts me to sleep," Mr. Maxwell said.

We ate in silence while Mr. Maxwell talked about one of his other cases. I didn't do much talking, having already stuck my foot in my mouth. I was also tired.

***

"Mrs. Jameson, you are the leader of an organization called Truly Feminists, correct?" Laura Smith asked.

"Yes, I founded it ten years ago to advance the causes of women," Mrs. Jameson, a middle-aged woman, replied.

"And abortion is one of these important issues?"

"Yes. Truly Feminists officially opposes abortion."

"How can that be?" Laura asked. "What about the right to social equality, the right to privacy, the right to reproductive health, the right to sexual fulfillment . . ."

"All of that is nonsense. Conspiracies against women."

"Conspiracies against women?"

"Yes, take the social equality right—"

"That's an important right to women . . ."

"Oh yes, it is. Women have a right to social equality, but abortion doesn't help women achieve it. In fact, it widens the gap of social equality."

"How so? According to Dr. Austin, child rearing is time consuming-and makes it harder for women to compete in the business world."

"And when you make abortion the solution to this problem, you widen the social gap because you're emphasizing the woman's role in child rearing while ignoring the man's responsibility. What kind of social equality are we talking about here? The true solution is a society where men have as much responsibility as women in protecting, nurturing, and caring for their children."[19]

"But women with children, no matter how much support they receive, still find difficulties in the workplace. Correct?"

"Are you saying these women should kill their own children? You see, in reality, abortion is a cheap solution designed to ignore women's rights. Women really want equal pay, flextime, job sharing, health-care maternity benefits, and affordable child care. Abortion rights don't help women achieve those things."[20]

"What about the right of women to personal fulfillment?"

"What is personal fulfillment for a woman? It's now measured by what men find fulfilling. What men don't do doesn't count. Pregnancy, childbirth, and nursing have been characterized as passive, debilitating, animal-like. Women's unique biological capacity has been denied, despised, and suppressed under male domination. Unfortunately, many women have fallen for the fallacy."[21]

"Dr. Austin mentioned two specific examples. The first is the sexual fulfillment of women."

"Give me a break! A more male-oriented model of erotic or amative sexuality endorses sexual permissiveness without long-term commitment or reproductive focus. Erotic sexuality emphasizes pleasure, play, passion, individual self-expression, and romantic games of courtship and conquest. It is assumed that a variety of partners and sexual experiences are necessary to stimulate romantic passion. This model of sexual life has often worked satisfactorily for men. But for the average woman, it is quite destructive. Women can only play the erotic game successfully when they are young, physically attractive, economically powerful, and fulfilled enough in a career to sacrifice family life. Abortion is also required. Because our society endorses this male-oriented, permissive view of sexuality, it is all too ready to give women abortion on demand. Abortion helps a woman's body be more like a man's. It has been observed that *Roe vs. Wade* removed the last defense women possessed against male sexual demands."[22]

"The other example she gave was the right not to have an unwanted child," said Laura.

"That's also ridiculous. Abortion rights activists promised us a world of equality and reduced poverty—a world where every child would be wanted. Instead, child abuse has escalated, and, rather than producing a more equitably shared responsibility for children, a greater part of the already heavy burden has shifted to women."[23]

"But is it fair for a woman to be forced to have unwanted children?"

"Truly Feminists agrees that every child should be wanted. A world with only wanted children would be an idyllic place in which to live. No one could quarrel with that as an idealistic goal. Wouldn't it also be a wonderful world if there were no unwanted spouses, no aging parents unwanted by their children—in fact, no people at all who are unwanted? Let's all try to achieve this, but also remember that people have clay feet and, sadly, the unwanted will probably always be with us. That's why we work so hard to support adoption,"[24] Mrs. Jameson said.

"But don't you agree that abortion, also, helps us achieve this idealistic goal of having everyone wanted?"

"Should we achieve this goal by killing children? The saying, 'Every child a wanted child,' shouldn't be completed with 'and if unwanted, kill!' For that's exactly what that slogan means," Mrs. Jameson replied. "And since when does anyone's right to live depend upon someone else wanting them? Radical feminists are outraged by the idea that a woman's worth can be determined by whether or not a man wants her, yet they're supportive of a woman's right to assign worth to her unborn child based on whether or not she wants *it*. It's a blatant contradiction."[25]

"Yes, it's unfortunate that some people's values depend on others wanting them, and that unwanted fetuses would be disposed of, but that's why our world is not an ideal place. That's reality," Laura Smith said. She was now playing the devil's advocate.

"To reflect on the current reality, we don't just kill unwanted. It is only recently the U.S Supreme Court and the governments in many other nations have, for the first time in modern history, granted to one citizen (the mother) the absolute legal right to kill another, if that first person does not want them."[26]

Mrs. Jameson straightened her back. "Do you have children, Ms. Smith?"

"Yes. Three." Laura was obviously taken aback.

"Think of your own pregnancies. Was each planned, or was one of them a surprise? Were you really happy each time, in the first month or two? Be honest. In the first few weeks or months, were all your pregnancies really wanted?"[27]

Laura Smith didn't answer.

"But now look at your children. Are you glad you have them? Would you give any back, or have any of them killed?"[28] Mrs. Jameson said.

"What about a woman's right as moral agent?" Laura Smith asked, avoiding the questions.

Mrs. Jameson laughed. "If you believe a person is a moral agent, then you'll provide her all the essential facts, and allow her to make her decision. But, in abortion, women are encouraged to believe that the 'right' choice is the one that suits them best, discounting the interests of anyone else involved. Women are told that it's OK to shirk moral responsibility."

"So, are you saying that if women are given all the facts in an unbiased manner, then they can be the sole moral agents?" Laura asked.

"No, I'm saying that this right is not respected by abortionists themselves, yet they hide behind it."

"What about the right to privacy?"

"Oh yes, another conspiracy to widen the social gap and make women poorer and poorer."

"The right to privacy does that?" Laura asked.

"Women need more social support and changes in the structure of society. They need increased self-confidence, increased self-expectations, and increased self-esteem. Society in general, and men in particular, have to provide women more support in rearing the next generation, or the devastating feminization of poverty will continue. But if a woman claims the right to decide by herself whether the fetus becomes a child or not, what does this do to paternal and communal responsibility? Why should men share responsibility for child support or child rearing if they have no say in the outcome of a pregnancy? For that matter, why should the state provide a system of day care or child support, or require workplaces to accommodate women's maternity needs and the needs of child rearing, if the woman could've chosen to abort her child? Permissive abortion, granted in the name of woman's privacy and reproductive freedom, ratifies the view that pregnancies and children are women's private individual responsibility. The larger community is relieved of all moral responsibility."[29]

"So abortion doesn't serve women?"

"Abortion hurts women. Abortionists try to say it provides social equality to women so they can avoid working on the real issues that bring social equality. They say abortion protects a woman's privacy so they can strip her of the support the community owes her. They say that abortion fulfills her sexual needs so she can immerse herself in a destructive lifestyle that only serves the needs of men. They try to tell her that abortion is a right to protect her body when they hide information from her that can hurt her. They try to say she is a moral agent, but at the same time, they're destroying her self-esteem . . . " Mrs. Jameson paused, catching her breath. "Instead of being empowered by their abortion choices, women who have abortions are trying to escape the debilitating reality of not being able to count on a committed male partner, not accepting responsibility for their own actions, and the gruesome guilt that goes along with murdering another human being. Women are hardly going to develop the self-esteem, self-discipline, and the self-confidence necessary to confront a male-dominated society through abortion."[30]

"Thank you Mrs. Jameson. I have no further questions." Laura went back to the table.

Mr. Nicholas got up from his seat. He looked tired. He walked toward the stand. "Mrs. Jameson," he said, "we have discussed all these rights before. Whether or not they benefit the woman is left for each woman to decide, but there is one important right you have not discussed."

"That's just it," Mrs. Jameson interjected. "The decision should not be made by the woman, alone—"

"What I'd like to discuss," Mr. Nicholas continued as if he hadn't heard her, "is the woman's right to control her own body."

"Since when has it been out of control?" Laughter erupted in the courtroom.

"I don't mean that her body is out of control, Mrs. Jameson," Mr. Nicholas continued patiently, "but that she has the right to control what is inside her body."

"This is another cliché that abortionists use. Abortions don't happen because women are concerned that their bodies are being used to feed an infant for nine months, but because they don't want to bring a child into a society that's unsupportive. How can women control their rights by killing their babies?" Mrs. Jameson leaned into the microphone. "For women to successfully combine childbearing, education, and careers, society has to recognize that female bodies come with wombs. By denying abortion and embracing this, women will thereby demand that society learn to accommodate them."[31]

Mr. Nicholas continued to cross-examine Mrs. Jameson, and she, in turn, continued giving him good answers. She was passionate about her beliefs. What she said resonated with me. As a matter of fact, it convinced me. To be honest, as a man, I wanted abortion to be legal so I could meet my own sexual needs. Abortion seemed to serve men more than women. Women wanted commitment and security, and abortion helped men to avoid giving them these. Abortion got men off the hook.

Court adjourned for the day and we headed out to Mr. Johnson's van.

"A challenging day, huh?" Mr. Johnson asked no one in particular.

"You got that right," Mr. Maxwell replied. He rested his head on the back of his seat.

"Laura, you did a great job," Mr. Johnson said.

"Thank you, Mr. Johnson," Laura replied, smiling.

"Why didn't you answer her questions about unwanted pregnancies?" Victoria asked.

"Victoria!" said her father, openly rebuking her. "Don't ask personal questions."

"I'm sorry," Victoria said.

"It's OK. Because you asked, all of them were . . . how should I say it? . . . not unwanted pregnancies but problematic ones—pregnancies with challenges." Laura sighed. "The first one was when my husband and I were in college. We didn't have much money or time to deal with the birth of a child. The second one was the first month after I'd started my law career. I wasn't excited about the timing. I thought it would be a bad start for my career, but it worked out."

"That's good," Victoria said.

"The third child was conceived a month before my husband passed away."

"I'm sorry," I said.

"Thank you. It's challenging—being a single mom. I love my children, but I'm grateful for my mother, who helps in raising the kids, and for Mr. Johnson."

"Oh, I don't do as much as I should," Mr. Johnson replied.

"No, allowing me to work from home two days a week and giving me a flexible schedule is what makes it possible for me to work *and* take care of my kids at the same time."

"God bless you," Victoria said. "I do feel for you. It's hard to bring kids up alone."

Laura nodded but was quiet.

As we left the van, Victoria motioned to me to wait for her.

"Do you feel sorry when a ten-year-old is killed?"

"What?"

"Do you feel sad when you learn that a ten-year-old is killed?"

"I guess so. Why?"

"How does your 'civil society' make you feel sad?"

"Because it's wrong, and because of what I told you. I feel sad when something wrong and bad happens," I replied.

"It doesn't make sense. I understand you may feel guilty if you commit a crime, but to feel sad when someone else kills a ten-year-old boy is not a response generated by civil society."

"It could."

"How could a contract in a civil society create the feeling of compassion and sadness?"

"Alright, then, I *don't* feel sad when a ten-year-old is killed," I replied.

"I don't believe you. How come you feel sad when imaginary characters in your dreams are killed?"

"I've got to run right now," I said. "Bye, Mr. Johnson." I nodded my head and left the van.

Why *did* I feel sad when a ten-year-old was killed? Another thing to think about later. For now, I was tired and I couldn't think of anything but sleep.

Chapter 19
Agent X

I stood in the middle of the room, staring at the RMs. I looked carefully at each one, but all I could see was a wasted life. When I looked at the RMs, I didn't see a meaningless number. I saw Kevin, George, Manny. I could hear their silent screams. Among them were potential doctors, lawyers, teachers—bad men and good. *What can justify so many wasted lives? Can the lives saved by these body parts excuse such horrible means? Can the satisfaction of Farm employees validate this system?* No, there was nothing whatsoever that could justify the wasting of one RM's life. The good that could come from the sacrifice of an RM didn't outweigh the evil.

But the RMs couldn't think, feel, communicate—they couldn't even go to the bathroom. It was more valuable for these kids to be cut into pieces and that, in fact, was the only contribution they were guaranteed to make to society. Why take a chance on letting them develop and make their own choices? This way, at least, they were sure to give to the common good.

Still, that didn't justify the system. I remained

unconvinced, the atrocity of it forcing my brain to search for some logical answer. *How could people be so blind to the inherent value of human life? How could they sleep at night? How had we come to this point?*

The Farm and Factory weren't just committing a crime against RM 8645-23, though. They were committing crimes against the whole human race, and a crime against me, personally. I was wronged because my human race was disrespected, insulted, and injured. I had the right to act.

I walked toward the RMs and put an earpiece behind each of their ears. I let the computer program run the simulations. I watched as they acted the plan out, and lost myself in my thoughts once more.

How had we come to the Human Farm and Body Parts Factory? It all started at the fertilized egg stage. We failed to acknowledge that the zygote was fully human, and that rights of a potential person existed at that stage. We didn't know that there were technologies out there, ready to turn a zygote into an RM. The biotechnology outgrew our understanding of bioethics. We were stuck calling each other names, using rhetorical tricks, avoiding any meaningful debate, and then the technology drove us directly here. Now, we didn't have the moral capacity to fight against the biotechnology. In this not-so-distant future world, we had only two choices: to accept our destinies or to hide in the camp.

The plan was going better than I'd expected. I'd easily taught the RMs several new words, and they had memorized the maps of the Farm. I divided the RMs into several groups— red, green, blue, and yellow—each responsible for evacuating a specific Farm area on the day of the attack. My job was to take care of the employees working at the time of the escape, and to set the Factory on fire. The computer program provided all the instructions the RMs needed to perform their tasks, but I needed more time to perfect the plan. We only had two weeks until July 4. I had to be ready.

"All employees must assemble in the Hart Auditorium!"

The speaker above my head startled me. I immediately stopped the exercise I'd been working on with the batch and sent the RMs to their afternoon nap. Then I walked to the auditorium.

The auditorium was teeming with employees. The best biscuit in the world was offered on tables near the entrance, but I was too curious to eat. A short, portly man stepped up to the podium on the stage.

"Ladies and gentleman, we are happy to have with us today the CEO of our fine company, Mr. Smith."

The crowd erupted in applause, and I found myself clapping my hands with them. Everyone stood and I followed suit.

"That's the good boss," Charles whispered in my ear as he joined me.

"Ladies and gentlemen, thank you very much," Mr. Smith said. People were still clapping. "I'm here today to launch a new program called 'SAFE SPORTS.'"

"A new program!" Charles raised his eyebrows.

"Through research, we've noticed that most of the body parts we sell are to replace those injured in sporting activities. Since our company is in the business of saving lives, we will begin actively encouraging safe sports in the country. We'll provide a free sport kit to every student in every high school and elementary school in this country. The kit will contain safe, high quality sports equipment—such as skateboards and tennis rackets—and instructional videos on how to keep sports safe."

Everyone applauded anew.

"The good news is that by helping our kids, we'll double the value of our stock."

The applause grew to shouts and whistles.

"We'd all better start buying more shares," Charles said out of the corner of his mouth.

"Thank you very much," Mr. Smith replied while the crowd was still applauding. "I will be happy to answer any of your questions."

A woman sitting in the row ahead of me pressed on the screen next to her seat and started talking from a microphone. Her picture was shown on all of the small screens next to our seats and on a big screen behind the stage.

"How much is it going to cost for us to give the safe sports kits to everyone?"

"Not a penny," Mr. Smith answered, beaming. "The kits are being distributed compliments of the government." The crowd murmured excitedly. "We've convinced our favorite senators that this is an important product for the protection of our children, and they agreed that the cause is more than worthy of our tax dollars. Also, we won't be needing parents' consent to give their children the kits."

"But how does this strategy increase the stock price?" a young man asked.

"Well, if we want to continue this business, we need to encourage sports among the population. We can't remain competitive if we rely on things like heart attacks and age-induced failures to meet sales quotas—we need more sports injuries."

"But, we're promoting *safe* sports," the young man persisted.

"Yes, but everyone knows that there's no such thing as entirely safe sports. We're utilizing a strategy here that has worked in the past, namely, by 'family planning' organizations. When those organizations started promoting safe sex and distributing free condoms, the abortion part of their business benefited."

"Mr. Smith are you saying that we're deliberately causing injuries so we can sell more body parts?" an old woman asked.

"Oh no, not at all. Kids will always play sports, whether they have this kit or not. That's what kids do, right? But when we give them a kit, we're promoting safety and probably saving lives, and that shows the community that we're a company that cares. And let me remind you: the reason we need our stock to go up is because we want to stay in the business of saving lives. Let me share with you a letter I received yesterday from a young woman."

Mr. Smith took a piece of paper from his pocket and started reading.

"'Dear Mr. Smith, my father had a car accident two weeks before my wedding. I always wanted him to walk me down the aisle, but I thought his accident would destroy my dream. When my father was sent to the hospital, the doctor told us to contact the Human Farm and Body Parts Factory. In a few hours, you delivered all the body parts my father needed. My father is now doing well. Yesterday, he walked me down the aisle. Thank you for saving my father's life. Thank you for being part of my wedding.' Signed Mary Nelson."

The crowd exploded in applause. I looked at the old woman who had asked the last question—her picture was still on the screen—and I could see tears leaking from her eyes.

The boss continued reading letters and giving examples of satisfied customers whose lives had been improved by our products. The clapping and hollering continued with each story, but I couldn't join in. With the RMs on my mind, I couldn't listen to the stories any longer. The distinction between RMs and free people seemed like nothing but an excuse to empower people, like Mr. Smith, to assign price tags to one another. Why was the life of the father who had the car accident more important than the life of the RM? Who decided the prices, and didn't those people realize that their resale values could be marked down just as easily?

Suddenly, the applause stopped. I looked at the screen to see what was going on, and I was surprised by what I saw. It was a picture of *me*, and I didn't look too happy. I immediately smiled.

"Now, we will move to the new employee introduction," the boss said.

I sighed.

"Mr. Randy Livingston has joined our company this month," the boss said. Then, turning to face me in the crowd, he added, "Welcome to the Human Farm and Body Parts Factory.'"

I nodded my head, trying to look pleased to be there, and the clapping began again. I waited, the smile stuck on my face for what seemed an eternity, until my picture was gone from the screen.

As I was leaving the meeting, I saw Lisa—the guide from my tour—for the first time since my initial visit to the compound.

"Hi!" she said when she saw me. "How do you like your job so far?"

"I love it, especially being in the business of saving lives." It wasn't exactly a lie—I was in the business of saving RMs' lives.

"Well, would you like to join our afternoon break?"

"Sure, I'd love to."

"I need to go to my office and get some things first."

"I'll wait for you in the cafeteria. What department do you work in?" I asked as we exited the auditorium.

"Retention and Records."

"What do you do there?"

"We keep records of all the RMs," she replied.

"What kind of information do you keep about them?"

She smiled at my interest.

"Do you want to come to my office so I can show you?"

"I'd love to," I answered and followed her to a wing of the main building that I'd never been to before.

When we got to her office, Lisa started the computer and opened a database.

"See, it keeps track of each RM's birthday, which we designate as the date it leaves the incubator. Each RM is assigned a unique number from the day it gets fertilized. Even if it dies in the incubator, it still retains this unique number. The death date," she said, pointing to another spot on the screen, "is the date it dies, obviously, which can be any day after fertilization."

"What's this 'mother cloning' column?" I asked.

"Well, each fertilized egg comes from an egg. This column tells whether the woman who owned the egg was cloned or not. The DNA structure of the egg is also included. And the agent column tells us the source of the eggs."

"Wow, you keep quite a lot of detailed information," I observed.

"We keep more data than this. We keep information about all the cloning that takes place, all the food the RMs eat, any extraordinary incidents they experience . . . everything."

"Can I take a look at the database for the RMs in my hall, batch 8645?" I asked.

"Of course." She entered a couple of key words in the

computer and showed me my RMs' information. "Take a look at the table, but don't touch anything," she told me. "I'll be back in two minutes."

Once she'd left the room, I looked closely at the information on my batch. A "No" was listed in the mother cloning column. *Does that mean that the parents of the RMs weren't cloned?* I'd thought everyone in this world had been cloned. I looked at the agent column and saw a large "X" filling the box. Curious, I followed the search procedure that Lisa had performed moments earlier, using old dates of fertilization, trying to find the agents of the other batches so I could compare. After some investigation, I discovered that the agent source had initially been EGGSO, but in the last several years, the agent for all the batches had become Agent X. *Who's Agent X?* I wondered. *Who, besides the camp residents, remained uncloned?*

Before Lisa came back, I managed to write down most of the DNA numbers of my RMs. When Lisa did reappear, I thanked her for the tour and left immediately for the camp, in search of Agent X.

Chapter 20
Miriam Hessian (Court Day #3)

"Miriam Hessian," said Martina Massy, identifying the picture projected on a portable screen in the courtroom. The face was that of a beautiful young woman about twenty years old. She had shiny, rich-looking brown hair, large hazel eyes, a smooth white face, and an enchanting smile.

"Miss Massy, you were Miriam Hessian's roommate, right?" Mr. Nicholas asked. Martina, also a very attractive twenty-something, had straight blonde hair and large blue eyes.

"Yeah," she replied.

"How long have you known Miss Miriam Hessian?"

"Let's see . . ." She sighed. "About seven years."

"So you met before college?"

"Yeah, in high school. She was my best friend. After high school, we decided to go to the same college and become roommates."

"What kind of student was she in high school?"

"Very smart," she answered. "She aced every subject. She was valedictorian of our class and won a full scholarship to the university."

"What about at college? What kind of student was she there?"

"She was studying premed, so she was working really hard. She spent most of her time studying or volunteering at the hospital."

"As a person, how would you describe her?"

"Funny, loving, outgoing, but at the same time, conservative and honest. I've never met anyone quite like her."

"Tell us what happened to Miriam Hessian on April 12 of this year."

"She killed herself," Martina replied, her voice shaky.

"Why would such a beautiful woman—who seemed to have everything going for her—kill herself?"

"She was pregnant."

"She killed herself because she was pregnant?"

"She couldn't deal with it. It wasn't her choice. She'd been raped."

"The pregnancy was the result of rape?"

"Yes."

"When did the rape take place?"

"March 28."

"Did she describe to you the events that led to her rape?" Mr. Nicholas asked.

"Yes. It was Thursday night, around eight. She was coming back from volunteering at Christ Hospital . . ."

"She volunteered at Christ Hospital?"

"Yes, twice a week."

"Please, go on."

"After getting off the bus," Martina went on, "a drunk, homeless man asked her for money. She told him she didn't have any and kept walking toward the dorms, which are about four minutes away. He followed her, and as she turned onto a side street, he jumped her, then raped her at gunpoint."

"What happened afterward?"

"I had been out on a date and came back to our room around nine. Miriam was taking a shower and I could hear her crying. She'd locked the door, so I couldn't get inside the bathroom to help her. I was really scared, so I told her I was going to call a doctor. She came out of the bathroom right away and told me not to call anybody. Then she told me she'd been raped." Martina paused for a few seconds, looking at Miriam's picture. Tears rolled down her cheeks. "It was horrible," she continued with a taut voice.

"Did she tell you how she felt after the rape?"

"She said she felt awful. She was emotionally devastated. She felt like it was the end of the world. She couldn't go to class. She couldn't do anything but cry. She had nightmares. She acted weird. Sometimes, she said she felt like she was dreaming. She couldn't think about anything but the rape."

"She then learned that she was pregnant?"

"Yes."

"How did this affect her?"

"It was the blow that led to her death." Martina looked back at the screen. "Miriam came from a very conservative family. Until the rape, she had been a virgin and was keeping herself for marriage. She was a little bit different than the rest of us. She didn't party. She didn't drink. And she didn't have a boyfriend."

"How did she say the pregnancy made her feel?"

"The pregnancy shattered her dreams. No man from her religious background would marry her, she said. In her religion, it's shameful for a woman to become pregnant outside of marriage. She told me stories about how they killed some girls back in her native country when they became pregnant. It was a question of honor. Her life would be in danger if she continued the pregnancy. Her cousin was also attending the same university, and she said he would tell on her if he found out. She couldn't continue her studies and be pregnant at the same time. She lost all hope of becoming a doctor. Not only was she pregnant by force, but she was pregnant with the child of a rapist, a loser, a criminal . . ."

"Did she consider abortion?"

"Yes, we talked about it. She had a serious dilemma. She wanted to do what was ethically right, but she was so afraid of her family's reaction. That's why she wouldn't report the crime to the police—she didn't want anyone to know about her." Martina took a deep breath and continued. "She was also concerned that she was pregnant with a child of a rapist, probably a murderer, even. She worried what the child would feel when he found out how he was conceived."

"What happened next?"

"I eventually convinced her to have an abortion. It was the right thing to do to save her sanity—to save her child from a miserable life—and to save Miriam herself."

"And did she have an abortion?"

"No."

"Why not?"

"I told her to go to Christ Hospital, since she volunteered there— maybe someone there could help her."

"Did she go to Christ Hospital?"

"Yes," Martina answered, "and the next day, she committed suicide." Her tears began again.

I looked at Victoria. She had tears in her eyes too. I found myself thinking it was impossible to think of abortion in black-and-white and not look at each case separately. How ignorant it was to reduce abortion to a political issue, when it was really about a woman and her life.

"Miriam would have been alive if she'd been allowed to have an abortion at Christ Hospital," Martina sobbed. "She just couldn't go through hell for nine months—and the rest of her life—for the sake of carrying the child of a rapist. Why should we allow a rapist's child to live? By continuing the pregnancy, Miriam would've suffered for the rest of her life." Mr. Nicholas was silent, so Martina continued. "The rape was in her past, but the pregnancy and its product were going to be a permanent reminder of it. And what about the child? Why would we want to bring a person into the world at a moral disadvantage? How horrible to know that your father was a criminal—that a horrific crime led to your creation! The child would be destined to be just like his father."

"Thank you, Miss Massy," Mr. Nicholas said. "I have no further questions for this witness."

"Mr. Johnson, do you want to question this witness?" the judge asked.

"Yes," Mr. Johnson replied, moving toward the witness stand. "Miss Massy, I'm sorry for the loss of your friend Miriam. It must be difficult for you to cope with this loss." He paused briefly. "Now, you testified that Miriam did not report the rape to the police. Is that correct?"

"Yes. She didn't want anyone to know about it."

"Did she see a doctor after the rape?"

"No."

"Did she tell you what happened when she visited Christ Hospital?"

"They told her that the fetus was a human being, and it had a right to live. They said abortion was murder. They made her feel guilty." Martina paused and looked at Miriam's picture, once again through tears. "She was very distressed and said she couldn't take it any longer, so she took her own life. It's awful to accuse a woman of murder when she's a victim herself. Miriam was no murderer."

"Miss Massy, did Miriam tell Christ Hospital about her

rape?"

"Not that I know of."

"Then what reason did she give them for wanting the abortion?"

"She didn't tell them she was pregnant. She acted as if she was just trying to get general information, so she could see if she could have the procedure done secretly."

"Your Honor," Mr. Johnson said, turning to the judge, "the hospital's records show that Miriam was not admitted as a patient during this time. She was seeking general information, and the hospital gave it to her."

"But the general information was devastating to her," Martina objected. "You can't do this to women. You need to take each woman's case separately and study it and—"

"Your friend was not admitted as a patient but was asking for general information, wasn't she?"

"Yea, but—"

"Miss Massy, when did Miriam talk to you about her family honor and her fear that she was going to be killed by her relatives if they found out about her rape?"

"Immediately after her rape."

"Miss Massy, did you ever tell anyone about Miriam's rape?"

Martina did not reply.

"Miss Massy, I have a report from campus police. According to them, you reported the rape that very night." Mr. Johnson slid the report in front of Martina.

"I had no choice. I thought I was doing the right thing."

"How could this be the right choice, given the consequences Miriam had described to you if anyone found out about her rape or pregnancy? Couldn't the report have easily spread to her cousin, who was, as you told us, attending classes at the same university?"

"First of all, I didn't feel safe with a rapist running around campus. He might've tried to rape other women. He had a gun and was obviously dangerous."

"But why did you write your friend's name on the report? You could have left it anonymous."

"I did it for Miriam's sake."

"Didn't you believe her when she told you her life was in danger because of her family?"

"I did, but what if the man raped her again? As a result of my report, the university installed an emergency phone at the bus stop. There's no telling how many people that's saved." She paused. "Besides, she needed help from someone . . ."

"Are you saying you were concerned for her mental state, and that's another reason you went to the police?"

"Yes, and the police were working with me, keeping her under surveillance to make sure she didn't try to harm herself."

"Can you read aloud the date of the report?"

"March 29."

"Why would you fear for her safety? After all, the report date is before she discovered she was pregnant."

"She had been acting suicidal from the first day she was raped. I wanted to protect her."

"So, let me get this straight. Are you saying she was suicidal *before* she learned about the pregnancy? That the rape alone could have driven her to suicide?"

"The pregnancy made it worse. It was difficult to hide the rape."

"And are you saying that hiding and denying the rape could have saved her life?"

"Probably."

"Miss Massy, are you a professional counselor?"

"No."

"Do you have previous experience dealing with rape or suicide victims?"

"No."

"What are you studying at college?"

"Finance."

"Objection, Your Honor. Miss Massy is here as a material witness, not as an expert," Mr. Nicholas interrupted.

"That's alright, Your Honor," Mr. Johnson said before the judge could respond. "I have no further questions for this witness."

Martina Massy left the stand. Miriam Hessian's picture was removed. Everyone was quiet in the court for a few seconds. I was feeling uneasy. I didn't want my beliefs to strip me of compassion and lead me to generalizations. I didn't want to ignore the individual stories of women like Miriam.

Mr. Johnson broke the brief silence after Martina Massy left the stand.

"Your Honor, I would like to call my next witness, Dr. Eleanor Gina."

I was well aware of Dr. Gina's credentials. She had a Ph.D. in psychology and had been working with rape victims and their children for the past twenty years. She was widely published on the subject. It was time to hear an expert opinion.

"What are the aftereffects of rape on a victim?" Mr. Johnson asked once Dr. Gina was seated and qualified as an expert witness.

"Rape is an outrageous crime that leaves its victim feeling extremely violated—physically, emotionally, and mentally. After a rape, the victim tends to feel dirty and disgusted. She may blame herself for the events, though she was not at fault. She may feel deeply embarrassed or shameful. She may become depressed and isolated. Rape victims often have trouble trusting anyone after the attack, even family members. They may also develop a lack of emotion or inability to feel love. Many women also experience a feeling of numbness, detachment, or 'unrealness' about everything.

"On top of that, a victim may experience flashbacks, frightening dreams, an inability to sleep, a lack of concentration, mood swings, outbursts of anger and crying, and a change in eating habits. Many victims try to avoid anything that may trigger a flashback, and that includes talking about the attack. In a nutshell, rape turns a woman's life upside down. Unfortunately, it's not uncommon for a victim to attempt suicide as a result of rape."

"Dr. Gina," Mr. Johnson asked, "are the above symptoms experienced only by those who get pregnant as a result of rape, and not by those who don't get pregnant as a result of it?"

"Of course not! All women who go through it experience the same traumatic effects." She paused. "Rape is a heinous crime that devastates *all* women, whatever their cultural background, political beliefs, acquaintance with their attacker, or whether or not the rape results in pregnancy. Rape is always wrong, and it always harms the woman."

"But wouldn't these effects be more severe for those who get pregnant as a result of the rape?" Mr. Johnson asked.

"Not really. The act of rape is, in itself, very violent—the damage has already been done. The pregnancy might add additional complications, but it can also contribute positively to the healing process if the woman chooses to continue the pregnancy to term." She looked at Martina Massy, then added, "Pregnancy will not make the situation so severe that a woman who never thought of suicide would end up killing herself because of it."

"Let's consider those cases in which the victim becomes

pregnant as a result of rape," Mr. Johnson said. "Does abortion contribute to the healing process you described earlier? For instance, does abortion reduce a woman's depression, improve her self-esteem, or reduce her likelihood of committing suicide after a rape?"

"Not at all. You see, the cause of these negative effects is not the pregnancy but the rape. *Abortion doesn't undo the rape*, and it's outrageous to think that abortion can heal a woman and make her forget all the trauma she went through." She paused. "If a pregnant woman can heal after rape by getting an abortion, what can heal women who don't get pregnant? Do you think one medical procedure can heal such a heinous and ugly crime?"

"Dr Gina, I do understand that rape is a violation of any woman. But we're talking about whether or not abortion helps women who become pregnant as a result of a rape. I'm not asking if abortion heals her completely or totally erases the memory of rape, but if it minimizes the effects of the rape," Mr. Johnson replied.

Mr. Johnson had warned me about Dr. Gina—he'd said she'd be a difficult witness. Her mission in life, as an extreme feminist, was to speak out about women's issues, using science and statistics to support her beliefs. She didn't put words in women's mouths—she let them speak for themselves.

"Dr. Gina, does abortion ease the pain of rape?" Mr. Johnson asked again.

"No. Evidence suggests that abortion often prolongs the healing process." Dr. Gina hesitated. "In a research study I was involved in, a number of rape victims—ones who had become pregnant after the attack—were interviewed. Seventy percent of the victims refused to have abortions. Many of the women interviewed after delivering their babies said they were more inclined to overcome the rape. Initially, most of the women didn't want their babies and resented their presence. Later on, however, they got used to the pregnancy, and not one of them reported regretting her decision. On the other hand, those who went ahead with abortions regretted their decisions afterward. This suggests that the women who kept their babies were able to heal faster than those who did not."

"How does abortion prolong the healing process?" Mr. Johnson asked.

"Abortion is not a simple procedure. It involves a stranger examining a woman's organs, followed by a violent operation. The procedure can remind a victim of her rape. In addition, research shows that the side effects of abortion—whether or not the pregnancy was the result of rape—include guilt, depression, feelings of being 'dirty,' low self-esteem, resentment of men, and suicide. What's remarkable is that these effects are identical to those a rape victim suffers. Unfortunately, on top of those emotions, a woman who opts for abortion generally feels the added guilt of having murdered her own child. Abortion seems to remove the responsibility for the crime from the rapist and put it all on the victim," Dr. Gina said. "It's very deceptive to tell a woman that abortion will help her heal. Many women go into an abortion thinking that way, and later find out that abortion increases the pain of the attack instead of easing it."

"And how does continuing the pregnancy help the victim heal?"

"Suppose you're an excellent employee and your supervisor does something to you that you don't deserve, and that ends up hurting you emotionally. You go home and can't sleep. The whole night, you just think about what he did to you, letting the events roll over in your brain, again and again. In the morning, you fear going back to work. You feel hurt and violated. You feel distressed and emotionally betrayed. How can you overcome the experience, especially if you can't undo what's happened?" Dr. Gina paused briefly. "You forgive. See, when you forgive a person, you gain control of yourself and your situation. This can be seen, for example, in the relatives of murder victims. Many of them have reportedly found healing through forgiveness. The offense that your boss committed is wrong and made you a victim. But you can choose to avoid being a victim. You can choose to surmount the offense. In the case of rape, even if the rapist ends up spending years in prison, the victim has still suffered the results of the crime and is probably still hurting. When a rape victim chooses to continue with an unintended pregnancy, the selfless act of giving life to an innocent child helps her overcome the effects of her attack."

Mr. Johnson nodded his understanding. "One more question, Dr. Gina. In your opinion, would abortion have saved the life of Miriam Hessian?"

"No," Dr. Gina answered firmly. "What would have saved her life is good counseling. Her pregnancy could have been easily prevented if she had seen a doctor immediately." She looked at Martina Massy. "I have counseled people coming from cultures like Miriam Hessian's. I've worked with doctors and the police, and both are sensitive to the issues surrounding female sexuality and unwanted pregnancies. In fact, two of the cases I worked with the police on involved pregnancy. In each case, the woman carried her child in a private location—using a private name—then gave her baby up for adoption. Both women are doing very well." She looked at Mr. Johnson. "You have to keep in mind, Mr. Johnson, rape is involved in less than 0.06 percent of all abortions performed every year in America. In my opinion, in the case of rape, abortion only harms the woman."

"Thank you, Dr. Gina," Mr. Johnson said. "No further questions."

Mr. Nicholas stood up to cross-examine Dr. Gina.

"All this talk about forgiveness is nice," Mr. Nicholas began, "but it's hard to believe a rape victim wouldn't be helped by an abortion."

"Yes, it's difficult to believe because the public wants to believe that abortion solves these problems," Dr. Gina responded. "Unfortunately, sexual assault victims are left out of this debate, and the public viewpoint is based on prejudice and fear. The public wants to believe that abortion is a cure-all for pregnancies that arise from rape. But rape is very complicated. Often the public blames rape victims as well as their attackers. Many times, the victim is made to feel she's at fault, and people aren't comfortable dealing with her because of this dual blame."

"Dr. Gina, are you opposed to abortion?" Mr. Nicholas asked.

"Objection," Mr. Johnson shouted, rising from his chair. "Dr. Gina is not here to discuss her opinion on abortion but to discuss the effect of abortion on rape victims."

"Overruled," replied the judge.

"Thank you, Your Honor," Mr. Nicholas said with a slight smile. "This is important to establish the credibility of the witness and her opinion."

"Your Honor," Mr. Johnson pleaded, "are we going to rule out the expertise of our witnesses because of their positions on abortion?"

Before the judge could respond, Mr. Nicholas spoke out.

"Your Honor, Dr. Gina is not a real expert. Psychology is not an absolute science, like biology or medicine, and anyone can have his or her own theories, depending on what he or she believes," Mr. Nicholas said.

"I agree, counselor," the judge responded. "Please continue."

"Excuse me!" Now Dr. Gina was throwing in her two cents. "Psychology is a social science that is—"

"Dr. Gina, let's not discuss the nature of psychology in this court," the judge interrupted. "Please answer Mr. Nicholas's question. Do you or do you not support abortion?"

"In the case of rape, I strongly recommend against abortion. It does more harm than good."

"Isn't it harmful for a woman, over the space of nine months, to carry a child who will continually remind her of her rape?" Mr. Nicholas asked.

"Rape victims remember their attacks for many years, regardless of whether or not they become pregnant." Dr. Gina was clearly not intimidated by Mr. Nicholas's question. "Abortion will *not* undo the rape nor erase its memory, Mr. Nicholas."

"So you recommend that a woman carry the child of a rapist?"

"Yes, but you must remember: that baby is her child too."

"True, but its father is a criminal."

"Are you saying we should punish the child for the crime of his father? The victim certainly isn't allowed to kill her rapist, so how can we justify killing an innocent child?"

"The last thing I would call this child is innocent," said Mr. Nicholas with a hollow laugh. "He's nothing but an aggressor who deserves to be removed from the woman's womb."

"Mr. Nicholas, the aggressor is not the child but the rapist. Again, as a counselor, my job is to help the mother. Killing the child simply increases the violence to which the victim is exposed. *A second wrong will not correct the initial wrong.*"

"You say that doing the right thing helps the woman, and what you define as right is to carry the baby to term. But that's your own definition of what is right and wrong in this case."

"What is right is not to think of the child as the rapist's, not to think that abortion is a capital punishment for the rape, and not to think that the child is an aggressor. Most women—when they have the right perspective—choose not to abort. As a matter of fact, as I stated earlier, 70 percent of the women I see refuse abortion because they already believe it's morally wrong. Most of the other 30 percent who choose abortion regret their decision later."

"But when a woman comes to you, you force her to remain pregnant by telling her that abortion is wrong?"

"When a rape victim comes to me, we do not immediately discuss abortion. We first focus on the rape and how she's feeling. The rape is the problem most in need of attention, not the pregnancy. The effects of pregnancy are minor compared to those of rape. I counsel rape victims. My expertise is in rape, not unwanted pregnancy."

"OK, then, Dr. Gina," Mr. Nicholas said, "how many women are raped each year?"

"Each year, about twenty thousand women in the U.S. report being raped. That says nothing of those who remain silent and do not report the crime."

"I've read your research, Doctor, and, in each one of your studies, you report less than three hundred women raped. How could your research have any statistical significance when the number of participants, compared to the actual number of victims, is so small?"

"Keep in mind, Mr. Nicholas, that pregnancy caused by rape is rare. Also, pregnancy from rape is 100 percent preventable if the woman seeks immediate medical attention." Dr. Gina continued. "So, if you're trying to justify abortion based on the demand of rape victims, you have no case. All you're doing is exploiting victims for the sake of some political agenda."

"No further questions," Mr. Nicholas grunted, clearly unhappy with Dr. Gina's last statement. But her last remark made sense to me. To argue for abortion solely because rape victims want it was like arguing to eliminate speed limit laws because they might be broken during a medical emergency. It just wasn't a strong case. [32,33,34,35,36]

***

After court adjourned for the day, we walked to the van. Today, Mr. Maxwell and Laura Smith weren't with us—they'd stayed at the office, preparing for the next day of trial. I sat in the front seat.

"In the case of rape," I said, "the woman had no choice in the pregnancy. It doesn't seem right to hold her accountable."

"No one's blaming the woman," Mr. Johnson replied.

"Think of it like this," said Victoria, speaking up from the back of the van. "Imagine you're in an airplane, and suddenly you discover there's a child next to you in a seat that was supposed to be empty. Someone put him in that seat without your permission. What's the ethical thing to do: throw him from the plane, or wait until the plane lands, then send him to the appropriate authorities?"[37]

"That's a good point, Victoria," her father said. He was obviously proud of his daughter.

"So, you're saying that the ethical thing to do is carry the baby to term, but that the woman is not obliged to take care of it after it's born?" I asked.

"I think, in this case, the whole community has to help out in rearing the child. I don't mind if she gives it up for adoption. If it were me, though, I wouldn't give him up for adoption."

"Why not?" Her father was listening to his daughter attentively.

"Because what if the adoptive parents raised him to be like . . . like . . . like Randy, for instance?" Victoria replied.

"Victoria!" her father scolded.

"I'm sorry."

"That's OK. I'm sure she didn't mean it, Mr. Johnson," I said, a bit surprised. I turned back to Victoria. "What's wrong with me?"

"I don't want my child not to know why it's wrong to kill a ten-year-old boy," she replied with a smile.

"Randy knows why it's wrong to kill a ten-year-old boy," her father said, clearly still embarrassed by her earlier comment.

"Mr. Johnson, it's a continuing private debate between Victoria and me," I said.

"A debate about a ten-year-old boy?"

"Something like that." With that, we all sat silently for the rest of the ride. I knew that a big lecture from Victoria awaited. She was blunt, but I didn't mind it. In fact, I got a kick out of it. But her father obviously felt differently. We arrived at the office, and walking to my car, I said good-bye. I had to find an answer to her question before I saw her again. Otherwise, I'd never hear the end of it.

***

Erick was in the kitchen when I got home. He was grilling meat on a small indoor grill.

"Do you want some?" he asked, pointing to a package of raw steak sitting on the counter.

"Sure, thanks."

"How was your day today?"

"OK."

"You don't seem to be OK."

"I'm just worried about Victoria."

"Victoria, your new girlfriend," Erick said, mockingly.

"She's *not* my girlfriend."

"What's she up to now? Is it another ten-year-old dying?"

I couldn't help but laugh. "No, it's the same ten-year-old. The civil society argument couldn't explain to her satisfaction why we feel sad when he's killed, even if we didn't kill him ourselves."

"I don't feel sad," Erick replied.

"You don't?"

"No, I don't. Maybe women are too emotional about everything—they feel sad whenever an actor dies in a film. Men are different. They're realistic. Men don't cry when a ten-year-old boy dies."

Was the problem with me? Was I too emotional? Was I less of a man than Erick? Maybe that was why Erick didn't have a problem with abortion. He had no problem when a ten-year-old dies, either.

"Are you capable of killing a ten-year-old boy?" I asked him.

"Is my answer going to be used against me in any way?" Erick joked. "You know, you *are* a lawyer, or nearly one. I've got to be careful."

"It's off the record. I promise."

"Everyone is capable of killing."

"Then why do I feel sad when a ten-year-old is killed?"

"You don't feel sad. You feel angry because it reminds you that, as a man, you were unable to stop or prevent it."

"What?"

"I don't think you understand your emotions," said Erick, looking up from the grill. "How you feel about things is a combination of factors—how you were raised, your biological makeup. For centuries, we've been brainwashed into thinking that killing is wrong, and that plays a part in how we feel when someone does it."

"You're right. How could I let Victoria get away with this?"

"Yeah, don't let them get to you, those right-wing fanatics."

I smiled. I couldn't believe that Victoria was able to make me feel the way I did. Why did I feel sad if a ten-year-old boy died? *Because I've been brainwashed into thinking that killing is wrong.* It was a part of my biological makeup—the result of millions of years of evolution. I still didn't need God. I was off the hook.

Chapter 21
Samantha (Court Day #4)

"Mrs. Lucky, when did you get pregnant with Samantha?" Mr. Nicholas asked the witness.

"About three years ago," she replied.

"Did you see a medical professional to confirm your pregnancy?"

"Yes."

"What was the name of the doctor?"

"Dr. George Miller."

"When was the first time you saw Dr. Miller?"

"It must have been sometime in January 1999."

"Why did you get pregnant with Samantha?"

"Why?"

"Let me rephrase. Was your pregnancy planned or unexpected?"

"My husband and I wanted a child," she replied.

"Was your child wanted, then?" he said, persisting.

"Definitely. It was our first child and we were looking forward to it."

"But, two months into your pregnancy, you sought to have

an abortion." Mr. Nicholas paused. "Why the change in plans?"

"Shortly after my pregnancy, I became sick and was diagnosed with rubella."

"And what did the doctor recommend, in terms of your daughter?"

"He suggested therapeutic abortion would be best for all of us. He said our child was at a very high risk of being born handicapped."

"What happened next?"

"I talked to my husband about it, and we decided to terminate the pregnancy."

"Why?"

"I didn't want my child to suffer through life."

"Mrs. Lucky, did you then have an abortion?"

"No."

"Why not?"

"I went to Christ Hospital with my doctor's referral to abort my child."

"Why Christ Hospital?"

"It's two blocks from my house."

"What happened when you went to the hospital?"

"They took me to a room and made me hear the heartbeat of my baby. They told me my baby was already a human being, and that I would be a murderer if I aborted her. They said I would be a sinner."

"Did that change your mind?"

"Not entirely. They also told me that if I had the abortion, I would run a higher risk of developing breast cancer, that I would feel miserable and depressed after the abortion, and that my chances of infertility would be increased. Then they made me sign a paper, saying I was aware of the consequences of having a handicapped baby, but that I was choosing not to abort."

"Did you change your mind?"

"I did, until I went home and told my husband what had happened."

"What did your husband say?"

"He said he had been reading articles about the risk of having rubella kids, and he said the risk was unacceptable to him."

"So what did you do?"

"We were about to make an appointment with another hospital when Christ Hospital called us."

"Who at Christ Hospital called you?"

"A counselor."

"It wasn't a medical doctor?"

"No, just a social worker."

"What did the counselor tell you?"

"She talked to my husband, telling him the same things I was told earlier—that we would be murderers if we aborted the baby, and that we would be putting my health at risk if we aborted. She told us to come to see her the next day."

"And what happened the next day?"

"They made us see the ultrasound and proved to us that the fetus had a heart. They showed us pictures of aborted fetuses." She paused. "They made me feel so bad—I felt intimidated by everything they said. They forced their beliefs on me, and I gave in."

"What happened then?"

"My child was born."

"Mrs. Lucky, can you please show the court your child?"

Mrs. Lucky got from her seat to get her child. She took a child from an older man, probably Mrs. Lucky's father. When she returned to the stand, she made her daughter sit on her lap. The child was obviously handicapped. One of her eyes looked permanently damaged, and she was making unpleasant noises.

"Mrs. Lucky, can you describe the condition of your child?"

"My daughter, Samantha, has congenital rubella. She contracted it from me during the first trimester. She's completely deaf. One of her eyes is damaged, as you can see. The other one doesn't look damaged, but she is almost blind out of that eye. She can only see shadows with it. She is also mentally retarded. She will never be able to speak. Her life expectancy is normal, however, so she will remain in this condition for several years."

"Mrs. Lucky, how are you coping with your daughter's condition?"

"It's very hard." Tears began streaming down her cheeks. "She's in a very bad situation. None of the schools in the state accepted her into their programs—her disability is too severe. I can't afford a private institution or a nurse, so there's no one to take care of her except me and her grandfather. This makes keeping a steady job extremely difficult. My husband couldn't deal with Samantha, and he left us. I'm constantly in severe emotional pain, seeing my daughter like this and knowing I could've prevented all this misery, all this suffering, if I had aborted her. She would've been much better off aborted than living in this horrible condition."

"Mrs. Lucky, you were the one who chose not to abort the fetus, then?"

"Yes, but I didn't know better. I expected Christ Hospital to give me medically sound advice, not religious beliefs and accusations. I went to a hospital, not to a church. I feel now that I'm worse than a murderer by allowing a person to live in such a miserable state. I don't think you can quite understand what it feels like when your own child is mentally retarded, blind, and deaf, knowing you could've prevented it all. Even if what Christ Hospital said is true, I'd rather be labeled a murderer and increase my risk of whatever diseases they claim that abortion causes than allow my own child to live a miserable life. I don't care about the nonsense about whether or not a fetus is human. A human should have the right *not* to be born."

"One more question, Mrs. Lucky," Mr. Nicholas said. "How could what happened to you be prevented from happening to other women?"

"I think that someone has to oversee this hospital and not allow it to operate in this area without accountability."

"Do you think that if Law 1105_ILCS_12.9 were enforced, such an incident could have been prevented?"

"Definitely."

"Thanks, Mrs. Lucky. No further questions, Your Honor."

Mrs. Lucky remained on the witness stand while her daughter made a wailing sound. Samantha was about three years old and horribly deformed. As she got older, her various handicaps could grow even worse. *Abortion in this case must be justifiable,* I thought. I still believed a fetus was human, but that human has rights too—the right to live normally. *Who gives us the right to force lifelong miseries on other human beings?* In Samantha's case, we weren't talking about abortion on demand. We were talking about a human life that could be spared misery. This woman seemed to want the best for her child. She wasn't a teenager who wanted to get rid of her baby. She wasn't irresponsible. She wasn't selfish. All this mother wanted was the best for her child.

"Does the defense want to cross-examine the witness?"

"Yes, Your Honor," Mr. Maxwell replied, getting up from his seat.

"Mrs. Lucky, you can return your child to her chair," Mr. Maxwell said.

The old man previously holding Samantha jumped from his seat, ran to the witness stand, and took the child from her mother. He carried her back to his seat, kissing her. His face was full of joy while carrying the child.

"Mrs. Lucky, you said your daughter is deaf, blind, and mentally retarded. True?" Mr. Maxwell asked.

"Yes. In addition, she has other problems. She might not be able to walk like everyone else. She will never be able to speak. She can't learn language because of her mental capabilities and deafness, and she's also incapable of speaking. The only thing she can do is make noise. She has a bladder problem that the doctors expect to last throughout her life. She will always need someone to take care of her, as if she were an infant."

"Mrs. Lucky, did Samantha acquire this disease after her birth, or prior to it?" Mr. Maxwell asked.

"Before her birth. Otherwise, why would I seek an abortion? My ex-husband and I wanted a child badly. Abortion would never have crossed my mind if she was going to be born healthy."

"So, let me get this straight. Are you telling me that while Samantha was in the womb she had the same problems that would make her physically and mentally retarded?"

"Yes," she replied.

"Mrs. Lucky, after her birth, did you see any improvements to her health?"

"Not at all."

"Are there any technologies or medical procedures available to improve her health and quality of life?"

"Objection," Mr. Nicholas said, standing up. "My witness is not an expert in this area."

"Objection sustained," the judge replied.

"Mrs. Lucky, do you agree with Mr. Nicholas that you are not an expert in this area?"

"I am not an expert in this area, but according to my best knowledge, there is nothing that can improve the health of my child."

"So, would you say that since she was born, you haven't seen any improvements in her health?"

"Yes, that is correct."

"What about the quality of her life, other than her health?"

"It's getting worse."

"If it's the same person, the same problem, or even worse, why can't we use the same solution?" Mr. Maxwell asked. "Mrs. Lucky, why can't you end Samantha's life right now?"

The old man jumped from his seat in objection to the question.

"Objection, Your Honor," Mr. Nicholas said, again standing. "Mr. Maxwell is assuming in his question that the unborn fetus, which is just a glob of tissue, is equivalent to a child."

"Objection sustained," the judge replied.

"Mrs. Lucky, has anything changed about your child to increase her *personhood* since she was born?" Mr. Maxwell asked.

"Objection, Your Honor," Mr. Nicholas stood up again. "Mrs. Lucky is not a philosopher, a medical expert, or a legal expert, and she is not qualified to answer such questions."

"Objection sustained," the judge answered. "Mr. Maxwell, please refrain from such questions."

"Your Honor, let me rephrase my question," Mr. Maxwell answered. "Mrs. Lucky, you said that the health of your child has not improved, and that you see your child's life as meaningless. Is that true?"

"Yes."

"So, would you allow someone to kill your child to solve this current problem?"

"Absolutely not!"

"Why not?"

"Because that would be murder."

"Mrs. Lucky, earlier you said something that struck me. You said that even if Samantha was a human while she was in your womb, she had the right not to be born. If a human has a right not to be born, how much more right to die does she have after her birth?"

"Objection, Your Honor," Mr. Nicholas said.

"Mr. Maxwell, I have asked you to stop this line of questioning with the witness. She is not an expert on these issues," the judge said.

"Yes, Your Honor." Mr. Maxwell looked back at Mrs. Lucky. "Mrs. Lucky, you said earlier this morning that you were willing to be called a murderer and suffer the negative consequences of abortion—"

"Objection, Your Honor. Mr. Maxwell is implying that these side effects are established facts."

"Your Honor, I'm only trying to repeat what Mrs. Lucky said this morning," Mr. Maxwell argued.

"Objection overruled," said the judge.

"Mrs. Lucky, you did say earlier that you were willing to be labeled a murderer and accept all negative side effects of abortion for the sake of sparing your own child this life. Why?"

"Because I'm a parent. To see your own child suffer in misery tears at my heart every day. No one wants to see her child go through what Samantha is going through."

"Mrs. Lucky, is your child unhappy?"

She laughed loudly. "Would you be happy if you were in this condition?"

"This is a report from Samantha's psychologist." Mr. Maxwell took a paper from his briefcase and read it aloud. "It shows that, in spite of all her physical and mental problems, her psychological state is far from miserable."

Mrs. Lucky didn't respond.

"What if you knew in advance that your daughter would be handicapped but would also be happy, as this report indicates, would you still consider aborting her?"

"Of course," she replied.

"Even if she's as happy as any other toddler?" Mr. Maxwell asked.

"She can't be happy in this horrible condition," Mrs. Lucky insisted.

"Mrs. Lucky, are you an expert in psychology?" Mr. Maxwell asked.

"No, but–"

"Then I want you, for a moment, to assume that Samantha is happy. Would you still abort the baby?"

"Yes, I would."

"Why?"

"Because I'm not happy."

"Why wouldn't you be happy if your child is happy?"

"I have to care for a handicapped child for the rest of my life. It's expensive. I have fewer friends. I'll never have a chance to experience what normal mothers experience in life–I'll never hear my daughter call me 'Mom.' I'll never see her grow up to become a beautiful woman. I'll never attend her wedding–"

"So, the issue here is *your* happiness, not Samantha's?"

Mrs. Lucky didn't reply at first. She put her head down,

then began sobbing. "I love my child, Mr. Maxwell. It's so hard to be a parent of a severely handicapped daughter."

Mr. Maxwell plucked a tissue from a box on his table and handed it to Mrs. Lucky. The court was quiet for a few moments. Aborting a handicapped child, I realized, was not always about a loving parent wanting to save the child from misery. It was about parents who didn't want to be inconvenienced by the hassles that handicapped kids bring with them. I didn't blame Mrs. Lucky for wanting to abort her baby. *The world would be much happier without handicapped kids*, I decided.

As I was thinking this, my eyes caught Victoria's, and immediately I felt guilty. No, I was wrong. The world would be much worse off without someone like Victoria. Samantha's moaning interrupted my thoughts, and I looked at her sitting with the old man. He was hugging her and playing with her. The expression on his face made it clear he really loved Samantha. Looking closer at him, I saw he was frail and weak. *How could he have run so fast to pick her up from the witness stand? How could he even carry her?* His love for that child must have motivated him. Maybe love could also empower a parent to deal with all the hassles of caring for handicapped children.

"Mr. Maxwell, are you done with the cross-examination?" the judge asked.

"Not yet, Your Honor," Mr. Maxwell replied, turning toward the witness. "Mrs. Lucky, when you went to Christ Hospital for an abortion, did you meet with Dr. Emanuel?"

"Yes, I did."

"What did she say when you asked for the operation?"

"She said that the hospital doesn't perform abortions unless the mother's life is in danger."

"Did she tell you that if you aborted the baby, you would

be called a murderer?"

"No, but she made me feel that way by saying that abortion is the murder of a human life."

"But did Dr. Emanuel tell you that you would be a murderer if you had an abortion?"

"No, but—"

"What *did* Dr. Emanuel tell you?" Mr. Maxwell persisted.

"Not much. She examined me and explained the hospital's policy on abortion. She said the fetus was human, so she implied that I'd be a murderer if I killed it."

"So, Dr. Emanuel specifically told you that the fetus was human?"

"She didn't say it in those exact words, but she went over the development chart with me, showed me the ultrasound of my baby, and let me hear her heartbeat."

"Mrs. Lucky, were you then convinced your baby was a human?"

"They convinced me by manipulating my decision."

"Mrs. Lucky, are you telling us that the hospital is guilty because they convinced you that the fetus is human?"

"Yes."

***

The court was dismissed for lunch. Mr. Johnson asked me to take Victoria to the cafeteria because he had some errands to run in the courthouse.

I found an empty table in the corner and wheeled Victoria to it. She didn't seem to be her usual cheerful self.

"What would you like to eat?" I asked.

"Nothing. I'm fine. Thanks," she replied.

Her reticence was scaring me. She seemed to be in a bad

mood.

"Are you sure?" I asked.

"Positive," she replied, looking away.

"You don't mind if I eat, do you? I'm starving," I asked.

"Not at all," she replied. "Go ahead."

On my way to the counter, I passed the old man. He was holding Samantha closely. I stopped.

"Hello," I said. "Your granddaughter?" I nodded toward the little girl.

He nodded. "She's my first grandchild," he responded proudly.

"You're not your normal self today," I commented to Victoria when I returned to our table.

She stared at me.

"Were you affected by the discussion this morning?"

"I'd prefer not to discuss it," she replied. "You know what? I'm just tired."

"Why don't you want to discuss it?" I responded quickly. Then I reconsidered. "I'm sorry, Victoria, I don't mean to be rude or anything. I'd just really like to know what's bothering you."

"It's a very sensitive subject for me, OK? I might end up crying if we discuss it."

"You can cry."

"Who's going to wipe my tears?"

I took several tissues from my pocket and put them on the table.

"The tissues are ready, just in case," I said. Then, with a smile, I added, "By the way, they're clean."

She smiled for the first time that day.

"What Mrs. Lucky said bothered me," she began.

"What, exactly, bothered you?" I asked.

"The general topic bothers me . . . because I'm handicapped. It hurts me when someone says they want to abort their handicapped kid. I feel my identity as a human being has been attacked." She continued, "I mean, how can I put it? I get mad and afraid at the same time. What if it wasn't Samantha? What if it was me? Anybody can justify aborting me. I can't walk, use my hands, or do anything for myself. I can't take a shower on my own, I can't eat by myself, I can't read by myself, I can't clean my nose by myself, I can't dress by myself . . . I can't even wipe my own tears. I can't do the most personal things for myself, I mean, even though my parents love me, I feel humiliated each time they give me a shower. It's not easy. I've been living this way for 18 years, and I will continue living this way for many years to come. My parents won't always be there for me. They will get old and need someone to take care of them. I'm lucky my father owns a law firm. But what if I don't succeed as a lawyer? What if I'm not able to find a job? How am I going to take care of myself?" She paused and looked around the cafeteria again. "In spite of the pain, in spite of the continuous humiliation and reminders of my disability, in spite of the unknown future and all uncertainties, I still want to live. That's what's hurting me—that my existence is considered a tragedy by others, a long life of misery and torture. But I'm happy in spite of everything. If I were given the choice in the womb to be born or not to be born, I would choose to be born. Of course, if you ask another person who's not handicapped if he'd rather live like me or not be born, he'd probably choose not to be born. But you *whole* people don't feel empathy toward us. Empathy is not feeling sorry for us. Empathy is understanding that we want to live, that our disabilities don't reduce our value as human beings, and that we want you to see beyond our limitations. It's scary that someone could have looked at my handicap and made a decision to abort me. I feel insulted."

"Victoria," I replied, "your parents love you. Your parents would never abort you if they had to do it all over again. You're very lucky in that sense. You should take each case by itself. Your handicap is not that bad—your parents can deal with it."

"Oh no, Randy. My handicap is bad enough to frustrate anybody. You wouldn't be able to deal with it. What's the difference between Samantha and me? We're both handicapped, but one of us is aware of it, and the other probably isn't. My parents probably do more for me than Samantha's mother does for her. Samantha's mother doesn't have to hear her child nagging at her, crying, making fusses, feeling depressed, complaining about her condition. That peaceful, harmless child is much easier to deal with than a young woman. You look at the young woman and say she'll never get married, and still that woman has emotions that are hurt more easily than Samantha's. My parents have it as bad as—or even worse than—Samantha's. But the funny part is that many parents have it even worse than that, not because their children are physically or mentally handicapped but because their kids are spiritually and morally disabled. A woman whose son turns out to be a murderer has it worse. There are more parents out there whom we should feel sorry for, yet we don't justify abortion for them."

I had never seen Victoria so emotional. She was telling me that, in spite of everything, she'd rather live with her handicap than never live at all. Mrs. Lucky said that in spite of everything, she'd rather have her child aborted than let her live a miserable life.

"I don't want to argue with you, but I still see more value in your life than Samantha's," I commented.

"If a human has a right to life, then he has a right to live a relatively meaningless life. Maybe, by our standards, she has no value, but in truth, she has value. Mrs. Lucky got it wrong altogether. It's not a question of the right to be born or not to be born. It's a choice between dying or living with a handicap, and I bet you, from my own experience, I would always choose to live. I even bet you that Samantha would choose to live. Samantha may not see her life as meaningless. She's a happy kid. Life might be harsh on her in the future, the same as it is on 'whole people.' 'Whole people' commit suicide more than handicapped people. That rhetoric about meaningless life is something I don't appreciate at all."

"I'll accept your answer that handicapped people find their lives meaningful, regardless of their handicap," I replied. "But what about their parents? Don't you think this would devalue their lives?"

She seemed uneasy with the question.

"My parents work hard and put so much of their time, money, and effort into helping me do things that 'whole people' can do for themselves. They worry about my future more than they worry about my brother's. I feel bad about that, but my dad has told me that this is his cross in life, and through this cross, he has found meaning. Everyone has a cross. This is the cross that God gave us as a family."

I stared at Victoria and realized she had something in her that other eighteen-year-olds didn't have. The world needed many more Victorias. But could Victoria be *this* Victoria without her handicap? I doubted it. Something good had to come from her disability. She had touched my life more than any other woman. It would be the greatest mistake in the world not to allow a person like Victoria to live. My eyes became watery as this thought occurred to me. I grabbed a tissue and wiped my own tears.

***

Back in court, Mr. Johnson called another expert on handicapped children. He questioned him about the percentage of abortions performed to prevent handicapped children versus abortions performed for other reasons. The percentage was so small, the expert said, it would not be enough to justify the abortion policy. Mr. Johnson also asked about the lives handicapped children led. The expert presented scientific studies showing that there seemed to be no difference between handicapped and normal people in their degree of life satisfaction, outlook on the immediate future, and vulnerability to frustration.[38] He then gave some facts on the difficulties that parents have raising handicapped children. He told us that more than 80 percent experience depression.

By the end of his testimony, I was convinced that the abortion of handicapped children was not done to end the suffering of a child but to end the suffering of a parent. It had nothing to do with the children. *But why should the parents be made to suffer? Didn't they have a right to a happy life too? Why was there suffering in this world? Where was God?*

Chapter 22
Martha

"Selling our eggs to EGGSO?" Martha repeated my question with disbelief. "No, no way, Randy." With her beautiful black eyes, she stared at me for a few seconds. "But we do donate our eggs."

"You donate your eggs?!"

"We don't sell them—"

"How could you?" I asked with disgust.

"Randy, we have no choice. We need to help each other. We do it for the sake of our camp."

"How does donating your eggs to the outsiders help the camp?" I asked.

"Wait a second. We don't donate them to the outsiders," she replied. "Randy, 60 percent of couples that get married can't have children, so we help them out by donating eggs."

"You expect me to believe you guys don't sell—or *donate*—eggs outside of the camp?"

"We've been living in the underground for years. We don't see the real sun. Even the air we breathe isn't natural. This is a hard life, and we do what we can to help each other out, but we don't go outside. Not without going through the Boss."

"Have you ever donated your eggs?" I asked.

Martha put her hands on mine and squeezed. "I try to do it as often as I can. I do it for the camp. You know that our greatest weapon is increasing our population. If only 40 percent of our couples can have children, we'll never be able to achieve our dreams. Children are our best hope."

I sat quietly, looking at the floor. I was confused.

"Randy, I hope this doesn't bother you," Martha replied, still holding my hand. "If you want, I'll stop donating my eggs, just for your sake."

I looked up at her, disbelieving. A month ago, she'd tried to call the camp police on me, and now she was willing to do something huge just for me, even though it wasn't in the best interest of the camp.

"Randy, I love you."

I was shocked. I definitely hadn't expected that. She looked at me hopefully, I suppose wanting me to say something in return. But the only thing I could tell her was that if I were part of that world, I would have married her, but I was not.

"I can't be with you. I love Victoria," I heard myself saying. I think my answer surprised me more than it surprised her.

"Victoria?!" She seemed surprised and hurt. "Which one? There are lots of Victorias in the camp."

"She's not from the camp."

"You're in love with an outsider?" She looked away, searching.

"No—"

"I should have known! How could I ever compete with a beautiful, cloned, white woman?"

"Martha, listen to me. She's not from the outside." I grabbed her shoulders and turned her to face me. "She's probably dead by now."

"Dead?"

"She's a memory from before my coma," I replied. "I don't know if she's real or a figment of my imagination, but I know I can never fully love anyone but her."

She seemed relieved.

"Martha, I don't know what I'm talking about; I'm just exhausted." My head was swimming, mostly with images of Victoria, whose very reality I was so uncertain of. "I can't commit to anyone right now. My life has to be devoted to the RMs."

She was obviously still hurt.

"At the Human Farm and Body Parts Factory, they raise the children like animals. They're cloned to look exactly the same. They never leave their room their whole lives. They never experience love. They don't know what a flower looks like. They never call anyone Dad or Mom. And then they accomplish their mission by getting killed, so someone can make money from their body parts."

"I know it's awful!" Martha replied. "That's why the camp will revolt one day."

"What's worse is that the eggs used to create the RMs come from uncloned people. Where else could they come from but the camp?"

"Impossible."

I didn't say anything.

"Impossible," Martha repeated. "No one in the camp would do something like that. No one. There must be a mistake . . ." Martha paused for several seconds. "You know what? I think I know what it is."

"What?"

"They could be using old eggs—frozen ones from years ago. That would explain it."

"I have the list of DNA numbers from my batch. Do you have a list of the numbers of the residents?" I asked.

"The camp police has that information, but it's confidential. No one can access it but them," Martha replied.

"I have to get a hold of that list," I said quietly.

"There's no way on earth—"

"There is," I interrupted, "and I need your help."

"My help?"

"Yes. I can break into the camp police station, and—"

"What?"

"You told me there's no other way, didn't you?" I said.

"But you'll get caught. They'll imprison you."

"I have to take my chances."

"I'm sorry, Randy," Martha said firmly. "I won't be able to help you."

"You don't need to help me break in," I insisted. "I want you to do something else."

"What?"

"I want you to go to the outside world, and—"

"Outside world! Randy, I've been down here my whole life. I've never—"

"There's a first time for everything."

"I'm a black woman. I'll get killed by the outsiders." Her expression was serious and frightened.

"I'm not saying it wouldn't be dangerous. We'd have to be careful."

"Why would you need me to go outside the camp? What could I possibly do?"

"I want you to take my watch and go to my apartment," I replied, "just in case someone's tracking me. I want the police to think I'm home while I break into the station."

Martha hesitated, looking deep into my eyes.

"I don't believe you. You're talking as if the police are the enemies."

There was no time for further discussion, not now that the plan was playing out in my head.

"Listen, I want you to dress like a man and make sure to hide your face. Just leave here around nine tonight and come back before two. I'll be waiting by your apartment."

Martha seemed as nervous as I was pretending not to be. I knew I was putting her life in danger, but I also knew she was intelligent and could handle the task. I gave her my watch, jacket, and hat, and headed to the police station.

Chapter 23
Father Matthias (Court Day #5)

"Can someone be in love and not know it?" I asked Erick the next morning.

"No. It's not possible." He poured more cereal into his bowl.

"What if you don't know that you're in love, but something tells you that you are?"

"So you think you're in love? Then you are."

"No, someone told you that you're in love, but you don't feel like you are."

"Then you're not," Erick said, putting a spoonful of cereal into his mouth.

"But, what if that someone who told you is you?" I persisted.

"Me?" he said with his mouth full.

"No, me," I said, pointing to myself. "I said to myself that I'm in love."

"You said to yourself that you're in love, and you don't know if you really are?" Erick got up from his chair and put the milk in the fridge.

"Who's right? Me now or me then?"

"Randy, cut to the chase," Erick interrupted. "Are you in love?"

"I didn't think so, but yesterday I dreamed—"

"Not your dreams again," he said, rolling his eyes as I slid into the chair across the table from him.

"That I was in love," I continued. "Well, in my dream, I said to another person that I was in love with this girl."

"Aha!"

"In the dream, I was surprised by what I'd said."

"You know what?" Erick put his spoon down. "Maybe you are in love, but you don't know it."

"So, it *is* possible to be in love and not know it?"

Erick brushed his hands. Sarcastically, he asked, "And who would this lucky woman be?"

"Victoria."

"Victoria! Your boss's daughter?" Erick started to laugh.

"You know what? Forget it!" I started to get up from the table. Erick put a hand on my arm.

"Seriously, I think you *are* in love. I mean, who else would bother finding answers to her silly questions?"

"But it's not possible," I replied. "I can't love her. She's young."

"A six-year age difference isn't that much."

"She's a quadriplegic."

"That could be a problem."

I nodded my head. I couldn't be in love with a severely handicapped person. Besides, I never thought of Victoria. It was just that stupid dream that put the idea in my head.

***

That day, the plaintiff's attorney called a priest to the stand.

"Father Matthias, you do not support the pro-life movement, do you?" Mr. Nicholas asked.

"No, I don't. The pro-life movement is a political cause that aims at making abortion illegal, and, hence, to restrict the rights of others to make their own moral choices." In response to Mr. Nicholas's questioning look, he added, "Don't misunderstand me—I *am* against abortion."

"How can you be against abortion and not be part of the pro-life movement?"

"We should not lose the distinction between moral and legal law, and therefore between sin and crime,"[39] Father Matthias replied. "It's not the obligation of the state to prohibit everything that the moral law prohibits. There can be little freedom if we lose sight of the vital distinction between moral questions and legal ones."[40]

"Father, why not?" Mr. Nicholas persisted. "Why shouldn't we prohibit everything that's sinful?"

Father Matthias laughed. "For one, we'd start imprisoning everyone who commits adultery, everyone who doesn't pay their tithe, everyone who utters white lies, and the list goes on. Our society is a pluralistic one, and different people have different beliefs about what constitutes a moral law. Furthermore, morality is a private issue. After all, our country *is* based largely on a separation between church and state."

"So, it doesn't bother you that abortions are being performed in America?"

"As much as it bothers me that people are not attending church. But I don't go to the government asking for laws forcing people to come to my church. Our laws allow everyone to practice their faith as they wish. If you believe abortion is wrong, no one is forcing you to have one. Morality is a decision each individual must make for himself. No one should impose their moral laws on others."

"Thank you, Father," Mr. Nicholas said, turning to the judge. "Your Honor, I have no further questions for Father Matthias."

Mr. Maxwell stood.

"Father, you said something about the distinction between moral and legal law, as I recall. You are a Christian, are you not?"

Father Matthias nodded his head.

"Does your moral law prohibit murder?"

"Yes."

"So, would you agree that, just because a religious group takes a position on a certain issue, such as rape or murder, that doesn't exempt the issue from public legislation?"

"Abortion is different than murder," Father Matthias replied.

"Father, please answer the question," Mr. Maxwell insisted. "Do you agree that because a religious—"

"Some issues can be both moral and legal. That's true," the priest conceded.

"So, the fact that something, such as murder, is a moral issue doesn't mean we shouldn't make it a crime. Do you agree with that, Father?"

"Yes, in the case of murder." Father Matthias was obviously trying to qualify all his answers.

"So, Father, when, in your opinion, should a moral law become part of the legal system?"

Father Matthias, rubbing his eyes, put his hands together and stared at the ceiling before answering. "When it affects other people's individual rights, I guess." He paused and took a deep breath. "Or when it affects society's peace and order, or when it's commonly accepted moral law by the majority of society."

"Why do you oppose abortion?"

"Because it destroys a sacred human life," the priest replied.

"And you don't believe that this unique, sacred life deserves to have his or her rights respected—especially the basic right to life?"

Father Matthias didn't reply for a few seconds.

"It's not as simple as you're putting it," Father Matthias answered, leaning forward. "I believe abortion is wrong because it's the destruction of human life. But the majority of society doesn't agree. In fact, many believe a fetus is just a glob of tissue, and nothing more. The problem is, because of our pluralistic society, we don't have a broad moral consensus on this issue."

"So, because there's no moral consensus on certain issues, those issues should not be subject to legislation?"

"Exactly. When there's no moral consensus on a particular issue, the government must allow its citizens to make the moral decisions themselves."

"Should there have been laws to protect the Jews from the Nazis, even though some believed they were a drain on society? Should we have allowed slavery laws to continue, even though half the country believed their religion or morality permitted them to own slaves? Should we allow polygamy because some believe that men should have multiple wives?" Mr. Maxwell paused. "How much moral consensus did we need for each of those cases? Is common acceptance proof of moral acceptability?"

"In the case of abortion, everyone should have the chance to practice their own moral convictions. If you believe it's wrong, then don't have an abortion." Father Matthias was growing impatient.

"But then, why not keep slavery legal? If you believe it's wrong, don't own a slave. Why don't we lift the laws against polygamy? If you believe it's wrong, just marry one woman," Mr. Maxwell replied, looking around the room. "If a person sincerely believes that abortion is murder, it makes no sense to tell them it's permitted under the law. Don't you think people have a right to protest and to demand that government protect them against such a heinous crime?"

"People do have the right to protest. Until we get this issue clarified, the government must remain neutral," Father Matthias replied.

"Father, a government that legalizes abortion hardly seems neutral.[41] Don't you see? Legalizing abortion implies that fetuses aren't humans."

"Which is what a great portion of society believes anyway," the priest retorted.

"So, would you agree that, as things stand today in our pluralistic society, the government has chosen to espouse the religious beliefs of one segment of society, and ignored your own personal belief that fetuses are human and that abortion kills humans?"

"There might be some truth to that, I suppose."

"Father, thank you. I have no further questions for you."

Father Matthias left the witness stand. His air of confidence had clearly diminished. I realized then that Mr. Maxwell saw every witness as prey, and every trial as a hunt. He was relentless. He never tried to make things easy for witnesses.

The prosecution rested its case, so we were given a fifteen-minute recess.

After the short break, Mr. Maxwell called his first witness to the stand—a philosophy professor named Dr. George Thomas.

"In our society, we seem to agree that murder is wrong and that rape is wrong. Why is it so difficult for us, Dr. Thomas, to agree on abortion?"

"Father Matthias said a moral law becomes a legal law when it involves human rights," Dr. Thomas began. "That's exactly the problem with our society. We think the government's purpose is to protect and secure the equal rights of all individuals, to allow us to pursue happiness, however we understand it. In changing our governing philosophy to think about individual rights, we've trivialized moral law into a simple system of contracts. When morality becomes a question of contracts, life becomes full of contract breaking. For instance, marriage became a legal contract, and the number of divorces increased significantly. We've forgotten that individual rights were not derived from contracts but given by God," Dr. Thomas answered.

"How does that result in a moral consensus about murder, but not about abortion? How does individualistic morality make it so hard to agree on abortion?"

"Because of the precise nature of the mother-fetus relationship. Rather than being a contract entered into willingly by both parties, the duties of the mother bind her to the fetus in ways to which neither has specifically consented. There really is no active, legal agreement to adhere to. The matter is further complicated when morality is thought of in terms of securing individual rights. Then moral consensus becomes impossible."

"Dr. Thomas," continued Mr. Maxwell, "if you're suggesting that we should not think of morality in terms of individual rights or contractual agreements, how *should* we think of it?"

"That's a very good question," Dr. Thomas replied.

"Morality consists of the acceptance of unexpected events that life presents. Responsiveness and responsibility to things unchosen define one's moral capacity. Morality is not confined to contracted agreements of isolated individuals. Yes, one is obliged by implicit compacts and involuntary relationships in which persons simply find themselves."[42]

Mr. Maxwell wasn't satisfied. "But why should we accept your definition of morality, and not the definition that involves individual rights and contractual agreements?"

Dr. Thomas considered this for a moment. "Four reasons," he began, ticking each off on a finger as he spoke. "First, individualistic morality doesn't work. Like it or not, we live in a community, and becoming embedded in a family, a neighborhood, or a social system brings moral obligations that have never been entered into with informed consent.[43] These moral obligations originate simply in the sorts of reciprocal relatedness that constitute being a human. The mother- fetus relation is characterized by obligations of this sort, as all parent-child relations.[44]

"Second, individualistic morality discourages personal sacrifices and encourages, at best, a minimal appreciation of the virtue—and even the necessity—of constructive suffering. Our culture has a low tolerance for the burdens and failures of life, and tends to deny that life has value when conducted in irremediably painful conditions.[45]

"My third problem with this type of morality is that moral and social dilemmas are regarded as the business and the burden of individuals, to be resolved, or borne, alone."[46]

"And that consequence is clearly seen in abortion?"

"Exactly. One consequence of the individualistic view of the pregnant woman as moral agent—besides the obvious one of minimizing restraints on her free power of self-discrimination—is that it reduces the obligations of other individuals or the community to offer support during and after a burdensome pregnancy. Society often seems to see parents as responsible for avoiding the births of defective (and hence burdensome) children, and, as a result, society's willingness to provide assistance to severely handicapped individuals and their families decreases correspondingly."[47]

"What's the fourth problem with this type of morality?" Mr. Maxwell asked.

"It can lead to values that conflict with our previously established values. Liberal pluralism then becomes a sort of confidence game in which, in the guise of showing respect for individual rights, we are, in reality, asked to consent to a new kind of society based on a new set of beliefs and values,"[48] Dr. Thomas explained. "By making the moral purpose of government the securing of individual rights, liberalism was able to secure political peace in a morally pluralistic and fragmentary society. Its deepest advantage is to remove from the political arena all issues that might be too deeply divisive of the citizenry. The ideal of liberalism is thus to make government neutral on the very subjects that matter most to people, precisely because they matter most."[49]

"But what happens to the individual's right to pursue happiness? Are you saying the individual doesn't matter?"

"That's the problem with individualistic morality," Dr. Thomas said, leaning forward. "It's self-defeating. We've become obsessed with individual rights, and that obsession has made us miserable. We're no longer happy at work, or in our marriages and other relationships—no longer happy at all. We know that the world is full of pain and suffering, and if we don't find meaning and happiness despite these elements, we're miserable. Who wins in that kind of society? The most outspoken—that's who. That's why special interest groups are winning. They speak the language of rights, yet the rights they advocate aren't natural rights, nor even deserved privileges, but destructive power that they're seeking to destroy the moral fabric of our society."

"So, you're saying that when we debate abortion, we should think of morality in a broader way than individual rights, or women's rights?"

"Yes. If we're able to foster a sense of duty to others and to our common society—a duty that precedes and grounds our own rights as individuals—then it becomes possible to envision a moral obligation to support cohesion in the human community of even its weakest members, those with the least forceful claim to consideration, whether they be the unborn, the sick, the poor, or the socially powerless."[50]

"Thank you, Dr. Thomas," Mr. Maxwell said. He turned to the judge. "No further questions, Your Honor."

Mr. Nicholas chose not to cross-examine Dr. Thomas.

What Dr. Thomas said made sense to me. He'd made clear why there's no moral consensus on abortion. Personally, I could attest to the fact that individual morality had made me miserable in many of my past relationships. It had clearly made Mrs. Lucky miserable. That obsession with our rights was actually keeping us from happiness.

Chapter 24
A Man Behind the Bush
(Court Day #6)

The defense called Dr. Marc Marcello as its next witness. When he took the stand, he looked in my direction and smiled.

"Dr. Marcello, is a fetus a person?"

"That depends on what you mean by 'person.' There are hundreds of definitions out there, some claiming a fetus is a person when there's a heartbeat, when it can feel pain, when it can think on its own, when it's aware of its own existence, and the list goes on . . ."

"Are you saying there is no universal definition of 'person' that people agree on?" Mr. Maxwell asked.

"That's correct. All these definitions are philosophical in nature, and as long as personhood is defined by philosophies, we'll continue to disagree on a universal definition," Dr. Marcello said. "However, if we put philosophies aside and consider biological science alone, the definition of personhood will no longer be subject to individual philosophies and preferences."

"How does science define a person?"

"Simply as an individual human being," Dr. Marcello replied.

"An individual human being!" Mr. Maxwell repeated.

"Yes, all of us can agree on that, can't we?" Dr. Marcello asked. "An individual human is the best term to describe a person. It's stripped from all philosophical biases. This definition, I must add, is also the one you'll find in an English dictionary."

"In light of this definition, is a fetus a person?"

"Of course it is."

"Equal in personhood to the mother?"

"Absolutely."

"How could this be, when the fetus doesn't relate to others as adults do, doesn't have dreams of his own, and so on?"

"You have to put the philosophical terms aside. An individual human is an individual human," Dr. Marcello insisted, emphasizing each word with a pound of his fist. "What I mean is, if you use the philosophical definitions of a person, you can be a good person or a bad person, for example, but when it comes to the scientific definition, you can only be an individual human being or something else. The phrase 'more or less of an individual human being' is meaningless."

"So, the question, then, is whether a fetus is an individual human being?" Mr. Maxwell asked.

"And the answer to the question is definitely yes," Dr. Marcello replied.

"Why?"

"Mr. Maxwell, may I ask you a question?" Mr. Maxwell nodded. "Are you a person?" This was the argument that had convinced me that life started at the moment of conception.

"Yes," Mr. Maxwell answered.

"Were you a person yesterday?"

"Yes."

"When you were one year old?"

"Yes."

"Were you a person the day before you were born?"

Mr. Maxwell did not answer.

"Has anything changed, aside from normal growth, since the day before you were born? Did you suddenly become an individual human being at your birth, or were you an individual human being a day before you were born?"

"I would say I was definitely a person one day before I was born."

"What about two days before you were born? One month before you were born?" Dr. Marcello continued. "Common sense tells us humans are constantly developing. Within such a continual growth process, it's hard to logically defend any demarcation point after conception at which an immature form of human life is so different from the day before or the day after, that it can be morally or legally discounted as a nonperson. Even the moment of birth can hardly differentiate a nine-month fetus from a newborn."[51]

Mr. Maxwell seemed to consider this. "So, you're saying that the zygote is a person because the newborn is a person, and the newborn develops from the zygote during a continuous process?"

"Yes, exactly!" Dr. Marcello was clearly excited.

"Your Honor, I don't have any further questions for Dr. Marcello, but I'd like the right to recall him."

"Very well," the judge replied. "Mr. Nicholas, would you like to cross-examine the witness?"

"Yes, Your Honor." Mr. Nicholas stood up and walked toward the stand as Mr. Maxwell took his seat.

"Dr. Marcello, according to secular forms of reasoning, continuous processes of change can fundamentally alter what undergoes change, so that what exists at the end is not the same sort of being as existed at the beginning. Through a continuous process, acorns develop into oak trees, but we don't conclude that 'acorn' and 'oak tree' are different words for the same thing. Do you agree?"[52]

"OK," said the doctor suspiciously.

"Doesn't it follow, then, that just because we have a continuous process of growth from the zygote to the newborn, the zygote is not necessarily a person because the newborn is?"

"Ah, but Mr. Nicholas, the gradual change does not always produce a change in essence,"[53] replied Dr. Marcello, smiling.

"No, but in this case, it clearly does."

"Then can you please explain why a human ovum always results in a human being, and any other ovum always results in another organism? For instance, no human being originates from a duck's egg?"[54]

"Well, again—"

"Isn't it because in each ovum, the essence has already been fixed, and only the appearance changes during development?"[55]

"Again, if something becomes a person later, that doesn't mean it's a person all the time." Mr. Nicholas was clearly caught off guard.

"Then what is a fetus, Mr. Nicholas?"

"A fetus, Doctor, is simply an organized society of single-celled individuals."[56]

"We are all made of an organized society of cells, Mr. Nicholas. If a fetus is not a person, what defines it?"

"It's a potential person," said Mr. Nicholas, smiling as he walked back to his table and sipped some water. "A fetus is not a person but a potential person. The life that pro-life advocates refer to is non-personal. It's sub-personal animal life only. The mother, however, is a person, and that's not debatable."[57]

"Potential person?" Dr. Marcello was getting angry.

"It's like a man coming to buy your house. You call him a buyer, but in reality, he's not a buyer at that stage but a potential buyer. The point here, Doctor, is there's a difference between a 'buyer' and a 'potential buyer.'"

"Mr. Nicholas, the term 'potential person' is meaningless and—"

"As meaningless as 'potential buyer,' a term used in business—"

"Meaningless when we talk about personhood. The young fetus has no alternative. It either dies or develops distinctively human traits and carries on human activities.[58] A person becomes a potential buyer by working hard, saving money, applying for a loan, and making a decision to buy a house. There's simply no comparing the two."

"Doctor, you've clearly shown that a fetus is a potential person. I agree with you on that point. But you've failed to show that the fetus is a person in its current stage," Mr. Nicholas continued. "You're assuming that a gradual change doesn't produce a change in *essence*."

"Scientific facts show that there is no change in essence and that the fetus is a human at the moment of conception."

"The facts show that the fetus has none of the qualities we have in mind when we proclaim our superior worth to the chimpanzees or dolphins. It cannot speak, reason, or distinguish between right and wrong. It cannot have personal relationships, without which a person is not functionally a person at all—"[59]

"Mr. Nicholas," Dr. Marcello interrupted, "first, the newborn baby wouldn't meet your criteria. As a matter of fact, your 'standard of personhood' is so high, half the human race couldn't meet the criteria during most of their waking hours, let alone their sleeping ones.[60] Finally, you're just throwing out philosophical arguments and not scientific facts."

"Why should we use your biological definition of personhood? After all, we're talking about society here"

"Mr. Nicholas, I don't expect us to agree on a definition of personhood," Dr. Marcello said. "Fortunately, a universal definition isn't necessary for abortion to be illegal."

"What?"

"It's not necessary to describe a fetus as a person. Rather, it's crucial that the fetus be recognized as a human individual. It's en route to becoming personal, but at all times, it possesses the full sanctity of human life. Thus, the two arguments are interwoven. First, biological data, especially at the stage of segmentation, establish human individuality. Second, Christian faith insists that the dignity of human life is not founded upon an individual's utility but is a dignity conferred by God irrespective of relative degrees of worth."[61]

"Wait a second. Why should personhood not be required? This is your own philosophical worldview that personhood is not needed."

"Not my own worldview. This is consistent with all our ethics and rules."

"What ethics and rules?"

"For instance, when a homicide occurs, it's because someone killed a human. The degree of personhood, such as relationality, intelligence, etc., will not affect the classification of the crime. All the standards acceptable today for determining death are based on physical or biological criteria, the breakdown of the three basic human systems of circulation, respiration, and brain function. Some might want to define death only in terms of brain death, but all these understandings of death, and tests for the presence of death, follow an individualistic model. Imagine what would happen if we proclaimed death when human relationships dissolved, rather than basing death on biological data. Why can't we use the same standard for a fetus?"[62]

Mr. Nicholas was ready with a response.

"Suppose we follow this line of reasoning. You were never able to show that a fetus is an individual human being. So, when would you say that individuality is present?"

"When completeness is present. For instance, an unfertilized egg is not an individual because it's not a complete human. It can unite with millions of sperm and produce different people. On the other hand, a fertilized egg's genetic makeup has already been determined."

"What about identical twins? I mean, here we're talking about a fertilized egg that divides into two eggs—two potential persons."

"Yes, but both are humans."

"Not individuals at that point?"

"Individuality *has* been determined. Both identical twins will have the same genetic codes. Individuality means that the fertilized egg has at least one complete human. It could later become two humans, but for now, we know there's at least one complete being with a well-established genetic structure."

"Dr. Marcello, it seems very crude to identify individuality with the gene combination. To say that the entire life of a person is determined by heredity is a theory of unfreedom that can only be regarded as monstrous.[63] The problem with your biological approach, at any point on its spectrum, is that it treats personhood as if it were purely a biological reality. Yet, personhood signifies a spiritual, transcendent reality, which is the basis for the sacredness of persons.[64] Consider, for instance, that identical twins are different individuals, each unique in consciousness. Though having the same genetic makeup, they will have been differently situated in the womb and hence will have received different stimuli. For that reason, if for no other, they will have developed differently, especially in their brains and nervous systems, and therefore personhood cannot be a function of genetic makeup only, can it?[65]"

"I agree that the environment and other factors shape human personality—that's part of the growth process. We grow and change as people, but this change doesn't change the fact that we're human. Biology will determine the existence of a person, but won't completely determine what kind of person he or she will be."

"And what about a person in a persistent vegetative state? He or she has a functioning spinal cord and brain stem, but not a functioning cortex. Though he's alive and has a human genetic code, he lacks all distinctively human abilities,[66] and it's not considered murder when family members discontinue life support. So, clearly, biological indicators are *not* the only ones used in determining death," Mr. Nicholas said. "And aren't the biological factors the same for a fetus? Shouldn't a family decide whether or not life support should be continued?"

"Mr. Nicholas," Dr. Marcello answered, "in this case, the fetus is temporarily, not permanently, incapable of engaging in distinctively human activities. Just as we don't deny personhood and the right to life to the temporarily unconscious, we should not deny personhood and the right to life to the temporarily immature.[67] Unlike the person in the vegetative state, the fetus could, given time, be capable of engaging in human activities." Dr. Marcello sighed. "We can argue day and night about whether the fetus is a person, whether the fetus is a potential person, and whether the fetus is an individual or a human. All these questions are important, even if we don't agree on the answer. But abortion is still wrong."

"Why, Doctor? Because we remove a few unwanted cells of material from a woman's body?"

"Because human life has intrinsic value. Morally, the fight against abortion is not primarily to protect the human dignity of the unborn but is, above all, to safeguard the dignity in all people. Does a pro-choice public policy tend to cheapen or enhance human dignity and the value of human life, generally speaking?"[68]

"The pro-life definition of 'person' cheapens human dignity. If God creates a person every time an ovum is fertilized by a sperm, then persons must be cheap and disposable, because approximately 58 percent of all fertilized ova spontaneously abort prior to implantation,"[69] Mr. Nicholas said.

"Mr. Nicholas, natural death takes place at every stage. Just because natural death occurs, that doesn't give us a license to kill."

"Dr. Marcello, we're talking about 58 percent of the population. Since nearly one-half of the fertilized ova die early as a result of failure to implant in the uterine wall, failure of implantation would be the gravest medical problem facing humanity if the concept of personhood or humanity were extended to include zygotes."[70]

"And more than 60 percent of those in their eighties die, but that doesn't mean they're not individual humans. At the very beginning of human life, or at the end of human life, we are, obviously, not dealing with life in its fullest realization. Instead, we're dealing with the bare minimum necessary for individual human existence."[71]

"Sir, those in their eighties can think and talk and relate

to others, while a fetus can do none of those things."

"A fetus is an immature, dependent form of human life that only needs time and protection to develop. Surely, immaturity and dependence are not crimes punishable by death."[72] Raising his voice, Dr. Marcello continued. "The fact is that abortion kills an innocent life. Either we're going to value embodied human life and humanity as a good thing, or take a nihilist position that assumes human life is just one more random occurrence in the universe such that each instance of human life must explicitly be justified to prove itself worthy to continue."[73]

"No further questions, Dr. Marcello."

***

Court was adjourned for the day. I walked Victoria to the car. I had a severe headache from listening so intently to the heated courtroom exchanges.

"Both groups had good arguments," I confided to Victoria. "It makes it hard to know what to believe. If I were a professor, I'd give both of them good grades."

Victoria smiled but looked worn out. "The problem is that the issue is not equivalent to grading a paper. It's a question of whether or not you're allowed to kill a certain entity."

"But, you have to admit it's hard to agree on these issues because both sides have so many good, compelling arguments."

"It might be hard to decide what to believe, but it's not hard to decide what to do."

"What do you mean?"

"Abortionists have doubts regarding their beliefs. I think we should act on those doubts. If there's a doubt whether or not life is present, the benefit of the doubt must be given to life,"[74] Victoria said. "Feelings of uncertainty about whether abortions early in pregnancy kill a person should lead us to refrain from abortions, just as uncertainty about whether a movement in the bushes is caused by a person or a deer should lead a hunter to refrain from shooting."[75]

Chapter 25
Knock Knock, Boss

When I got to the station, it was surrounded by at least twelve guards. Cameras were mounted all over the place. It was going to be a tough place to break into. *I must do it.* I entered the station and was immediately stopped by a guard.

"Can I help you?"

"I need to see Victor," I answered, recalling the name of one of the first guards who had interrogated me.

"Wait here," the guard ordered.

I waited in the lobby until the guard returned and asked me to follow him.

We walked down a long corridor and I realized I didn't remember seeing any of the station in my last visit, thanks to my well-applied blindfold. We passed a room called "Camp Records," and I knew right away it was the room I was looking for. Shortly thereafter, we entered a small office with a metal desk, behind which sat Victor.

"Mr. Livingston." He stood. "What brings you to the station?"

"The Boss," I replied.

"The Boss?" Victor was astonished. "The Boss never surprises us. He would have told us if he sent you."

"It was an emergency," I lied. "He wants to know if these DNA numbers belong to the camp." I slid a paper from the Farm in front of him.

He studied the sheet for a moment, then looked at me apprehensively. He got up from his desk.

"That wouldn't make sense, but it doesn't hurt to check."

"Exactly," I replied.

Victor stared at me.

"He's testing me." I smiled.

"I see."

Victor led me to the records room. Once we got there, he went directly to the nearest computer and started searching.

"Hmm, all right. Yes, these numbers belong to people in the camp," he said. "In fact, one of them belongs to your friend Martha." He looked at me distrustfully.

"Martha?" *Oh no.*

"OK, Mr. Livingston, I'm on to you. The Boss doesn't work this way."

"How does the Boss contact people?" I asked, ignoring his accusation. "When will he contact me?"

"When you least expect it."

Victor, apparently giving up on getting an easy confession out of me, started to log off the computer. But before he could, a phone rang in his office and he hurried to answer it.

As we were leaving the records room, I saw Martha headed down the corridor in our direction. She was clearly surprised to see me. *How stupid of me,* I thought. *Of course she's part of the camp police.* It was all coming together. *She was the one who gave me the tour my first day there. She had access to the submarine. What had I been thinking?*

"Martha," said Victor, greeting her heartily when he looked up from the door. The phone in the office had gone silent. "Apparently, your DNA is included on the list that the Boss gave to Mr. Livingston," he said jokingly.

Martha froze.

"Well, I guess I'd better get back to work . . . at the Human Farm and Body Parts Factory," I said, trying to remind Martha of the implications of donating her eggs. "Who knows who'll be slaughtered next? Martha, by the way, I forgot my jacket at your place. Would you mind taking me back there to get it?" I wanted to give her the option of explaining to me, in private, what had brought her to the station.

"Sure," she said softly, her eyes shifting to the floor. "Can you wait here for a minute while I talk to Victor?"

I agreed and watched as the pair walked into Victor's office and shut the door.

Might as well use my time wisely, I thought, and returned to the records room. I sat at a computer and began searching for the identities of camp prisoners.

The list was long, so I narrowed it to include only those imprisoned before age ten. The search returned only one prisoner: Steven Adams. I wrote down his DNA and clone codes, then logged off the computer. A moment after I left the room, Martha and Victor reappeared in the corridor, but their serious expressions couldn't dampen my mood. I thought to myself, *I, too, can contact the Boss when he least expects it,* and smiled as I met up with them.

***

"Martha, I thought you loved me," I said with mock disappointment. "But, sadly, all that talk was just part of your spying on me." She stopped walking just outside the front doors to the station.

"I had no choice," she replied. "The only thing I care for is the camp, Randy. The camp is the great hope of my family and friends. What do you expect me to do when someone shows up from the middle of nowhere and tells me that, until recently, he's been in a lengthy coma? Do you expect me to believe him? We had to keep an eye on you to be sure you weren't an agent."

"An agent?"

"An agent to the outside world, like the person who steals our eggs." She looked defeated.

"My son is in your batch?" She looked at me with desperation in her eyes. "What does he look like? Does he look like me?"

"He has your eyes," I lied. I couldn't tell her he was cloned to look like everyone else. "I promise you, I'll make sure he doesn't get processed."

"Processed?" Martha replied with fear in her eyes.

"Victor shouldn't have told you," I murmured.

"What? Of course he should've! I'm a mother, after all." Then she started laughing hysterically. "I have a son who lives in the outside world!"

Not really, I thought. *He lives on the Farm, where he's more a prisoner than his mom. Everyone in this world is a prisoner.*

When we reached Martha's apartment, she handed me my watch, jacket, and hat. I bid her good-bye and promised I would look after her son. Despite her deceit, I cared for Martha. She'd been made a prisoner the day she was born, yet she hadn't lost hope of creating a better world for future generations. Our ways of gaining that better world were just vastly different.

But as I left the underground, I thought about the truth I had uncovered just that afternoon. Corruption had entered the camp like sewer water entering a well. Would the camp erupt in a flood of waste?

On my way home, I stopped by the "outsider" library and searched for Steven Adams in the computer system. A picture popped up of a young boy lost at age eight, but after that, there was no information to be found.

I then searched using the DNA and clone numbers I'd written down. The computer turned up a Mr. Adam Lincoln, owner of a Fortune 500 company. There was a great resemblance between his photo and that of eight-year-old Steven Adams. According to an article listed in the search results, Mr. Adam Lincoln had died in a car accident—*ten years ago.*

Chapter 26
Abortion on Trial (Court Day #7)

"Good morning," said Mr. Johnson, greeting me when I got to the office. "Maxwell and Victoria are already in the van waiting for us."

I climbed into the van and sat next to Victoria. I felt uneasy. She, on the other hand, was staring at me and smiling. Her smile made me even more uncomfortable.

"*What?*" I asked after a few minutes. Her wide smile was driving me crazy. "Well?" Her eyes opened wide and she started giggling.

"What is it, Victoria?" her dad asked. He looked at Mr. Maxwell. "She woke up happy and has been smiling ever since."

"Would you care to share with us what's making you so happy today?" Mr. Maxwell asked laughingly.

"I'm always happy," Victoria replied.

"Very true," her dad responded, "but today seems special."

"I had a dream," Victoria replied.

"A dream!" I couldn't hide my surprise.

"Randy, you're not the only person who dreams or who

250

remembers their dreams," she said. Mr. Maxwell laughed loudly.

"What was the dream about?" Her father was more serious.

"I dreamed I was wearing a white dress, just like a bride . . ." Mr. Johnson slowed down and looked at his daughter in the rearview mirror. "And I dreamed I got out of my wheelchair and could walk."

"Wow," Mr. Maxwell said. Mr. Johnson and I remained silent.

"I could walk and walk," Victoria continued. "It felt so good."

"I bet it was a great feeling," Mr. Maxwell said.

"Yes, but . . ."

"But what?" Her father was still serious.

"But Dad and Randy—"

"*Me?* I was in your dream?" *It wasn't possible we'd both dreamed of each other, was it?*

"Were not allowing me to walk," she continued. "You kept saying, 'Victoria, come back and sit in your chair,' and I was saying, 'Why? Why? I like it. I like to walk. It feels good and I like it.' You said, 'Come back. You'll fall.' But I just kept walking. Oh, it felt so good."

We were all silent.

"I can still feel it—I can still feel my legs walking. What a great feeling to walk and walk and walk." Victoria closed her eyes.

The rest of the ride, Victoria quietly smiled, still thinking of her dream, I guessed. I sat quietly next to her, thinking of my dream, her dream, and of her. I knew that after today, it wasn't going to be the same between Victoria and me. Maybe I should just let go and allow Randy Livingston to fall in love.

But she was a quadriplegic. *Randy Livingston goes with his mind, not with his heart*, I thought. *I'm to be a lawyer, after all—a scientist, a logical person, and not a person swayed by emotions and dreams.* I was fighting with myself.

***

Mr. Maxwell called Dr. Marcello to the stand again.

"Is it accurate to say you have performed hundreds of abortions?" Mr. Maxwell asked.

"I would say thousands," Dr. Marcello replied.

"Can you describe to us what happens during the abortion procedure?"

"Many techniques are used to perform an abortion," Dr. Marcello said. "It depends on which trimester the pregnancy is in."

"Let's start with the first trimester. What techniques are used then?"

"A variety of techniques can be used—suction aspiration, dilatation and curettage, RU 486/mifeprex, or methotrexate."

"Which technique is most common?"

"Suction aspiration."

"Please describe this technique."

"Well," the doctor began, "a powerful suction tube with a sharp cutting edge is inserted into the womb through the dilated cervix. The suction dismembers the body of the fetus and tears the placenta from the wall of the uterus, sucking blood, amniotic fluid, placental tissue, and fetal parts into a collection bottle."[76]

"Are there any side effects associated with this technique?"

"Other than killing the fetus?"

"Side effects to the woman," Mr. Maxwell clarified.

"Putting aside the typical side effects of abortion, such as decreased fertility, the specific side effects include the possible puncturing of the uterus during the procedure, which may cause hemorrhaging and necessitate further surgery. Also, infection can easily develop if any fetal or placental tissue is left behind in the uterus. In fact, that's the most frequent post-abortion complication."[77]

"What about the other techniques? Can you describe them for us?"

"In the dilatation or dilation and curettage technique, the cervix is dilated or stretched to permit the insertion of a loop-shaped steel knife."[78]

As Dr. Marcello spoke, Mr. Maxwell selected an item from his table. He showed it to the doctor.

"Like this?" he asked.

"Exactly."

"Please continue," Mr. Maxwell said.

"The body of the fetus is cut into pieces and removed, and the placenta is scraped off the uterine wall. Blood loss from a D&C is greater than for suction aspiration, as is the likelihood of uterine perforation and infection."[79]

"So the difference between the two techniques is the device used to dislodge the fetus?"

"Yes. One uses suction, and the other uses a knife."

"What about RU 486?" Mr. Maxwell asked. "Is that the same as the French morning-after pill?"

"Yes, but it's actually made of two powerful synthetic hormones to chemically induce abortions in women five to nine weeks pregnant."[80]

"So, in this technique, a woman swallows some pills, and abortion happens in the privacy of her home without anyone knowing about it?"

"No, no, no," Dr. Marcello replied. "The RU 486 procedure requires at least three trips to the abortion facility."[81]

"Three visits!" Mr. Maxwell exclaimed.

"At least," the doctor replied. "You see, in the first visit, the woman is given a physical exam. If she has no obvious contraindications—red flags like smoking, asthma, high blood pressure, obesity, etc. that could make the drug deadly to her—she swallows the RU 486 pills. RU 486 blocks the action of progesterone, the natural hormone vital to maintaining the rich nutrient lining of the uterus. The developing fetus starves as the nutrient lining disintegrates."[82]

"So basically, RU 486 kills the baby by withholding food from him or her?"

"That's the first step. At a second visit, thirty-six to forty-eight hours later, the woman is given a dose of artificial prostaglandins, usually misoprostol, which initiates uterine contractions that cause the fetus to be expelled from the uterus. Most women abort during the four-hour waiting period at the clinic, but about 30 percent abort later—at home, work, wherever—as many as five days later. On the third visit about two weeks later, a doctor determines whether the abortion has occurred or a surgical abortion is necessary to complete the procedure."[83]

"So, there's a possibility that a surgical abortion will still be required?"

"Five to 10 percent of all such cases require surgical abortion."[84]

"But for the 90 percent of cases that don't require surgery, this procedure eliminates the side effects experienced by the other two procedures?" Mr. Maxwell asked.

"No," Dr. Marcello said. "There are several serious, well-documented side effects associated with RU 486 abortions, including severe bleeding that can last up to forty-four days—as well as nausea, vomiting, pain, and even death."[85]

"Death?"

"At least one woman in France has died so far," Dr. Marcello said, nodding, "while others there have suffered life-threatening heart attacks. In FDA trials conducted in 1995, one woman nearly died after losing half her blood and requiring emergency surgery."[86]

"Dr. Marcello, one woman's death hardly holds any statistical significance—surely not enough to conclude that death is a side effect of RU 486."

"On the other hand," Dr. Marcello responded, avoiding the question, "we don't have nearly enough statistical evidence to tell us this drug is safe."

"Is that so?"

"Long-term effects of the drug have not yet been sufficiently studied," Dr. Marcello explained, "but there are reasons to believe that RU 486 could affect not only a woman's current pregnancy but her future pregnancies as well, potentially inducing miscarriages or causing severe malformations in later children."[87]

Mr. Maxwell paused, considering this last statement.

"What about methotrexate?" he asked finally.

"The procedure with methotrexate is similar to the one using RU 486, but the hormones are administered through an intramuscular injection rather than with a pill."[88]

"Isn't methotrexate approved by the FDA for the treatment of cancer?"

"Yes. It was originally designed to attack fast-growing cells, such as cancers, by neutralizing the B vitamin and folic acid necessary for cell division. Apparently, methotrexate also attacks the fast-growing cells of the trophoblast, the tissue surrounding the embryo that eventually gives rise to the placenta. The trophoblast not only functions as the 'life support system' for the developing child, drawing oxygen and nutrients from the mother's blood supply and disposing of carbon dioxide and waste products, but also produces HCG—human chorionic gonadotropin—the hormone that signals the corpus luteum to continue the production of progesterone necessary to prevent the breakdown of the uterine lining and loss of the pregnancy. Methotrexate initiates the disintegration of that sustaining, protective, and nourishing environment. Deprived of the food, oxygen, and fluids it needs to survive, the fetus dies."[89]

"So, basically, this is another method of starving the baby?"

"Yes, and both expel the fetus from the womb. Three to seven days after the administration of methotrexate, a suppository of misoprostol is inserted into the woman's vagina to trigger expulsion of the fetus from the woman's uterus. Sometimes, expulsion occurs within the next few hours, but often a second dose of the prostaglandin is required, making the time lapse between the initial administration and the actual completion of the abortion as long as several weeks. A woman may bleed for weeks afterward—forty-two days in one study—and may abort anywhere. Those still pregnant in later visits, in this case at least one of every twenty-five women, are given surgical abortions."[90]

"What are the side effects of methotrexate?"

"Because of its high toxicity and unpredictable side effects, even doctors who support abortion are reluctant to prescribe methotrexate for abortion. Known side effects commonly include nausea, pain, and diarrhea, as well as less visible but more serious effects, like bone marrow depression, severe anemia, liver damage, and lung disease." Dr. Marcello paused and took a deep breath. "Even the manufacturer warns in the package insert that, while methotrexate has shown itself useful in treating certain types of cancer and severe cases of arthritis and psoriasis, deaths have been reported with the use of methotrexate. They recommend that its use be limited to physicians whose knowledge and experience includes the use of antimetabolite therapy. Researchers performing methotrexate abortions have dismissed such concerns because of the low dosage used in the procedure, but other abortion doctors have disagreed, and the package insert clearly warns that toxic effects may be related in severity to dose or frequency of administration, but have been seen at all doses."[91]

"Let's move on to the second and third trimesters, Dr. Marcello. What techniques are used at those times?"

Dr. Marcello took a sip of water from a glass beside him.

"The first one is called dilatation, or *dilation*, and evacuation," he answered. "It's used to abort unborn children as old as twenty-four weeks and is similar to the D&C. The difference is that, instead of a looped steel knife, forceps with sharp metal jaws are used to extract the fetus."

Mr. Maxwell selected a pair of forceps from his table.

"Like these?"

"Precisely." The forceps looked like pliers with teeth. "These are used to grab parts of the developing baby, which are then twisted and torn away from the uterus. Because the baby's skull has often hardened to bone by this time, it must sometimes be compressed or crushed to facilitate removal. If not carefully removed, the sharp, bony edges may cause cervical laceration. Bleeding from this procedure can be profuse."[92]

"Your Honor, with your permission, I'd like to present a brief video illustration at this time," Mr. Maxwell said, turning toward the judge.

"Very well. Keep it short, though," the judge said.

Mr. Maxwell played the video, muting the sounds. He leaned against the defendant's table.

"Dr. Marcello," he said as the tape began playing, "are you

familiar with this video?"

"Yes. I made it while performing the procedure—before I became pro-life."

"Please explain to us what's going on here," Mr. Maxwell said as images began to flash on the screen.

"We used ultrasound to view the inside of the womb," Dr. Marcello explained. "On the left side of the screen, you can see the operating room. On the right is a view of the inside of the mother's womb." On the right side of the screen, we could see the picture of a small fetus moving and sucking his thumb.

"This particular fetus was twenty-three weeks old," Dr. Marcello continued. "Here, I was explaining the procedure to students." Mr. Maxwell fast-forwarded the video. When he stopped, the doctor continued his commentary.

"The first step, as you can see, is to insert a long-toothed clamp inside the woman." The minute the forceps touched the walls of the womb, the baby recoiled, though the metal had not yet made contact.[93]

On the video, Dr. Marcello grabbed the fetus's leg, twisted it, cut it, and pulled it out through the vagina.

I heard Victoria gasp. Mr. Johnson turned and looked at her.

"Now, as you can see, I was grabbing body parts at random, then twisting them," Dr. Marcello said. "Because the developing baby already has calcified bones, the parts had to be twisted and torn away."[94] The video showed Dr. Marcello cutting a hand and pulling it out, followed by a leg. Finally, the forceps twisted and removed the whole body, sans head.

"The skull needed to be crushed first before removing it," Dr. Marcello explained.

When the procedure was completed, Dr. Marcello was again shown talking to his students. He looked tired. Mr. Maxwell mentioned his appearance, and Dr. Marcello elaborated.

"Believe me," he said, "this procedure is traumatic for doctors too. There's no way for the doctor to deny the act of destruction he's just committed. It's right in front of him. The sensation of dismemberment flows through the forceps like an electric current."[95]

"What about the other techniques?" Mr. Maxwell asked. "Are they as traumatic for doctors?"

"All of them are traumatic in their own way," Dr. Marcello answered.

Mr. Maxwell paused while the television was wheeled out of the room.

"Tell us about other procedures done during this time in the pregnancy."

"Well," Dr. Marcello sighed, "another method used is instillation."

"Instillation?"

"Yes. This involves the injection of drugs or chemicals through the abdomen or cervix into the amniotic sac. The chemicals cause the death of the child and his or her expulsion from the uterus. Several drugs have been tried, but the most commonly used are hypertonic saline, or urea."[96]

"Are these similar to RU 486 and methotrexate?" Mr. Maxwell asked.

"Not entirely. In the previous methods, you try to kill the baby by starving it and then expelling it. Here, you're trying to kill the baby by poisoning it and then expelling it."

"Poisoning it?!" Mr. Maxwell said.

Dr. Marcello nodded slowly. "This technique is used after sixteen weeks of pregnancy, when enough fluid has accumulated in the amniotic sac surrounding the baby. A needle is inserted through the mother's abdomen, and 50 to 250 milliliters—as much as a cup—of amniotic fluid is withdrawn and replaced with a solution of concentrated salt. The fetus breathes in, swallowing the salt, and is poisoned. The chemical solution also causes painful burning and deterioration of the baby's skin. Usually, after about an hour, the child dies. The mother goes into labor about thirty-three to thirty-five hours after instillation and delivers a dead, burned, and shriveled baby. About 97 percent of mothers deliver their dead babies within seventy-two hours."[97]

"Any side effects to the mother?"

"Hypertonic saline may initiate a condition in the mother called 'consumption coagulopathy'—uncontrolled blood clotting throughout the body. Severe hemorrhaging can also occur, as well as other serious side effects that affect the central nervous system. Seizures, coma, or death may result from saline inadvertently injected into the woman's vascular system."[98]

"And urea is about the same?"

"Sort of," Dr. Marcello replied. "Because of the dangers associated with saline methods, other instillation methods, such as hypersomolar urea, are sometimes employed. But these are less effective and must usually be supplemented by oxytocin or a prostaglandin in order to achieve the desired result. Incomplete or failed abortions remain a problem with urea methods, often precipitating the additional risk of surgery."[99]

"So, urea is less dangerous than the saline, but also less effective?"

"It still has side effects," Dr. Marcello said. "As with other instillation techniques, gastrointestinal side effects, such as nausea or vomiting, are frequent, but the most common problem with second trimester techniques involves cervical injuries, which range from small lacerations to complete detachments of the anterior or posterior cervix. Between 1 and 2 percent of women administered urea must be hospitalized for treatment of endometritis, an infection of the uterus lining."[100]

"What about prostaglandins? They're not poisons, are they?"

"No, they're not," Dr. Marcello responded. "Prostaglandins are naturally produced chemical compounds that normally assist in the birthing process. The injection of concentrations of artificial prostaglandins, prematurely, into the amniotic sac induces violent labor, and the birth of a child usually too young to survive. Often salt or another toxin is first injected to ensure that the baby will be delivered dead—as in instillation—because some babies survive the trauma of a prostaglandin birth and are born alive."[101]

"Are there any side effects to this method, which uses naturally produced chemicals?" Mr. Maxwell asked.

"Of course. There's the risk of retained placenta, cervical trauma, infection, hemorrhage, hyperthermia, bronchoconstriction, and tachycardia, as well as more serious side effects and complications from the use of artificial prostaglandins, including cardiac arrest and rupture of the uterus, which can be unpredictable and very severe. Death is not unheard of." [102]

"Hmmm," Mr. Maxwell considered. "And there is one technique left?"

"Actually, there are two: partial birth abortion, which is sometimes referred to as dilation and extraction, and hysterotomy."

"Hysterotomy?"

"Similar to the caesarean section, hysterotomy is generally used if chemical methods, such as salt poisoning or prostaglandins, fail. Incisions are made in the abdomen, uterus, and the fetus, after which the placenta and amniotic sac are removed. Babies sometimes born alive during this procedure, raising questions as to how and when these infants are killed and by whom."[103]

"So, in this technique, babies may be killed after they are born?"

"Yes."

"Is this technique risky to the mother's health?"

"Most definitely," Dr. Marcello replied. "This method offers the highest risk to the health of the mother, because the potential for rupture during subsequent pregnancies is appreciable. In the first two years of legal abortion in New York State, the death rate from hysterotomy was 271.2 deaths per 100,000 cases."[104]

"Do women still want this procedure performed on them?"

"Only if everything else fails."

"And what about the infamous 'partial birth abortion' procedure?"

"This procedure is used in women who are twenty to thirty-two weeks pregnant, or even farther into their pregnancies. Guided by ultrasound, the doctor reaches into the uterus, grabs the unborn baby's leg with forceps, and pulls the baby into the birth canal, deliberately leaving the head, which is kept just inside the womb. Then the doctor forces scissors into the back of the baby's skull, spreading the tips of the scissors apart to enlarge the wound. After removing the scissors, a suction catheter is inserted into the skull and the baby's brains are sucked out. The collapsed head is then removed from the uterus."[105]

"So, the baby is delivered halfway and is still alive?"

"Yes."

"Could it survive on its own if it were fully delivered?" Mr. Maxwell asked.

"Of course. After twenty-three weeks, the probability of survival is substantial."

"Dr. Marcello, do we know if the baby experiences pain

during this procedure?"

Dr. Marcello looked down at his hands. "Yes, it does. That's why I used to give the baby painkillers before the procedure."

"Painkillers?"

"Yes."

"Your Honor," Mr. Maxwell said, turning toward the judge, "may I present another brief video given to me by Dr. Marcello?"

"You may," the judge answered. The television was wheeled back into the center of the courtroom.

There was silence in the court. Even Mr. Nicholas didn't object to anything that had been said. Mr. Maxwell began the video, but this time didn't mute the sound.

On the screen, a woman was sleeping on an operating table. Dr. Marcello reached into her vagina. A moment later, he withdrew his hand, and a tiny foot appeared.

"Randy," Mr. Johnson whispered to me, "may I ask you a favor?"

"Sure," I replied, hoping for an excuse to leave the room.

"Can you take Victoria to the cafeteria? I don't want her to see this."

"Of course," I said.

"You can leave her there and come back."

I walked behind Victoria's chair, stooped over so as not to block anyone's view of the television.

"Where are you taking me?" she asked as I began to pull her from the table.

"I'll tell you later," I whispered in her ear, wheeling her from the courtroom. As I closed the door behind us, I could see the video. The baby's legs and hands were hanging from the mother's body.

"It's a boy," Dr. Marcello was saying in the video. His

students laughed.

"Couldn't you have waited a few minutes?" Victoria asked as we made our way down the hallway. "You made me miss the video."

"That's the point," I answered.

"What point?"

"Your dad didn't want you to see the procedure."

"Oh, come on."

"Listen, he's my boss and I have to do whatever he says." Victoria sighed.

"Besides, I'm happy to get out of there," I said.

We entered the cafeteria. It was empty except for a man sitting at one of the tables. We passed him and sat at a table across the room. I didn't know what to say to Victoria. I felt emotionally drained.

"You know, sometimes we're not thankful enough," Victoria said thoughtfully. "I mean, sometimes I complain about my condition, but look at those poor babies and what's happening to them. I can't believe their own mothers have them killed."

I didn't know what to say. Suddenly, she looked so beautiful to me. How come I'd never noticed it before? I'd always seen her as a good-looking girl, but today, she was gorgeous. Because of our dreams, though, I wasn't comfortable looking at her. I was self-conscious; I couldn't let my eyes meet hers without my heart racing.

"You know, you and I are lucky," she continued. "Our parents didn't make us go through that heinous procedure."

"We wouldn't have known the difference," I replied.

"Of course we would have," Victoria said. "Think of a ten-year-old."

"Another ten-year-old, or the same one?" I forced myself to chuckle, trying to lighten the mood.

Victoria laughed. "The same one. Suppose you were fifty, and someone said to you it was a good thing you weren't tortured and killed when you were ten. Does it make sense to tell them you wouldn't have known the difference?"

"It's not the same, Victoria." *Here we go again*, I thought.

"It is," Victoria insisted. "Even Dr. Marcello said so."

"He said so?" I tried to remember Dr. Marcello mentioning a ten-year-old.

"He said the fetus experiences pain when it's aborted, and that's why he gave it pain killers." Victoria caught her breath. "Just like a ten-year-old who's experiencing pain at the moment of his death. Though its suffering ends when it dies, that doesn't negate the pain it felt."

"You're right. We *are* lucky," I replied. I was amazed that a quadriplegic could consider herself lucky because she wasn't aborted. Victoria was truly amazing.

"Victoria, your dream that you told us about this morning . . ."

"Yes, of course!" Victoria became excited at the mention of her dream. Her face lit up and her eyes became wide and shiny. Her smile was radiant. It was a significant change from the sad, thoughtful countenance she'd maintained during our just completed discussion.

"Do you believe you will walk one day?"

Just as suddenly as it had come, her smile faded. She took a deep breath and closed her eyes for few seconds. "Yes," she said, opening her eyes again and looking as if she felt a bit foolish.

"Yes?"

"Maybe they'll find a way to restore a quadriplegic's abilities. Who knows?"

"Maybe," I said. "But what if they don't?"

Victoria was quiet for a moment. She looked around the empty cafeteria, then back at me.

"I don't mind not walking; I'd just like to gain some independence. I'd like to be able to take a shower on my own, flip the pages of a book on my own, eat on my own, cook on my own . . . " She smiled self-consciously.

"To cook on your own?" I was surprised at that dream.

"I love to cook whenever my mom lends me her hands. One day, by God's grace, I'll be able to cook on my own. We're working on it."

"Working on it?"

"My brother and I are doing experiments in our lab," she said, looking down at the table.

"You have a lab?"

"In our basement," she answered. "We're doing experiments and inventing things—to create ways for quadriplegics to be on their own."

"Interesting." There seemed to be no end to Victoria's ambition.

"Yeah. Give me a few years, and I'll be able to push this chair on my own." She smiled. She explained to me some of the devices they were working on. Apparently, she could already eat on her own, but in front of guests, she confessed, she avoided doing so—she still had a tendency to drop food on herself.

I quietly listened to her, amazed by her energy and vitality—by her love for life. Although she was quadriplegic, her soul was so free. I realized then that I did indeed love her. But I was so unsure of where this journey of love would take me. Was it just a crush, or was it true love? Whatever it was, I had to be careful. She was the daughter of my boss. She was also young, and I couldn't lead her on and later leave her. I had to be sure of my love. Nonetheless, I felt great joy, as if a weight had been lifted from my shoulders. I was happy to be in love with her, at least for this one moment.

Thoughts of Mr. Johnson suddenly pulled me from my reverie.

"Victoria, do you mind if I go and find out what's going inside the courtroom?"

"No, not at all," she replied with a smile.

I went to the courtroom, smiling a little to myself. As I opened the door, I set my face in a serious expression. Mr. Nicholas was cross-examining Dr. Marcello. I sat down next to Mr. Johnson and asked if I should bring Victoria back. He told me not to bother—the court session was almost over for the day.

"Dr. Marcello, have you ever cut a chicken?" Mr. Nicholas was saying.

"Cut a chicken? Yes."

"You have no problem cutting a chicken?"

"Of course not. It's only a chicken," Dr. Marcello replied, suspiciously.

"Regardless of what method you use to cut it?"

"Regardless."

"Because it's only a chicken, right?"

"That's right," Dr. Marcello replied impatiently.

"Then all this discussion about abortion methods is irrelevant, since a fetus, just like a chicken, is not a person." Mr. Nicholas turned toward the plaintiff's table.

"What?" Dr. Marcello was clearly taken aback.

"No further questions for Dr. Marcello," Mr. Nicholas told the judge.

***

Court adjourned for the weekend. I walked with Mr. Johnson and Mr. Maxwell to the cafeteria.

"Was his whole cross-examination like that?" I asked.

"No," Mr. Johnson replied. "He talked about how abortions are rarely performed during the second and third trimesters."

"And that partial birth abortions take place only to save the mother's life," Mr. Maxwell added. "He also talked about how all medical procedures have side effects and discussed the side effects of childbirth."

"So, he was good?" I asked.

"Not that good," Mr. Maxwell said. "He *did* bring in that chicken argument . . ."

Mr. Johnson laughed. "Speaking of chicken, I'm famished."

"Personally, I'm not sure I ever want to eat chicken again," Mr. Maxwell said.

We entered the cafeteria.

"Where's Victoria?" Mr. Johnson asked, scanning the room.

"Over there." I pointed to our table.

"Where?" Mr. Johnson asked again. I looked over to where I had left Victoria. She was gone.

I looked frantically around the room, but I didn't see her anywhere.

"She was right here, by this table?" I insisted, walking over to it.

"Maybe someone took her around to see something," Mr. Johnson said calmly.

We split up to look for her, but she was nowhere to be found. I began feeling really nervous. *Where could she be?* She couldn't move her chair by herself. Somebody must've taken her somewhere. Before long, even the judge and Mr. Nicholas were searching the courthouse with us. After more than 40 minutes, there was still no sign of her.

Finally, Mr. Johnson lost his cool. "Someone has kidnapped my daughter!"

Chapter 27
The Death of an RM

She was sitting in the wheelchair, facing the wall. Her long hair was down. I stood behind her and put my hands on her shoulders.

"Honey, we thought we were going to lose you," I said.

"I thought so too," Victoria said, still facing the wall.

"We won't allow this to happen again," I assured her. "I'll never leave you again, regardless."

The dream faded away when I opened my eyes. I looked across the room and saw Erick in his bed, deep in sleep. *How could we have left Victoria all alone in the cafeteria? Where did they take her? Why?*

Mr. Johnson and I were determined not to go home before finding Victoria. We scoured the courthouse for her well into the evening. We called her name by loudspeaker every several minutes, and security guards thoroughly checked everyone leaving the building before letting them pass. Victoria was nowhere to be found.

"I shouldn't have left her alone," I said with tears in my eyes.

"It's not your fault. It's mine," Mr. Johnson said. He broke down and started crying. "I didn't want her to see those pictures. Her mother and I were seriously considering abortion, and the thought that I even considered that heinous act makes me shiver. When the subject is discussed, I can't be in the same room with her without feeling guilty."

"Mr. Johnson, that was the past. Fortunately, you didn't abort her. You should forgive yourself and move on. Don't let unnecessary guilt ruin your life."

Mr. Johnson nodded his head reluctantly and took a deep breath.

"We'll find her," I assured him. "No matter what, we'll find her."

"The doctor said I'm very sick," she said.

"I'll be your hands, your feet, anything you want." I closed my eyes. "I love you."

"But it's my heart that hurts," she replied.

I sat up in bed, listening to Erick snore. After we'd looked for Victoria in the courthouse, we'd gone outside to search the grounds. There, by the entrance of the building, we found her empty chair. Mr. Johnson's jaw dropped at the sight of it.

I lay back in bed and turned my body to face the wall. She, too, was still facing the wall . . .

"What's wrong with your heart?" I asked her.

"I need a new one. I need a heart transplant," she replied. I wanted to turn her chair and get a glimpse of her face, but I couldn't.

"I know where she is." The judge came rushing at us, face white. "Get in my car and I'll take you there."

When we got to the hospital, she was lying in a bed with

wires all over her body.

"She's had a heart attack," the doctor said. "She needs a heart transplant, or she may not survive longer than a week." He paused, studying Mr. Johnson. "We put her on the waiting list, but the list is very long."

I'd never thought I would lose her so quickly. The only person I'd ever loved was now losing her life. I couldn't allow it to happen. I had to save her.

I listened to Erick's snoring . . .

"Sweetheart, what are you doing here at the Human Farm and Body Parts Factory?" I asked her, examining her long, thick, glistening hair.

"I told you, I'm sick. Very sick," she replied.

"Is there anything I can do for you?"

"Yes, find me a heart. I need a heart transplant."

"I'll give you the heart of the best RM we have here at the Farm," I told her.

"Please hurry. I feel like I'm dying quickly." And indeed, her voice was growing weak.

"Don't die on me. Wait for me," I begged, then rushed to find my batch.

I got out of bed, feeling like I'd had a nightmare. *I didn't want Victoria to die. I'd do anything to keep her alive. Anything?* My thoughts were scaring me. It was 2:00 a.m. and I couldn't take it anymore. I got up and took two sleeping pills, then returned to bed and waited for them to take effect.

I ran through the empty corridors. *We must save her life,* I thought. *She needs a heart. We must start processing the RM right away—there's not much time left.*

"Charles, there's a young lady in a wheelchair who needs a heart transplant," I said as I ran past him to my RMs' room.

"We're taking care of her," he answered with a reassuring smile. "We're processing her order, and we'll process an RM for her today."

"Good." I reached the room and didn't stop running until I was smack in the center.

"Beginstartstandupend!" I shouted. I needed to choose the best RM for Victoria.

I looked at each one of them standing before me, then dropped to the floor, crying. How cruel of me to allow such a thought to cross my mind. I wished I could reverse time and erase the thought.

"Begin New word . . ." The RMs became alert in anticipation of hearing a new word.

"Start . . . Sorry . . . End."

They repeated the word "sorry." I couldn't explain to them what it meant, but I chose to express it by kissing the hand of one of them. I continued kissing the hand of each RM, begging for forgiveness for the thought that had crossed my mind. Even Mr. Johnson wouldn't give his heart to his daughter—what made me think it was OK to take an RM's heart and give it to Victoria? Even Victoria didn't deserve that. I was so overwhelmed with guilt that I couldn't continue preparing the RMs for the attack. I stood there for an hour, paralyzed by my thoughts. Then I remembered Mr. Johnson saying to me that he couldn't forgive himself for considering an abortion for Victoria. I'd told him he needed to forgive himself and to concentrate on the mission of finding her. And I not only needed to forgive myself for my near mistake but to remember my mission to save the RMs' lives.

OK, Randy, back to action. I pulled out my laptop and

opened the simulation program. In a week or so, we would execute the plan and save all the RMs. *Good-bye Human Farm and Body Parts Factory.*

"I have good news for you," Charles said as he walked into the room.

"Yes?"

"We'll process your first RM today."

I stared at him with a frozen tongue, frozen mind, frozen heart—a frozen man.

"For what reason?" I asked.

"For the young handicapped lady."

"Oh, Victoria," I replied.

"I believe her name is Tracy."

"Oh, right. Hey, out of curiosity, why from my batch?"

"It's the decision of the boss. RM 8645-23 is already in the Factory, ready for processing." With that, Charles left the room. I started counting the RMs. Yes—there was one missing. It was Martha's son.

What luck! Why didn't I start the plan of attack yesterday? I could have saved Martha's son! I ran to the Factory.

RM 8645-23 was standing next to the processor when I arrived. The boss, Mr. Manson, and Charles were there. *Should I act right now?* I weighed my options. There were five workers here, along with the other three men. I couldn't win. I wanted to shout "Murderers!" but I held my tongue. I could lose the rest of the batch, but because of my promises, RM 8645-23 was especially important to me.

"Call 8645-23 . . . Begin . . . Mission accomplished . . . End."

The RM was led to the processing table. When he looked at me, tears sprang from my eyes. I couldn't handle looking back—I felt like I was leading an innocent man to his hanging.

What had he done to deserve this punishment? Why was Tracy's quality of life more important than the actual life of my RM? I couldn't watch the great unfairness, the great evil. *What can a man do to stop this great injustice, the murder and killing of an innocent child?* My mind was screaming at me, but words weren't sufficient to save the life of this dying boy.

I ran from the room and headed quickly down the hallway.

Then I saw her, still facing the wall. I turned her chair to make her face me. She was beautiful, but something ugly kept me from talking to her. Didn't she know that, to give her the heart she was looking for, we had to kill another human being? I wasn't a fanatic, but I was pro-life. I didn't condone the murder of innocent children.

"Change of plans," I said aloud when I reached my RMs' room. "We will execute the plan tomorrow," I said aloud. "I have so much work to do . . . we all have so much work to do."

I didn't have time to mourn my friend. I felt like I'd lost my own child, but there was no time to think about it—it was time for action. I needed to prepare the RMs. Tomorrow morning, the war would begin.

I closed the door to the room and put the Tracko device next to it. I went to my computer and quickly ran part of the simulations. Because I was now one RM short, I had to change the plan and modify the program slightly. 8645-23 had been one of the three who would help me put explosives around the Factory. I'd simply have to cover for him.

I sent the RMs to sleep—they needed rest and I needed to leave early. I had so much to do. I had to get the rental trucks to transport the RMs, and I needed them by morning. I also had to come back later that night to disable the alarm and install my new system, a system I'd spent the past month developing.

I left the RMs and went down to the processing room to see what had happened to 8645-23. When I got there, Charles and the boss were gone. The workers didn't seem to notice me, and I watched for a moment as they packed 23's body parts. His unusable remains were put into bags and thrown in a biological waste container.

"Do you mind if I help dispose of his remains?" I asked.

"Sure, just get PPEs from the storage room," one of the workers said. "Here, take this key."

I went to the room to pick up the gloves and apron that were required, using the key to let myself in. It was loaded with supplies, and I helped myself to a few white aprons, hats, and respirators. They would come in handy for the next day's explosive operation.

I went back to the processing room and gave the worker a different key from my pocket. I would keep his in case I needed more supplies. I salvaged what remains I could find, and instead of putting them in the biological waste container, I took them home.

Before I started anything, I properly buried Martha's son.

Chapter 28
Will the Fetus Take the Stand?
(Court Day #8)

I woke up early and went to the cemetery. I parked my car and walked among the graves. An old man was standing next to a tombstone, a bouquet of fresh flowers in his hands. As I passed him, I managed to read the writing on the stone: "Here lies my wife and friend, Thelma Thaxinon. 1940-1985." His wife had died more than twenty years ago, and here he was, still putting flowers on her grave.

I walked toward Victoria's grave. The grass that covered the small rise of earth above her coffin was fresh and green, causing it to stand out from the coarse, withered grass around the plot. The smell of newness reminded me of the freshness of the tragedy—the freshness of her abbreviated life. I could easily see newly picked flowers on her grave twenty years from now. Who could forget Victoria? She'd left more than an empty chair behind—she'd left empty hearts.

I took a ring out of my pocket. "Victoria, I never had a chance to offer you this," I said aloud, "but it belongs to you. I wish I'd had the chance to put this ring on your finger, to hold you, to . . . " I fell to my knees, sobbing. "I still hear your voice in my head, still speaking to me, still asking me your questions . . ." A few minutes passed as I gathered myself. "Victoria, you became a part of me, and they took you away from me. They violated me.

"Once, I asked my roommate if it were possible to be in love without knowing it. Now I know the answer. I love you. I wish I'd had the chance to tell you." I closed my eyes and sighed. "Victoria, I miss you. I miss our rides in the van. I miss your analysis of our days in court. I miss your stubbornness, your opinionated spirit. I even miss your evangelistic spirit.

"I promise I will avenge your death. I will bring the violators to justice." It made me feel better to promise her that. I felt I might actually regain some control over the situation. But there was still more to say.

"I promise I will seek God with an open mind, and I'll believe in him, if he shows himself to me . . ."

With that, I felt I'd finally put Victoria to rest.

I dug a small hole next to Victoria's headstone. I wanted to bury the ring. I wanted to bury it deep within the earth. No one should wear that ring but her.

"What are you doing?" a voice demanded from somewhere above me.

I jumped and looked up. It was Mr. Johnson.

"I . . . I . . . I . . ." I swallowed and caught my breath. "I was having a private moment with Victoria."

"What about this?" Mr. Johnson looked at the hole. I had no choice but to tell him the truth.

"A ring?" Mr. Johnson looked at me in a way I didn't understand. I felt uncomfortable. I took the ring out of my pocket and showed him, in case he doubted my story.

"Randy, we still have a few hours before court, so . . ." He motioned toward the grave.

"Court? I thought it was postponed until—"

"I wanted to get it over with." He looked at the headstone. "I can't put Victoria to rest until this case has ended." With a softer voice, he added, "Until I win it."

I immediately felt the intense pressure to win this case.

"What do you say to breakfast?" Mr. Johnson suggested, putting an arm around my shoulders and squeezing them slightly.

"Sure," I replied.

"Let's put Victoria's grave back to order," he said. "I don't think we should disturb her."

"I apologize . . ."

Mr. Johnson didn't reply. He covered the hole I'd created, rearranging the flowers and adding some new ones.

We walked toward our cars in silence. On the way to the parking lot, we passed the old man, still at his wife's grave. He looked up at us and nodded his head. His image lingered in my head for a few seconds. Could a man ever be happy after losing his beloved? Could life ever be the same? For the first time since Victoria's death, I thought of Mr. Johnson. For a moment, my self-pity subsided and my heart went out to him.

I followed his car to the restaurant he had suggested.

"This was Victoria's favorite café," Mr. Johnson commented as we were seated.

I nodded, unsure of how to respond.

"The ring," Mr. Johnson began.

"Yes?"

"Tell me more about it." His eyes opened widely, just as Victoria's did when she was excited.

"I don't know what to say . . ." I paused. "I . . . I . . . I fell in love with Victoria."

"You were in love with Victoria," Mr. Johnson repeated,

smiling. "Tell me more."

"I don't know what to say," I said again. Mr. Johnson was silent, so I tried to think of a way to explain.

"I recently discovered she was the woman I wanted to spend the rest of my life with . . ." Tears welled up in my eyes. Mr. Johnson handed me a tissue and we sat in silence for a few seconds.

"But she was a quadriplegic," Mr. Johnson said.

"Initially, I wasn't sure it would work out." I wiped my tears. "But, eventually, I was so in love with her mind and spirit, it didn't matter."

Mr. Johnson sipped his coffee. "Did she know?"

"I never got a chance to tell her."

"No?"

"It wasn't until the day she disappeared that I admitted to myself that I loved her," I replied.

Mr. Johnson looked into his coffee cup. I'd never seen him so thoughtful before.

"May I see the ring?" he asked me after a few minutes had passed.

"Yes." I handed it to him.

"May I keep it?" he asked, then added quickly, "I'll pay you for it."

"Mr. Johnson, it's my gift to Victoria, and I didn't buy—"

"I'd like to keep it," Mr. Johnson said, his eyes filling. "I never imagined that a handsome, educated young man like you would fall in love with my daughter. I had accepted that Victoria would always live with me and her mother. It never occurred to me that, one day, I might push her chair down the aisle." Tears streamed down his face and he smiled the same, self-conscious smile Victoria had given me when she told me of her dreams of independence. I nodded, agreeing to let him keep the token I'd intended for his daughter.

"Thank you." He got up and came to my side of the table. Leaning down, he hugged me.

He insisted on paying for the ring, but I refused. After much debate, he accepted the gift. He put the ring in his breast pocket. Patting it, he said, "I'll take good care of it." He sighed. "Let's go, Randy. We've got a lot to do before court resumes."

***

When we arrived at the courthouse, it looked the same as the evening we'd left it, but it seemed so different. In the courtroom, everyone was quiet. The judge made his entrance.

"The defense has asked that we adhere to the regular trial schedule as much as possible," he said once he was seated. "Counselor, the court is willing to postpone this case for some time if you need to take more time off." He looked questioningly at Mr. Johnson.

"Thank you, Your Honor." Mr. Johnson got up and moved toward the bench. He turned to face the people gathered in the courtroom. "Your Honor, may I address the court?"

"If you wish," he answered.

"Thank you all for your support through this difficult time. My daughter, Victoria, was eighteen years old. She is—" Mr. Johnson stopped himself—"she *was* quadriplegic. She was born that way, unable to control her body from the neck down." Mr. Johnson looked over to the spot where Victoria used to sit. "On the day of the accident, I sent her away from the courtroom because I didn't want her to see the horrific videos we were shown. I was trying to be a protective father, but instead of witnessing the murder of a child, she experienced death herself." Mr. Johnson removed his glasses and wiped at an eye with his index finger. "When my wife was pregnant with Victoria, we knew our child would be disabled. We seriously considered abortion."

The courtroom was silent.

"By the grace of God, her life was spared." Mr. Johnson paused for a few seconds. "No one brought more joy to my life than Victoria. When I think of the precious gift I would have lost to abortion, I feel ill."

The judge was obviously uncomfortable with the way Mr. Johnson's speech was progressing. The prosecutor shifted in his seat, clearly trying to keep himself from objecting. It was a tricky situation. Mr. Johnson was extremely emotional, addressing both the Christ Hospital case and Victoria in his speech. Suddenly, he started weeping. Before I could think twice about it, I was out of my seat and heading toward him.

"I would like to say . . . I would like to thank you, Mr. Johnson," I started over, "for *not* aborting Victoria. Thank you for choosing life. Thank you for your sacrificial love and years of service to your daughter. No one has influenced my life like Victoria." I was shocked by my own words, but I couldn't stop talking, and everyone's eyes were fixed on me. "Her life was valuable. When people consider abortion, they should remember that their child is not just theirs. She might become someone's wife, mother, lover, sister." I paused. "Your Honor, I would like to bring the fetus to the stand."

Across the silent courtroom, people's mouths dropped open. A few gasped.

"Will the fetus take the stand?" I shouted.

Mr. Nicholas finally stood. "Your Honor, I think it's clear we should postpone this trial. Mr. Johnson buried his daughter two days ago—"

"Will the fetus take the stand?" I interrupted.

"I agree, Mr. Nicholas," the judge replied, ignoring me.

Suddenly, I remembered what Mr. Johnson had said to me that morning. Victoria would've wanted the case to be resolved. I quickly tried to regain my composure.

"Your Honor, my apologies," I said, "but we insist that this case be resolved in a timely manner."

The judge hesitated. "All right," he said finally, "but one more outburst from the defense and I'll have to declare a mistrial."

"Thank you, Your Honor." I turned to face the gallery. "Will Dr. Lee please take the stand?"

"Are you OK handling the examination?" Mr. Johnson whispered to me.

"I'll try, Mr. Johnson." I squeezed his hand. "I have to do my best, for Victoria's sake."

"And for the sake of the unborn, Randy." Mr. Johnson patted me on the back and went back to his seat.

As Dr. Lee was sworn in as a witness, I quickly organized my thoughts.

"Dr. Lee," I began, "what qualifies you to represent a fetus?"

"Well—"

"Objection, Your Honor." Mr. Nicholas interrupted, standing. "A fetus is not a legal person and therefore cannot be represented in this court."

"Your Honor," I argued, "this fetus is not receiving any legal representation per se. He's only being called to the stand."

"Your Honor, this is ridiculous," Mr. Nicholas objected. "The defense should immediately cease these silly games."

"Samantha Lucky was allowed to appear on the stand when her mother was the representative—"

"Samantha's not a fetus," Mr. Nicholas countered.

"But she needed a representative," I persisted.

"Samantha was able to sit in front of this court, Mr. Livingston," the judge interrupted. "Where is this fetus?"

"On the stand," I replied. "Dr. Lee is pregnant." Mr. Nicholas was speechless.

"I'll overrule the objection for now," the judge replied reluctantly, "but I want you to address Dr. Lee, and not the fetus, Counselor."

"Thank you, Your Honor." I looked at Mr. Johnson. He was smiling.

"Dr. Lee," I began again, "can you please answer the question? What qualifies you to represent a fetus?"

"Well, of course, now you all know I'm pregnant—I'm four months along and expecting a beautiful baby girl." Smiling, Dr. Lee put her hands on her belly. "I'm also a professor of embryology at the Chicago Medical Center. I've been working in embryology for the last twenty years. I'm also a gynecologist and obstetrician who's delivered nearly a thousand babies."

I pulled a piece of paper from my pocket. I'd been scribbling questions on it throughout the trial.

"Dr. Lee, will you please describe the process of conception?"

"You mean fertilization?" Dr. Lee asked. "Conception is not a process, Mr. Livingston. It's an event. It's the result of the fertilization process."

"Forgive me," I said. "*Fertilization*—what happens at fertilization?"

"Fertilization involves a mature oocyte and a mature spermatozoon."

"Spermatozoon?"

"Sperm-at-a-zo-on," she sounded out. "The plural is *spermatozoa*. They're male gametes—germ cells."

"Germs," I repeated.

"Sperm," she said in clarification.

"Oh, of course, yes," I said. "Then the oocyte is the female egg?"

"Well, it's part of the egg. During fertilization, the egg is divided into unequal parts, and the oocyte is the part that fuses with the spermatozoon."

"So, what exactly happens at the moment of conception?"

"Let's start a month or two earlier," Dr. Lee suggested.

"A month or two earlier?"

"As I said, for conception to occur, we need a mature oocyte and a mature spermatozoon. These are produced and mature through a process called gametogenesis."

"Gametogenesis?"

"Yes, the process that converts primordial germ cells—or primitive sex cells—into mature sex gametes. In the male, these are spermatozoa, or sperm, and, in the female, definitive oocytes."[106]

"So, basically, just before fertilization, we start with a mature egg and some sperm?"

"Yes," she replied. "But one thing to point out about the maturation process is the reduction of the number of chromosomes. You see, all human cells contain forty-six chromosomes," Dr. Lee continued. "The oocyte and spermatozoon come from germ cells that are also made of forty-six chromosomes. However, for conception to occur, we need the oocyte and the spermatozoon to have only twenty-three chromosomes each, so they can fuse together and create a human being with forty-six. The ovum and the immature sperm must first go through a reduction process, which is called meiosis."

"Meiosis," I repeated, trying to follow along.

"Meiosis is a reductive division. During this process, the number of chromosomes in a cell is reduced by half. The resultant gametes have only half the number of chromosomes found in a somatic (or *body*) cell. This allows two gametes to fuse and restore the diploid number of chromosomes, thus creating a unique zygote."[107]

"So, in layman's terms, meiosis is cell division?" She was getting too technical for me and the court.

"Well, meiosis is not the typical cell division that's seen in an embryo or in adults, where the number of chromosomes is maintained in each new cell. In meiosis, the number of chromosomes is reduced."

"OK, let's recap. For conception to occur, we need an egg and a sperm with half the number of chromosomes found in a human somatic cell, so that when they fuse together, we end up with the necessary number of chromosomes for a human being. Correct?"

"Exactly. Gametogenesis occurs months or years before conception."

I wanted to stop her and ask her to talk about the point of conception only, but I was afraid I'd miss something important. I was beginning to think I wasn't ready for this examination, after all. How could I get her to say what I wanted her to say? With other witnesses, Mr. Johnson and Mr. Maxwell had made it look so easy.

"In males, the primitive germ cells are called spermatogonia. They are present at birth and are the source of all mature sperms. Spermatogenesis begins when the male reaches puberty and continues into old age. In this process, each spermatogonium produces many primary spermatocytes through mitosis. Each primary spermatocyte then undergoes the first meiotic division to produce two secondary spermatocytes. Secondary spermatocytes undergo the second meiotic division to produce four haploid spermatozoan or sperm. Spermatogenesis begins in the seminiferous tubules of the testis, after which the sperm move into the epididymis to be stored and become functionally mature. The entire process takes approximately two months and results in gametes that are either 23,X or 23,Y. The functionally mature spermatozoan is very specialized in structure, with a head and acrosome cap (containing enzymes), a neck, middle piece, and a motile tail."[108]

"Years before conception?" I desperately needed clarification.

"Yes. In layman's terms, a mature sperm is created from primitive germ cells. The mature sperm has twenty-three chromosomes. It can be either type X or type Y, and it takes about two months or so for the spermatozoon to mature."

"What about the egg?"

"Unlike the male, maturation of the gamete begins before birth. In the female fetus, the primitive germ cells are called oogonia. The oogonia differentiate into primary oocytes before birth so that the female is born with all the primary oocytes she'll ever have—about two million of them. After birth, no more primary oocytes are formed. These primary oocytes begin the first meiotic division, but are arrested at prophase, which is the first step in the process. They stay in prophase until ovulation, which begins at puberty. Before this time, many regress, so only about forty thousand remain at puberty. Then each month until menopause, one primary oocyte completes the first meiotic division to form one secondary oocyte and one smaller polar body. The secondary oocyte begins the second meiotic division, but again halts, this time at metaphase. During ovulation, it's released from the surrounding ovarian follicle and enters the fallopian tube. If, while in the fallopian tube, it's penetrated by a sperm, it quickly completes the second meiotic division to become a mature ovum and a second polar body. During meiosis II, the first polar body is also thought to divide, forming two polar bodies, so that a total of three polar bodies are formed."[109]

"Dr. Lee, help make this simple for us," I said. I was beginning to get frustrated. I was sure Mr. Johnson was growing impatient with my cross-examination.

"Dr. Lee, we're not scientists," the judge said to my surprise. "Counselor, please limit the technical information to the minimum necessary for your case. Let's move this along."

"Yes, Your Honor," I replied. I could feel the heat rising in my cheeks. Apparently, I wasn't the scientist I thought I was. Dr. Lee had showed me that what I knew about science, especially the science of embryology, was nothing compared to what I didn't know. How arrogant of me to think I could form opinions about the status of an embryo without bothering to look into the complex science surrounding it.

Dr. Lee, apologizing for using such complicated terminology, continued: "Every month, a woman ovulates. At that time, the egg, which contains forty-six chromosomes, is released to the fallopian tube." She indicated the fallopian tube on a chart that sat on an easel next to her. "During fertilization, one very lucky sperm out of hundreds of millions will penetrate the outside layer of the ovum and fertilize it. The surface of the ovum changes its electrical characteristics and prevents additional sperm from entering. After fertilization begins, the reduction of the oocytes occurs."[110]

"So," I asked, "the first step of fertilization is completing the reduction of the number of chromosomes of the egg?"

"Yes."

"What happens next?"

"The oocyte and the spermatozoon fuse together, forming a new, unique entity called the zygote."

"The zygote is another name for the fertilized egg?"

"No. The term 'fertilized egg' is an unscientific and inaccurate term. After fertilization, the egg ceases to exist. A new entity is formed that is different from the oocyte and the spermatozoon."

"How different is it from the spermatozoon and the oocyte?"

"The spermatozoon and the oocyte each possess 'human life,' because they are parts of a living human being, but they're not whole living human beings themselves. They each have only twenty-three chromosomes, not the required forty-six for a single, individual member of the human species. Furthermore, a sperm can produce only sperm proteins and enzymes. An oocyte can produce only oocyte proteins and enzymes. Neither can produce a human being on its own."[111]

"How do you characterize the zygote?"

"How do I characterize the zygote?" Dr. Lee repeated the question. "It is a human being."

"A human being?"

"Well, it has the complete number of chromosomes of a human being, and its gender has already been determined. It immediately starts directing its own development. It's a unique human being."

"What happens after the zygote is conceived?"

"Five days after its conception, the zygote travels down the fallopian tube toward the womb." Dr. Lee pointed to the picture of the female reproductive system. "It begins to attach itself to the wall of the womb. Twelve days after conception, the blastocyst has fully attached itself to the endometrium—"

"The endometrium?" I interrupted.

"The lining of the womb," Dr. Lee explained. "If instructions are followed exactly, a home pregnancy test may reliably detect pregnancy at this point or shortly thereafter."[112]

"So, twelve days after conception, a woman can detect

pregnancy?"

"Yes, and that's why many people, especially those in the pro-choice faction, consider that point the start of pregnancy," Dr. Lee continued. "We know the pregnancy starts earlier, but the limitations of our detection devices make it impossible to discover it before then."

"Does that mean abortion can't take place until twelve days after conception?"

"Not exactly. Abortion can happen before twelve days have passed. But less than 14 percent of all abortions take place before seven weeks after conception."[113]

"Seven weeks after conception," I repeated. "Dr. Lee, Can you share with us some milestones that occur up to seven weeks of a pregnancy?"

"The greatest milestone, Mr. Livingston, is conception. After that, there are many developmental milestones because the human body is so complex. One milestone occurs at approximately eighteen to twenty-one days after conception—that's when the heart begins beating."[114]

"That's only around three weeks."

"Your Honor," Mr. Nicholas said, standing up. "Objection. Relevancy? If the defense claims that personhood starts at conception, why does it matter when the heart starts to beat?"

"Please approach the bench," the judge said.

"Your Honor," Mr. Nicholas said when we reached the judge, "Law 1105_ILCS_12.9 requires Christ Hospital to perform abortions at every stage of pregnancy. As a matter of fact, 80 percent of abortions are performed after the fetus's heart starts beating. Whether or not there's a heartbeat should have no bearing on this case."

I kept quiet. Dr. Lee had made my point.

"There's no sense in objecting now," the judge decided.

"Get to the point, Counselor," he said, sternly looking at me.

"Yes, Your Honor," I said.

I tried not to let the judge's reprimand affect me.

"Dr. Lee, you said your own fetus is now four months old. Is that correct?"

"Yes. Her heart has been beating for the past three months."

"So, you're saying a lot of our understanding of embryonic development is greatly limited by the capabilities of medical equipment. Is that also correct?"

"Unfortunately, yes. State-of-the-art equipment has helped us understand embryonic development, bur we can't use this equipment every day on every pregnant woman—partly because some of the equipment emits high levels of radiation, and partly because some of it is very expensive. But scientific research has detected a baby's first heartbeat as early as eighteen days[115] after conception."

"That's very interesting, Doctor. What other milestones occur before seven weeks?"

Dr. Lee flipped the diagram next to her to reveal a fetal development chart. "At five weeks, arms, hands, and fingers start to form. Fingerprints can also be detected then. At six weeks," she continued, "the embryo has both eyes, and its mouth and nose start to form."[116] Dr. Lee then flipped to a chart of embryo development.

"At two months, some of the brain function begins to develop. The embryo responds to prodding. At ten weeks, its face is distinguishable, and its gender is detectable."[117]

"I thought you said the gender was determined at conception."

"Of course. But, at this point, we're able to detect the gender in the doctor's office."

Dr. Lee pointed to the five-month stage in the

development chart. "At five months, the fetus is generally about twelve inches long and weighs about one pound. It has hair on its head, and its movements can be felt. Halfway through this month, the lungs may be developed to the point where the fetus can survive if forced to live outside the womb."[118]

"So, at five months, a fetus can survive without its mother?"

"Not exactly. Five months is when it can live on his own without the help of a respirator. It can survive outside its mother's womb long before five months—in a test tube, for example," Dr. Lee explained.

"At six months, the fetus is typically around fourteen inches long and weighs up to two pounds. The lungs' bronchioles develop. Interlinking of the brain's neurons begins. Some rudimentary brain waves can be detected. In the past, state laws outlawed abortions at this stage, except under very unusual circumstances.[119]

"At seven months, as you'll see here," Dr. Lee pointed to the chart, "the fetus can be sixteen inches long and weigh around three pounds. Regular brain waves are detectable, which are similar to those in adults.[120]

"By the time it reaches nine months, the fetus is generally around twenty inches long and weighs, on average, seven pounds. It's at this time that the fetus is born."

"Dr. Lee, as an embryologist, when do you believe personhood starts?"

"Definitely at conception. There's no doubt in my mind about it."

"Thank you, Dr. Lee. I have no further questions, Your Honor." I went back to my seat. Mr. Johnson looked downcast, but patted me on the shoulder in a congratulatory way.

"Mr. Nicholas, would you like to cross-examine the

witness?" the judge asked.

"Yes, Your Honor." Mr. Nicholas approached Dr. Lee. "Dr. Lee, can you please show us the fetal development chart again?"

"Sure," she said, flipping to the appropriate diagram.

"Which is the image of the fetus at seven weeks?"

"This one," she replied, pointing at an illustration that, from where I sat, looked an awful lot like a lima bean.

"Wouldn't you agree that that looks more like a pig than a human?"

"I'll agree that it doesn't look like an *adult* human," Dr. Lee said coolly. "But it looks exactly like what a human should look like at seven weeks."

"And at four weeks, would you say it looks like a fish?" Mr. Nicholas said, ignoring Dr. Lee's comment.

"Again, at four weeks, it looks exactly as a four-week-old human embryo should look."

"Come on, Dr. Lee. Do you honestly believe that creature is a person?"

"Yes," Dr. Lee snapped. "As I said before, all humans look this way at these early stages of development. The fetus continues to carry the correct number of human chromosomes and to produce DNA of a human, not that of a fish or a pig." Dr. Lee paused. "In my twenty years as an embryologist, I haven't come across a case yet where a woman delivered a pig or a fish." Muffled laughter rose up from the courtroom.

"What's the size of a fetus at about one month of age?" Mr. Nicholas asked.

"At six weeks, it's about half an inch."

"Half an inch!" Mr. Nicholas went to his table and grabbed a ruler. He gave it to Dr. Lee. "Please measure the size of your fingernail," he commanded.

Dr. Lee took the ruler and grudgingly measured the nail on her pinky finger.

"How does the size of a fetus, at age six weeks, compare to the size of your smallest fingernail?"

"It's about the same," Dr. Lee mumbled.

"The same?" Mr. Nicholas repeated loudly.

"About the same," Dr. Lee repeated. "Maybe a tiny bit smaller," she added reluctantly.

"So, is this entity, which looks like a pig and is smaller than your fingernail, really a human being?"

"Yes!" Dr. Lee was clearly frustrated. "Mr. Nicholas, have you ever even *seen* a newborn human being?"

"Of course."

"Then you know that it was about twenty inches in length—that's less than the size of your head." The laughter in the courtroom rose above a quiet rumble.

"Dr. Lee, we're talking about a pig-looking, one-month-old fetus, whose size is less than your fingernail."

"Personally, I'm glad it's smaller than my fingernail. Obviously, it's going to grow to about twenty inches by its birth. Women's bodies can't handle more than that. Pregnancy already adds an average of thirty pounds to a woman. How many extra pounds do women need to carry to convince you that a fetus is human?"

"I wouldn't wish a woman to carry any more than is necessary. But, Dr. Lee, what I find odd is that you expect us to believe a fertilized egg is a human."

"The zygote."

"Whatever you call it. It has no limbs, no head, no brain. It doesn't have the ability to see, hear, smell, taste, or touch. It lacks internal organs, self-consciousness, the ability to think, reason, sense its environment. Even at the age of one month, it can't be distinguished from the embryo of a cat or dog."[121]

"*You* may not be able to distinguish it from the embryo of a cat or a dog—you're not trained to do that." For the first time that day, I heard Mr. Johnson laugh. "The question as to when a human being begins is strictly a scientific one," Dr. Lee continued, "and should be answered by human embryologists, not by philosophers, theologians, politicians, movie stars, or obstetricians, and *especially* not by lawyers like yourself. After twenty years in the field, I can assure you that a human being begins at the moment of conception."

"Dr. Lee, I agree with you that human *biological* life starts at conception, but personhood doesn't—"

"I'm an embryologist, Mr. Nicholas, and I'm not here to discuss philosophical questions but to provide the court my expertise on embryology."

"Forgive me, Dr. Lee," Mr. Nicholas said insincerely, "but are you saying that embryologists cannot determine when personhood starts because it's outside their expertise?"

"Not at all. As a matter of fact, embryologists are better suited to do this than philosophers. In embryology, personhood is synonymous with biological life."

"That's an embryologist's opinion, isn't it?"

"I'm sure that many of my colleagues agree with this concept of personhood. An embryologist's opinion is based on science and is consistent with common medical practice," Dr Lee continued. "My husband is a medical doctor. He writes death certificates regularly. He's never written a death certificate based on the fact that a person cannot reason or respond to his environment. Death outside the womb is based on the failure of biological components of the body. Unless, of course, we want to change our practice to include those with low IQ, the poor, the handicapped, the elderly, the sick . . ."

Dr. Lee paused, as if waiting for an answer to her suggestion. "Whether or not we choose to protect the unborn," she continued, "doesn't alter the fact that the fetus, from the point of conception, is a human being."

Dr. Lee had clearly made her point, and her conclusion was the key argument of our defense—abortion was wrong because it killed human beings, and not because it killed "persons." The important question that people should've been asking was not whether or not a fetus was a person but how did we want to define murder? We needed to answer that question carefully. If we chose to define murder in terms of killing *persons* and not simply human beings, then we had divorced security and married unpredictability. Unlike the definition of a person, the definition of a human being was set in stone, scientifically proven to be the moment of conception. That fact was indisputable. Why not choose such a solid definition for personhood? Why were we insisting on making it harder than it had to be?

Chapter 29
The Boss

I left the truck parked behind a row of trees; I didn't want anyone to see it and get suspicious. At the entrance to the Farm stood a sign, reading "The Human Farm and Body Parts Factory. Established in 2015." *And it would be demolished today, on June 20, 2060.* I entered through the gate and the electronic greeter welcomed me in its computer-generated voice.

I headed toward my batch room, paying close attention to my surroundings to ensure that everything was in place. I entered the batch room and began to order the command for them to wake up, but something was wrong. They weren't there.

I left the room and hurried toward the cafeteria. Everyone I passed seemed to look at me curiously.

"Randy Livingston, please come to room four twenty-three," shouted a voice through the loudspeaker.

Kept from my search for the RMs, I felt irritated, but I went immediately to the assigned room anyway. The sign on the door read "Mr. Smith, CEO." *The boss wants to talk to me.*

I knocked on the door.

"Come in, Randy."

The boss was behind a table, with Mr. Manson sitting across from him.

"Take a seat," Mr. Smith ordered.

I sat.

"Take a look at this." Mr. Smith handed me a batch processing record. "Read the comment section."

I read the comments: "RM 8645-23 kicked during the processing. Called Randy's name, and used new vocabulary."

I smiled.

"Mr. Livingston, apparently, you were not following the rules and regulations of the Farm," Mr. Smith said. "We were forced, prematurely, to process your entire batch."

I didn't reply

"Here are the batch records for the rest of the RMs." Mr. Smith handed me more files.

"How many have you processed?" I asked.

"All of them."

"You processed the whole batch?!" I stood up. "You murderers. You pigs!" I slammed my fist on the table. "Death to the Human Farm and Body Parts Factory!" I yelled, then stormed out of the room.

The minute I left, I heard the boss calling security. I ran quickly down to the hiding place, picked up the truck, and drove to the camp.

***

The streets were empty except for a young black boy who appeared from one of the alleys. It was the same boy who had first led me to the camp.

"You!" I shouted. "Stop!"

Just like the last time I saw him, he began to run.

"Stop!"

This time I wasn't going to let him get away. I ran as fast as I could and caught up to him. I grabbed him by the shoulders.

"Hey, didn't I tell you to stop?" I demanded, panting. The boy looked at me. His eyes were full of fear. I heard footsteps behind us.

"C'mon." I pulled the boy behind a nearby garage, just in time to see Charles hurry past. *How does he know where I went?* I watched as Charles disappeared through a doorway into a small house.

"I need to get to the camp safely," I murmured.

"Mister, I know how to. At 6:13." He looked at his watch.

"6:13?"

"Yeah, the perfect position; the cameras won't get you, and no one knows if you're leaving or entering."

"What's your name?" I asked, grasping his wrist and holding it firmly.

"Adams Lincoln II."

That name was familiar. Where had I heard it? *Of course*, I recalled. *It was the Boss's name.*

"Who named you that?"

"My daddy and mommy, o' course."

"I'd like to meet them," I said.

"Can't," he replied. "They're in prison."

"Where do you live?"

"Alone. I work alone."

"Doing what?"

"Freedom stuff."

I looked at him quizzically.

"I want to free my parents and everyone so they can live outside—in the real world," he explained.

"But you're black and—I assume—uncloned."

"That doesn't matter. They just tell us that to keep us in prison. They're liars."

I wasn't sure what to think. I didn't think anything else in this world would surprise me.

Ten minutes later, a door opened and Charles left the house, carrying a large container.

"He comes twice a week," the boy said, "carrying the same container."

"Agent X," I murmured. "Getting all the eggs. Hey, why are your parents in prison?" It suddenly occurred to me to ask.

"Those liars said my daddy's a threat to camp security," he said. "My daddy is smart; he taught me all the tunnels in the camp."

"The tunnels?"

"Yep, they're everywhere, and no one can see you sneakin' around. I go once every week to the camp police."

"And?"

"And I snoop around. I update my dad with information, so we'll be ready for the great revolution."

"The great revolution?"

"When we free the prisoners of the camp."

"The great revolution is today, son," I said.

"Are you sure, mister?"

"Very sure." I patted his head. "I need your help."

"Yes, mister."

"I need to give a speech to all the campers."

"'Bout what?"

"About freedom."

"Yes, mister."

"How can I gather all the people in Freedom Square?"

"Easy—you just start the siren. They got the party one, the emergency one, and the town meeting one."

"How do you start the siren?"

"It's in the camp police station. It takes a code to open it."

"I've got to break into it," I said, thinking aloud.

"No need to, mister. Besides, the police alarm will go off and those liars'll arrest you," the boy replied. "I know the code."

"You know the code?"

"It's 6:10," he said, looking at his watch. "Follow me."

I let go of the boy's wrist and followed him out from behind the garage. For several minutes, I tried to imitate him as he jumped, ran, or kept low. I followed all his maneuvers, and we soon reached a door.

"Shush," he said, pointing to his mouth.

Through the door came the unmistakable sound of men talking.

We tiptoed to the end of the room, where the boy pulled back a metal disk covering a hole. He told me to go down and he followed, recovering the hole behind us. Before the light disappeared, I saw we were in a tunnel.

We crawled silently for nearly twenty minutes before either of us spoke.

"Now, it is safe to talk, mister," the boy said finally, sitting down to rest. "I'll take you to Freedom Square. It'll take us an hour in the tunnels. Then, I'll come back to the police station. At 8:30, they close the control rooms for the squares. I'll activate the siren and microphones. Wait about half an hour for the people to gather." He looked at his watch, whose face was glowing in the dark tunnel. "It's 6:30 right now. We got two hours."

"Excellent." I patted the boy on the shoulder.

"What alarm do you want me to activate?"

"Emergency."

"Never been heard in the camp," he mused. "Well, I guess we'd better get going. Don't want to be late."

The boy continued through the tunnel and I followed. He stopped many times to look behind him, making sure I was still there. As we crawled, I thought about my mission at the Farm. It had been a failure because of timing—I'd needed one extra day to prepare. I could still complete my mission, though.

Finally, we reached Freedom Square. My knees were caked in dirt and aching from the crawl, but I supposed it was better than trying to dodge the police and tracking devices in the camp.

"The cameras rotate everywhere," the boy said. "Stay in the blind spot by the oak tree, under the mark of 'X.' No one can see you there."

"Thank you, Adam."

"No problem, mister."

The tunnel ended between some bushes. I emerged slowly, looking for the oak, and finally saw it across the yard. The square was mostly clear, so I left the bushes quickly. I easily found the large X carved into the bark, and I sat on a nearby bench below the tree, leaning my head on the mark.

Unlike the upper world, the streets of the camp were busy. Children played everywhere. Lovers held hands. Young mothers were walking with their children. All was calm; all was peaceful. *Why would anyone want to leave the underground?* I asked myself. Here, they could raise their families without worrying about anything. What was in the upper world that these people needed? Below, it was safe and sheltered. Why revolt against the camp's government and disturb such tranquility? Was I selfish in trying to force them into a revolution?

The sirens went off.

The happy people on the streets began looking around in confusion. I stayed in my place. I constantly looked at my watch to time 30 minutes.

Slowly, people started gathering in the square. Ten minutes after the alarm, what looked like more than a thousand residents had already congregated. When thirty minutes had passed, I moved to the podium.

"Residents of the camp," I began, my voice echoing loudly all around the square. The crowd's eyes fixed on me. "Fellow citizens, a few months ago, I joined your camp. In an attempt to aid in the revolution, I took a job at an evil place called the Human Farm and Body Parts Factory. In that place, they take humans, raise them like animals, cut their body parts off, and sell those parts for millions of dollars. How do you feel about a place like that?"

A large number of people gasped and shook their heads.

"I have evidence that shows that eggs used to produce the humans farmed there came from people in this camp." Everyone was quiet and I paused for a moment. "Yes, these are your children they're killing.

"The eggs that you have donated to your neighbors have been stolen by someone calling himself Agent X. They're being used to, ultimately, harvest body parts." I raised my voice. "It's time to put an end to the slaughter of your own children. It's time to act against the Human Farm and Body Parts Factory. Who wants to act?"

They remained silent for a moment, looking at each other to see who would make the first move. Then, slowly, hands began to creep into the air and people began to shout.

"You have been sheltered down here for more than twenty years. When are you going to fulfill your true mission? Silence is the greatest enemy of freedom. Isolating yourselves from the rest of the world keeps you in bondage. Postponing this war is causing us to lose it. Every minute counts. Every minute saved results in lives saved. You have formed a great society of more than fifty thousand people. What more do you need to conquer the Farm, where your own children are being slaughtered?"

Suddenly, I felt a hard hand grab my shoulder and pull me away from the podium. Two men wrestled my arms behind my back and cuffed my wrists together. I resisted as best I could, straining back toward the microphone.

"What are you waiting for?" I shouted.

The audience shouted and people raised their fists in support.

"Who wants to join the army of freedom?"

More shouts.

"Who wants to save the lives of your children?"

"Death to Agent X!" they shouted back.

The men pulled me away from the microphone, and I was forced to turn my back on the crowd.

"Where are you taking me?" I demanded.

The men didn't reply but led me to the police station. They chained my hands and feet to a chair and left me alone in an empty room. Twenty minutes passed before the door was opened and Victor appeared.

"Mr. Livingston, I'm afraid your behavior out there was extremely irrational."

I didn't reply.

"We're going to have to take away your privileges to go to the outside world. We must confine you to the lower levels of the camp."

"You can't do that to me," I shouted. "I don't want to be part of your camp!"

"In that case, we'll have to treat you as a trespasser. And since you pose a threat to the safety of the camp, we'll have to imprison you for life."

Just then, another man entered the room and whispered something in Victor's ear. Victor's eyes opened wide.

"Be ready in two minutes," the other man said as he left the room.

"Mr. Livingston," Victor began reluctantly, "The Boss would like to meet you."

"The Boss?"

"Let's get you ready to meet him." He tied a thick, black band across my eyes.

"Why are you doing that?"

"Procedure. No one knows the location of his office, with the exception of a few guards." He placed a headset over my ears. "You will hear the Boss's voice through the headset. It will be modified so you won't be able to recognize it. On your way to see him, you'll listen to music and be isolated from any sounds emanating from your surroundings."

Victor performed a body search on me, then briefly shuffled through a small stack of paperwork, stopping every few pages to scribble what I assumed was his name.

Several men came to escort me to the Boss. Loud instrumental music blared through the headset. As we began to walk, I started to count the number of steps I was taking, but the music's volume and rhythm were strange, and I was unable to concentrate.

About five minutes seemed to pass before the music stopped.

"Take a seat," came a voice from the headset.

A guard pushed me backward and I sat down on a hard chair.

"Randy Livingston." He seemed to be considering me.

"Are you the Boss?" I asked.

"Yes, and a very busy one. You know I have to manage the business inside and outside the camp." He paused. "I heard you've been stirring up trouble in the camp."

I didn't reply.

"Are you another computer simulation of some sort?" I asked after a minute. "Why can't I see you?"

"For your safety," the Boss replied.

"My safety!" I laughed.

"The standard answer is for the safety of the camp, but in this specific case, it is indeed for your own safety."

I continued laughing.

"If you were to see me, you would become a greater threat to the camp, and we would end up having to put you in a maximum security prison for life."

Adam Lincoln, II's father must have seen the Boss, I thought.

"Let me assure you that I am real—" a hand patted my back— "but if you insist on gambling with your freedom, I'll let you see me face-to-face."

"I would like that," I replied.

The headset was removed from my ears and the blinding shroud was taken from my eyes. It took a few seconds to adjust to the light in the room, but when my eyes had recovered, I saw in front of me a huge, elegant desk. Seated on a leather chair across from me was a large man, his back toward me. He slowly turned around and I saw his face. It was Mr. Smith, the CEO of the Human Farm and Body Parts Factory.

Chapter 30
Hypocrisy (Court Day #9)

"I solemnly pledge myself to consecrate my life to the service of humanity. I will give my teachers the respect and gratitude that is their due. I will practice my profession with conscience and dignity. The health of my patient will be my first consideration. I will respect the secrets confided in me. I will maintain, by all means in my power, the honor and noble traditions of the medical profession. My colleagues will be my brothers. I will not permit considerations of religion, nationality, race, party politics, or social standing to intervene between my duty and my patient. I will maintain the utmost respect for human life, from time of conception. Even under threat, I will not use my medical knowledge contrary to the laws of humanity. I make these promises solemnly, freely, and upon my honor."[122]

Dr. James, the president of Christ Hospital, folded the paper from which he was reading and put it in his pocket.

"Dr. James, this is the pledge every Christ Hospital doctor makes?" I asked.

"Yes. We pledge to protect human life from the moment

of conception."

"How does Law 1105_ILCS_12.9 affect you as a professional doctor?"

"It introduces professional hypocrisy. As doctors, we're supposed to save human life, not destroy it," Dr. James answered.

"What about your business? Does this law help or hinder your hospital?"

"It ultimately harms us," Dr. James said. "Patients don't trust doctors who perform abortions. In a nationwide survey, 64 percent of abortion doctors say that the non-abortion parts of their practices have suffered because of it. In the same survey, 69 percent said they're not respected in the medical community, 65 percent feel ostracized, 87 percent have been harassed, and 50 percent have problems retaining staff.[123] It's simply not fair to force a doctor to perform such an operation. For over two thousand years," he continued, "people have trusted their doctor to 'do no harm.' That trust has been seriously undermined by legalized abortion.[124] Please," he pleaded, "do not complete the destruction of this trust and confidence by forcing Christ Hospital to perform this atrocity."

"Thank you, Dr. James," I said. "Nothing further."

"Dr. James, let me ask you a question," Mr. Nicholas said, rising from his chair. "Which is better: two deaths or one murder?"

"Murder is never justifiable," the doctor answered.

"So, do you agree that it's not morally permissible for a doctor to kill an innocent patient to save another's life?"

"Yes, I would agree with that," the doctor replied.

"So, how do you justify abortion if a woman's life is in danger? In this case, does it become permissible to take an innocent life?"

"Yes. In that case, abortion is not murder—"

"Isn't this still the murder of an innocent life?" Mr. Nicholas interrupted.

"In that case, abortion is self-defense."

"Self-defense." Mr. Nicholas repeated. "Hmmm. Then, isn't abortion self-defense in the case of rape? Isn't it self-defense when a fetus is causing psychological, emotional, and economic stress in a woman's life? And, wouldn't it then follow that abortion could always be considered self-defense?"

"Listen to me," the doctor said, leaning forward. "We always try to avoid abortion, regardless of the circumstances. We try our best to save both lives, whenever possible. If not, we try to save at least one life rather than allow both to perish. It's not a question of murdering one life versus allowing two to die naturally."

"But, Doctor, are you saying that if you have to choose between the life of the woman and the child, you will choose the life of the woman?"

"Most likely."

"So, the mother's life is superior to the fetus's. Is that accurate?"

"If I tried to save the fetus's life," Dr. James replied, "then you'd accuse me of believing the fetus's life is superior to its mother's." He seemed to have Mr. Nicholas figured out. "Listen, this is a very hard case. As a medical doctor, I'd try to save both lives, but if not possible, I'd try to save the life whose chances of survival are the greater."

"What if the likelihood of survival for both the mother and the child were equal? Whose life would you save then, Doctor?"

"The mother's."

"Why? Is the woman now more important than the fetus? If so, shouldn't she be more important in every case of abortion?" Mr. Nicholas pressed. "Sometimes death forces us to see the truth." He turned his back to Dr. James.

"Do you have children?" Dr. James asked, seemingly out of nowhere.

Mr. Nicholas turned back to face him. "Yes," he answered.

"How old are they?"

"I have a four-month-old son."

"What's his name?"

"Dr. James, this is irrelevant—"

"Let me ask you," Dr. James insisted, "who has the right to decide which city you should live in? You or your son? Who has the right to choose what kind of food you eat? You or him?"

"Me, of course. But—"

"You're right, Mr. Nicholas. It can also be argued that your life is more valuable than your son's. You have to provide for your family. Your death would cause a greater burden to society. Similarly, a woman is considered more valuable than a fetus, or even more than a newborn baby, and, frankly, that's why this topic is hard. However, that doesn't give the mother permission to end her child's life, just as you, with all your rights, are not allowed to kill your son. When the child and his mother are in danger, one needs to prioritize who will be saved first, and then execute that decision, however difficult it may be. I believe everyone is in favor of the mother's life."

"So, are you, or are you not, saying that the mother's life is more valuable than the fetus's?" Mr. Nicholas demanded, exasperated.

"Not intrinsically but socially. Yes."

"Your Honor, I have no further questions for Dr. James."

I have to admit, every inch of me believed that, in Mr. Nicholas's example, the woman's life was more important. But if her life was more valuable, why wasn't abortion justified? Because only her physical life was more valuable, I supposed—

not her comfort, desires, career, dreams, or economic status. When the mother's life was in danger, abortion was, it seemed, a necessary evil.

"Your Honor, I'd like the opportunity to redirect the witness," Mr. Maxwell said, standing. I was disappointed he felt he had to question Dr. James further than I had. I listened intently to his interrogation, attempting to learn what I had missed the first time.

"Make it short, counselor," the judge said.

"Thank you, your Honor." He turned to the witness. "Dr. James, what percentage of abortions are performed because the mother's life is in danger?"

"Less than 2.8 percent," the doctor answered.

"Thank you. No further questions."

***

I went home that afternoon and told Erick what had happened in court that day.

"We were told that 69 percent of abortion doctors feel they're not respected in the medical community, 65 percent feel ostracized, 87 percent have been harassed, and 50 percent have problems retaining staff," I said. "Do you see things that way?"

"No, I don't," Erick replied. He had been my friend and roommate for years and, though we got along wonderfully, I could never understand his unwavering support for abortion.

"Will you continue to work at the clinic after you graduate?" I asked him, though I knew what his answer would be.

"Of course!" he replied predictably. "It's my dream job."

"*Dream job?!* Why?"

"Why?" he said, repeating my question. "You know, Randy, you've been my roommate for years, and you don't even know why I do what I do."

"All I've ever heard from you is rhetoric—'to save the woman's life' and blah, blah, blah . . ."

"I'm proud to be able to help women retain some control over their lives, and I'll do it a million times over, if I can."

"You're the *last* person in the world I'd want for a doctor," I said. "I just couldn't trust a doctor who has no respect for human life."

"You're the most arrogant person I've ever met," Erick said, getting angry. "You think you know everything." He stood, face flushed. "And you're selfish. You think the world revolves around you."

"What?" Where had this attack come from?

"You think you're the only one who ever lost someone he loves. I've been mourning all my life, Randy, but you don't see me taking my pain out on other people."

"What are you talking about? Your dad died when you were five years old. I just lost Victoria. But what does that have to do with anything?" My head was spinning, trying to figure out where Erick's anger had come from and where, more importantly, it was heading. "Wait. Because I've been mourning Victoria the last few days, I'm selfish?"

"At least I'm doing something to help humanity, not wasting my life trying to become a sleazy lawyer!"

"I might not be out to save humanity, but unlike you, I'm not out to destroy it, either."

"People like me never should have been born," Erick said suddenly. He sat down and stopped arguing. We were both quiet for a few minutes.

"Everything I told you about my father was a lie," Erick

said finally, breaking the silence.

"What do you mean? He didn't die in an accident?" As long as I'd known Erick, he'd told me his father had died in a car accident when Erick was only five.

"No, I never knew him." He paused. "He was never married to my mother."

"Oh." It was all I could think to say.

"He left her after she became pregnant. I always felt I was the reason for my mother's unhappiness," he admitted, looking up at me from the kitchen table. "When I was in high school, I made a vow to become a doctor—one who supported abortion and could keep other kids from going through what I went through."

"I'm sorry," I said softly. I sat down across from him.

"Don't cry for me," Erick said, becoming angry again. "I don't need your pity."

"I'm not pitying you."

We were both quiet again for a few minutes.

"I really miss her," I said suddenly.

"Victoria?"

"Yes. She had the right answers for everything."

"And the right questions," Erick smiled. "It's weird, but I miss her too. I miss the funny questions you shared with me. What was it? Why is it wrong to kill a ten-year-old boy?"

"Yeah." We both laughed.

"I'm hungry," I said when our laughter subsided. "You said you got Chinese food?"

Erick got up and started pulling paper cartons from a plastic bag on the counter. We loaded our plates, taking turns popping them into the microwave. As we ate, we talked about everything except his father and Victoria.

***

That night, both Erick and I went to bed early. I couldn't sleep—I was thinking of Victoria. *Would it ever get easier?*

"Erick?" I asked softly, "Are you sleeping?"

"No. What's up?" His voice was gravelly—a good indication he was lying about having been awake.

"Did you mean it when you said you wished you'd never been born?"

"I don't know," he replied after a few moments of silence.

"Really?"

He was quiet again. "It's more like I wish my circumstances were different," he said. "I wish my dad had married my mom and stayed with her, and not left because of me."

"So, you *don't* wish you were not born?"

"I guess not."

"You shouldn't become an abortion doctor," I said. "You should try to change people's circumstances instead."

"Like how?"

"Like being a doctor who heals people—who does nothing *but* heal people."

He didn't respond.

"Erick?" I thought maybe he'd fallen back asleep.

"Yeah?"

"*I'm* glad you were born."

"Yeah?" he asked, a smile obvious in his voice.

"For real."

"Thanks, buddy."

"Good night."

"Good night."

Chapter 31
The Death of Randy Livingston

"Ten years ago, a man by the name of Adam Lincoln wanted to destroy the Human Farm and the Body Parts Factory."

"The real boss of the camp," I said.

"I see you've done your homework, Mr. Livingston," remarked Mr. Smith.

"You murdered him," I said calmly.

"Mr. Lincoln made the same mistake you did. He wasn't satisfied just working for the camp. He wanted to save the RMs," Mr. Smith said, looking at me intently. "He sent a spy to work in my factory." He paused. "You know the spy, Mr. Livingston, don't you?"

"I wasn't here ten years ago," I replied.

"Ahhh, but he still works with us."

"Charles," I said. "Agent X."

"Good guess. Mr. Lincoln gave Charles a chip—like yours—to enable him to spy on my organization. I uncovered the plot," Mr. Smith said. "I bribed Charles to tell me everything, and I blackmailed Adam. Poor man, he had no choice but to keep paying me lots of money for the safety of the camp. I told him I was going to tell the government about his little underground operation. In 2049, EGGSO tripled its price for eggs, and our demand went up. I got a clever idea to steal the eggs from the camp. I got rid of the Boss, and I appointed myself his successor. I eliminated the few people who knew the former boss, and established different contacts within the camp police. Charles did a great job."

Mr. Smith looked at me and laughed, "Any questions?"

"How did you bribe Charles to betray the Boss and the camp?"

"I offered him one of the most extraordinarily beautiful women in the world." His smile faded. "Unfortunately, Mr. Livingston, you'll not be given such a choice."

"I don't want any of your ugly women."

"For the safety of the camp, I'll have to kill you."

I laughed.

"We'll give you the honor of dying in the same manner as the RMs, and as the original boss. Of course, your body parts are useless to us, but we'll save your skull." Mr. Smith took a glass container and put it in front of me. It contained a skull, below which was a gold nameplate: Adam Lincoln.

"I'll add your skull to my collection," Mr. Smith remarked wryly.

Two guards grabbed me, pulling me up from my seat. I tried to fight back, but my effort was in vain. Across the room was a HeadSeg, slightly smaller than the one at the Factory. The guards placed me on a moving belt. As I looked up into the machine, I could see the blood of the RMs coating it.

"Call Randy *Begin* . . . Mission unaccomplished . . . *End.*" the Boss laughed.

"You'll pay for this," I screamed.

"I look forward to adding you to my skull collection," the Boss said, grinning.

I decided to ignore him and to reflect on the last seconds of my life.

"He's got the whole world in his hands . . ." I began singing. The knife was coming down on my neck. "He's got the whole . . ."

Chapter 32
Mission Accomplished
(Court Day #10)

"You're having a nightmare," Erick was saying in my ear. I opened my eyes to see him kneeling by my bedside.

I sat up.

"You were screaming," he explained.

"They cut off my head."

"It was a dream. You're OK." Erick handed me a glass of water. "Here."

"What time is it?" I asked, accepting the glass and taking a long drink.

"2:00 a.m."

"Today's the last day of the Christ Hospital trial. Mr. Johnson asked me to deliver the closing statement." I took another drink. "I'm so nervous," I confessed.

"You'll do fine," Erick replied. "But you need to get some sleep."

I thanked him and sank back into my bed. I was shaken by the dream. As soon as Erick left, I sobbed quietly until I drifted back to sleep.

***

When I arrived at the office, Mr. Johnson and Mr. Maxwell were waiting for me in the van. I climbed in and saw that Victoria's chair was still in its place. This was the first time I'd been in the van since her death. My nervousness about court was quickly replaced by a deep sadness. I remembered our first conversation in the van—it was about why it was wrong to kill a ten-year-old boy. I laughed out loud, causing Mr. Johnson and Mr. Maxwell to turn and look at me.

"I'm sorry," I apologized. "I just remembered something Victoria said."

Mr. Johnson's expression changed from concern to something softer, more nostalgic. "What'd she say?"

"She asked me why it was wrong to kill a ten-year-old. But what's funny is that it was the first thing she ever said to me, and she wouldn't drop it," I explained.

"That ten-year-old boy," said Mr. Maxwell laughing.

"She asked you about him too?"

Mr. Maxwell nodded.

"One good thing about bringing Victoria to court was that, when we went home, she would give her mother a precise report of what had happened that day," Mr. Johnson said. "For a few weeks, I didn't have to deliver the report myself."

We all laughed.

"Mr. Johnson, on a serious note," I asked, "why *is* it wrong to kill a ten-year-old boy?"

"Because he was created in the image of God," Mr. Johnson replied. "That's the only reason I can think of. All other answers have some loophole."

Mr. Maxwell was quiet. I didn't know anything about his religious beliefs.

"But that's also the most difficult answer," I said. "It requires a belief in God."

"And I do believe in God," Mr. Johnson said. "These days, I believe in him more than before. He's the one who's making it possible for me to survive this whole ordeal."

"Forgive me, Mr. Johnson," I pressed, "but he allowed Victoria to die, didn't he? Aren't you angry about that?"

Mr. Johnson looked at me in the rearview mirror. His eyes were sad.

"He's good and loving. I trust him."

Why would anyone trust a god who brought a quadriplegic girl into the world, then allowed her to die in her youth? What kind of god who allowed such a thing to happen? Why trust him now? I wondered.

"Remember the dream she had?" Mr. Johnson asked, changing the subject.

"The dream about walking?" I asked.

"I remember it well." Mr. Maxwell spoke for the first time in several minutes. "She told us about it the same day as the accident."

"It was you and I, Randy, who wanted her to sit in the chair, but she wanted to walk," Mr. Johnson continued.

"Yes, I remember," I said.

"Randy, she did walk—she walked and walked until she reached heaven," Mr. Johnson said. With that, we were quiet until we reached the courthouse.

When we got out of the van, Mr. Johnson unhooked Victoria's chair and wheeled it down a ramp into the parking lot.

"What's that—" I began, but Mr. Maxwell motioned to me

not to ask. Mr. Johnson wheeled the chair into the courtroom, putting it where Victoria used to sit. I sat awkwardly in my seat next to the empty wheelchair.

"The defense has rested their case," the judge reminded the court. "Is the prosecution ready to deliver its closing statement?"

"Yes, Your Honor." Mr. Nicholas walked confidently toward the bench.

"Your Honor, today, women's rights are at issue. The defense wants us to believe that a single cell, a piece of tissue—that cannot think, feel, or be aware of its surroundings—is a person. Not only is this glob of tissue a person, but the defense will have you believe it is a person whose rights are equal to those of an adult woman. Imagine that! A single cell equivalent to a grown, mature woman! That's ridiculous. And why does the defense want us to believe that? For the simple reason that they are sexist. They want to allow a single cell to take away the rights of women—rights that women in this country have worked a long time to have recognized, rights that have already suffered years of neglect and abuse, like the right to social equality, the right to pursue happiness and personal fulfillment, the right to control one's own body, to name but a few.

"Is it reasonable to think that a piece of tissue should take away all these important rights? The defense doesn't care about women, or about the oppression they've suffered for centuries. It wants to force them to carry to term the product of rape, and the burden of handicapped and unwanted children. It wants to force these innocent women into lives of undeserved misery. Law 1105_ILCS_12.9 is necessary to protect women from institutions, like Christ Hospital, that discriminate against them. Whatever arguments the defense has made about the unborn, keep in mind that they are nothing compared to the irrefutable fact that the unborn is not a legal person. I repeat," said Mr. Nicholas, emphasizing each word, *"an unborn fetus is not a legal person.* And, as such, it has no protection whatsoever under the law.

"Law 1105_ILCS_12.9, which was passed by the Illinois legislature and signed into law by the governor of this state, requires that all hospitals in Illinois provide abortion services. Christ Hospital continues to disobey this law, continues to ignore the needs of women, and continues to discriminate against women. Although so much has been said about abortion in this court, let me remind you that this case is not about abortion but about an institution that is putting its religious beliefs above sound medical practices and, in doing so, is hurting women and their fetuses. I beseech you: do not let our hospitals be run by those with backward religious beliefs. Let's protect women's rights."

Mr. Nicholas sat down and Mr. Johnson motioned to me to get up. I stood and walked slowly to the center of the room, hoping I looked as confident as Mr. Nicholas had. I looked at Mr. Johnson. His smile encouraged me, but next to him, Mr. Maxwell looked worried. My eyes caught Victoria's chair and I imagined her there. She would be smiling, just like her dad, encouraging me to speak.

"Your Honor," I began, "a few weeks ago, I had a dream—a dream about a place called the Human Farm and Body Parts Factory." I paused. "It's a place where humans are engineered and manufactured through the cloning process, rather than conceived and born. It's a place where they're are subjected to quality control, property rights, and cruelty, and where they're the raw material used for the production of body parts. I know you're probably wondering what my dream has to do with this case. Unfortunately, abortion has everything to do with the

Human Farm. Once we abolish the moral laws that protect the smallest form of human life, anything is possible." I turned to face the people in the courtroom.

"In this trial, we've shown, through the use of science, that human life begins at conception. This entity, the one the prosecution keeps referring to as 'a glob of tissue,' has unique chromosomes—specific DNA. Scientists, like Dr. Lee, agree that human life begins at conception. The prosecution wants to avoid science by introducing the concept of personhood. But, how did they define personhood? Unfortunately, no concrete definition was ever given. Each expert witness the prosecution presented defined personhood in an arbitrary way. As a matter of fact, all their definitions, if applied in a nondiscriminatory way, would exclude half the human race! The prosecution's worldview—that humanity is not intrinsic to being alive but is endowed by other humans—is positioning us to accept things like the Human Farm and Body Parts Factory. As a matter of fact, Law 1105_ILCS_12.9 is forcing our hospitals to be something like the Human Farm and Body Parts Factory, where doctors are forced to use knives and forceps to grab the body parts of babies, twist them, tear them apart, and then pull them from their mothers' wombs. Law 1105_ILCS_12.9 forces the doctors of Christ Hospital, and other medical institutions in this state, to commit murder against their will. Christ Hospital will continue to uphold its ideals despite this inhumane law. It will refuse to turn itself into a Human Farm and Body Parts Factory.

"Your Honor," I said, turning back to the judge, "I hope you will support the hospital's mission to save lives. Misguided rhetoric about being antiwoman is merely a dishonest way to discredit the hospital. Christ Hospital respects women and their rights, and believes that these rights can still be protected. What it doesn't believe is that killing innocent children is the way to maintain women's rights. Thank you, Your Honor."

I returned to my seat. I was nervous, unsure of the effectiveness of my argument.

"I'll give you my ruling after a brief recess," the judge said. He stood and left the courtroom.

Mr. Johnson, Mr. Maxwell, and I paced silently in the hallway for what seemed like an eternity. After only a few minutes, though, the bailiff ordered us back into the courtroom. The judge reentered and everyone stood.

"Please be seated."

My heart was pounding in my ears. I leaned toward Victoria's chair and touched it. She should have been there.

"I believe that Law 1105_ILCS_12.9 must be modified," the judge said. I held my breath. "Christ Hospital has demonstrated that it believes abortion is murder. They've done this using science, and not religion, as the prosecution claims. No law should force the hospital to practice something it considers contrary to the ethics of its doctors."

Mr. Johnson turned toward me, eyes full. He squeezed my arm.

"That said," the judge continued, "abortion remains legal in this state, and is granted, by both federal and state governments, as a basic right for women. Therefore, I will require Christ Hospital to provide patients with the addresses of other hospitals, should such patients desire to exercise this right. With this, I am dismissing the case against Christ Hospital."

I should've been happy, but something still felt wrong. I wasn't satisfied with the judge's ruling. Abortion on demand was still legal. But I realized that nobody would be happy with a decision made in a courtroom. What was needed was a greater moral consensus on the issue. That consensus wouldn't come by legal action, but by educating the public, by choosing the right candidates for office, and by voting. Finally, I resolved to be happy that Christ Hospital wasn't forced to murder innocent children.

When we stood, Mr. Johnson hugged me.

"Excellent job, Randy," he said.

"Thank you, Mr. Johnson. I didn't do much—it was all you and Mr. Maxwell."

"No, Randy. You did a marvelous job," Mr. Maxwell said, shaking my hand firmly.

Doctors from Christ Hospital came over to us and shook our hands. Mr. Johnson was undoubtedly delighted, but there was still a sadness about him. I, too, felt this sorrow. Victoria was not there to celebrate the victory with us. When the courtroom had settled down and people began to leave, Mr. Johnson placed his hands on Victoria's chair and backed it away from our table.

"May I ask you a favor, Mr. Johnson?" I asked.

"What is it, Randy?"

"Will you allow me to push Victoria's chair?"

Mr. Johnson was hesitant. "You know what? Why don't we push it together?"

I grabbed one handle and we pushed the chair to the van. As in her dream, neither of us would let go of the chair. In the parking lot, Mr. Johnson asked me to come back to the office with him. I agreed, climbing into the van and taking my usual spot next to Victoria's chair.

"Randy, when does school start?" Mr. Maxwell asked.

"In two weeks."

"And you have one week left of this internship?"

"Yes."

"About that," Mr. Johnson broke in, "I was thinking that you should take the next week off. Consider it a paid vacation."

"But, Mr. Johnson—" I objected.

"No buts. You deserve it, Randy. And besides, I'm not going to put you on a new case just for one week. I'm taking next week off too," he added.

I thanked Mr. Johnson and went to gather my things from the office. I saw a box covered with gift paper sitting on my desk. I opened it. It was a Bible. *Who would give me a Bible?* I wondered as I opened the cover. Inside, a note was scribbled in nearly illegible handwriting. *Dear Randy, Please accept this gift from me. I hope you will read it.–Victoria.* It was dated the same day she died. I ran to Mr. Johnson's office.

"Mr. Johnson, Mr. Johnson!" I shouted.

"Yes, Randy?" He looked up at me from his desk.

"Have you seen this?" I pointed to the Bible. "When did she give it to me?"

"Randy, take a seat. There's something I need to tell you."

I did as he asked.

"Victoria was not kidnapped. She left on her own. She asked a person in the cafeteria to take her to a nearby bookstore. She wanted to buy you a Bible. The person, however, lost control of her wheelchair, and that's when the accident happened."

I sat there quietly, trying to comprehend what Mr. Johnson had said. I felt hot tears fill my eyes.

"I didn't want to tell you about it because I didn't want you to feel bad. Randy, I'm sorry." Mr. Johnson reached across his desk and grasped my forearm, squeezing it.

"It was my fault," I said, not wanting to believe the truth.

"Oh no, no. That's why I didn't want to tell you. She asked me to buy you a Bible, and I didn't do it. So, technically, it was my fault," said Mr. Johnson as he wiped his eyes. "Listen, it's not anyone's fault. She had to walk to heaven."

We both smiled.

"Randy, will you promise me . . ."

"I will read it. I will—I promised her at her grave that I would." I didn't know if I would ever believe in God, but I did know that, for Victoria's sake, I would look for him, and if he was there, I might find him. If not, I would put him to rest forever.

"Randy, I wasn't asking you to promise me to read the Bible. I can't make you promise me to do such a thing—that's completely a personal decision," Mr. Johnson said. "But, thank you for sharing that with me. You don't know how happy it makes me. I'm sure that's how Victoria wanted it to be."

I nodded my head.

"Randy, I want you to promise me you'll do one more thing."

"What's that, Mr. Johnson?"

"Will you promise to send me your résumé when you graduate—before you send it to anyone else?"

"I promise."

"I'm holding you to that." We stood, and Mr. Johnson hugged me.

"Randy," Mr. Johnson called as I was leaving, "one last thing."

"Yes?"

"Great job. Mission accomplished."

I smiled.

"Mission accomplished," I repeated.

Chapter 33
Welcome to Gentle Care Center

"Get up. You're late for work," Erick pushed me from bed. "I need a ride."

I got up reluctantly, still very tired. I couldn't believe Erick was waking me up like that.

"Are you out of your mind?" I asked. "First of all, this is the first time I've had a good night's sleep in a long time—no dreams or nightmares. Second of all, I'm done at the firm for the summer. And third, you know very well I'm no longer giving you rides to the abortion clinic. As a matter of fact, when I graduate and get my law license, I plan to prosecute you for murder." I lay back down and closed my eyes.

"There'll be no need," Erick replied. "I'm resigning."

I sat up. "What?"

"Yeah, I'm sick of being an abortionist," he explained.

I was shocked.

"Stop starring at me and give me a ride. I'm late."

We drove to the clinic through the usual scenery. Outside were the same protestors, all offering the same arguments on their signs. Winning the case hadn't made a difference to this crowd.

We went into the waiting room, where Erick left me to go talk with his supervisor. I looked around at all the young women and became despondent. I felt like I was back at the Human Farm and Body Parts Factory.

I sat next to a girl who looked to be in her early teens. I decided to start a conversation with her.

"How old is your baby?" I asked.

"I don't want to hear anything about that 'baby' stuff," she replied.

"I had a dream last night about your child," I remarked.

"Yeah, right!"

"Believe me. Do you mind if I share the dream with you?"

She didn't respond, but she seemed interested, so I told her the story of the RMs. At the end of the story, her eyes filled with tears.

"I don't know what to do with it," she said.

And it struck me: It wasn't enough to preach against abortion. I needed to find a way to help. With preaching came social responsibility. During the trial, we had talked about individual rights and the role of community. Yet, so many people—myself included, it seemed—were hesitant to actually help.

"I'll help you," I said.

"How?" she asked with a mixture of skepticism and hope.

"I'll take care of everything," I replied.

"How?"

"Trust me."

I held her hands and hugged her. Erick came by and interrupted.

"Hello," he said curiously.

"Oh, by the way, my name is Randy, and this is my friend Erick," I told the girl.

"Hi. I'm Jessica."

"Didn't we meet a Jessica the first time you were here with me?" Erick asked me.

"We did, but this Jessica is coming with us," I explained.

I held Jessica's hand as we walked to the car. Erick followed a few steps behind. As we walked, I saw the protestor who had looked so familiar to me.

"That man looks like someone I know, but I still haven't figured out who he is," I told Jessica.

"That's easy," she said. "He looks like your friend Erick."

For the first time, I could see the resemblance. It was uncanny.

"Erick, come here," I shouted as he caught up with us. "Get Jessica to the car, will you? I'll be there in a minute. Here's the key."

As Erick and Jessica started off, I approached the man.

"Hello, sir. May I talk to you?"

"What do you want?" he snapped.

"I see you here every day, and I always wonder whether what you're doing is worth all the time and effort."

He stared at me for a moment, then said, "When I was a teenager, I asked my girlfriend to abort our son. I don't know what happened to him."

"You don't?"

"No, but what happened has greatly affected me, emotionally."

"It did? But you're a man . . ."

"That's a lie, my son. It's a lie."

"What's a lie?"

"That abortion affects only women. It's a lie."

"Was your girlfriend named Juan Mary Frankston?" I asked.

The man opened his mouth in surprise.

"If your child was not aborted, would he have been born in April of 1981, in Ohio?"

"I guess," he replied. "How did you know all that?"

"I just guessed." I left the man with his mouth hanging open.

"Wait up. Hey!" The man followed me.

I thought he really was Erick's father, but I decided to pursue that later. I promised him I would come and see him another day. For the first time, I saw a smile creep across the man's face.

I returned to the car and looked at Erick. I couldn't believe the resemblance. Abortion had almost prevented my best friend from being born.

***

"Welcome to Gentle Care Center," said a very beautiful short, blonde-haired woman. "My name is Lisa. I will be your tour guide today."

"Thank you."

"Before we tour the place, I'd like you to sit in our café and have a chat. Is that OK?"

"Sure," Erick replied. He seemed just as curious about the place as I was.

The café was relatively small but cozy. Each table had a vase of flowers on it.

"Here are some biscuits and juice."

I took a piece of biscuit and ate one. It wasn't bad. I grabbed another one, then a third. I noticed that Erick and Jessica were staring at me.

"I didn't have breakfast today," I explained. I decided to stop eating.

"Well, let's start with why you're here," Lisa said.

I looked at Jessica and she seemed uncomfortable.

"Our friend Jessica is pregnant," I told her.

"How old are you, Jessica?" Lisa asked.

"I'm thirteen." Jessica's face turned red.

"How old is your baby?"

"I don't know. Maybe two months."

"Do your parents know about this?"

"Oh, no."

"Jessica, since you're a minor, we have to tell your parents."

"No." Jessica stood up in protest. "I don't want to go through this anymore."

"Jessica, please sit down," Lisa said calmly. "Let's talk."

I held Jessica's hand and assured her it would be OK. She slowly sank back into her chair.

"Jessica, do you want to abort your baby?" Lisa asked.

"No, I don't want to kill it." Jessica started crying. "But I don't want to keep it either. I don't want anyone to know about it. I don't know what to do."

"Jessica, you're in a dilemma because you're not in an ideal situation to start with. You cannot undo your pregnancy. The baby is there, and it's real."

Jessica nodded her head.

"Your only options are to either kill the child or carry it to term."

"I don't want to be a mother," Jessica sobbed.

"You don't have to be a mother," Lisa said.

"I don't?"

"No, and that's where we can help."

"You can help?"

"We help by placing your baby with a caring, adoptive family."

Jessica didn't respond for a while.

"I wish my mother had put me in an adoptive family," Erick said. We all turned our heads toward him. "Well, I'm the child of a single woman. I never saw my dad. I always felt my mom didn't want me. It hurt."

Jessica was listening attentively.

"I wished my mother had put me up for adoption," he said. "At least I would've been wanted by a family."

I was moved by Erick's openness.

"What if they treat my baby badly? I mean, who would want my baby when even his mommy doesn't?" Jessica said.

"I understand your struggles and questions," Lisa said. "But families that want to adopt want to do so because they long to have a child. They're sometimes the best parents, because they actively search out a new member of their family. Many of them wait years to adopt and spend thousands of dollars in the process.

"I have four children - two adopted," she continued, "and I can tell you, from experience, that I love them all the same. The adopted ones are as much a part of me and my life as the biological ones.

"Because you don't want your baby, you feel that no one else does. But there are a lot of loving families out there just waiting to give your baby a home. They're better equipped than you to provide for your child. Trust me, your baby is a wanted baby."

Jessica didn't respond. We were all silent.

"But I want someone just like you to adopt my baby," Jessica said, finally breaking the silence.

"Jessica, you can help us choose the family for your baby," Lisa said, smiling. Jessica beamed, but her smile quickly disappeared.

"But, I don't want my parents and my friends to know about it."

"What's the worst thing that could happen if your parents knew?" Lisa asked.

"They'd kill me."

"Kill you?"

"Well, OK. But they might kick me out of the house, or be mean to me."

"OK, that's the worst case scenario. If that happened, we could offer you a room in our special dorms. We'll give you a tour of those dorms in a few minutes," she added. "Now, what's the best case scenario?"

Jessica didn't respond.

"Isn't it that your parents would be supportive? Wouldn't you like that?"

Jessica nodded.

"So, what do you have to lose? As a matter of fact, you might lose more if you don't tell your parents than if you do. Besides, Jessica, they're your parents—they have a right to know."

"I think it's better if we tour the place first and talk about this later," I suggested.

We left the café. To the left was a corridor with several doors. Lisa opened one door to a small reception room.

"This is our clinic. We have several gynecologists who come here a few hours every day. They work in other hospitals, but they give us several hours of their time."

A woman with a white robe came into the reception room.

"This is Dr. Emanuel from Christ Hospital," Lisa said.

"Christ Hospital?" I said.

"Yes," Dr. Emanuel answered, approaching us.

"Randy just helped defend you at trial," Erick said.

"Randy Livingston?" Dr. Emanuel and Lisa said at the same time.

"How do you know my name?"

"Everyone in the hospital is talking about you," Dr. Emanuel said.

"The whole trial's been in the *Chicago Tribune*," Lisa said.

"What?!"

"Your closing statement was reprinted verbatim," Lisa said. "Don't you read the *Trib*?"

"He's a *Sun Times* person," Erick joked. "Actually, he lives in a world of dreams, and he knows nothing about the outside world." I gave Erick a dirty look, but I was still shocked that my name had been in the newspaper.

"I'm so pleased to meet you, Randy," Dr. Emanuel said. "And, you are?" She asked, looking at Erick.

"Erick Frankston." Erick extended his hand to Dr. Emanuel.

"Erick used to work in Sam—" Erick hit me—"Sam's Club," I said.

"I need to pay for medical school somehow," said Erick, shrugging and smiling sheepishly.

"You're in medical school?"

"Yes. I have one year of specialization left."

"What are you going to specialize in?"

"Gynecology," Erick answered quickly, his eyes flashing in my direction. I decided to keep my mouth shut.

"I'm looking for people to help out here. Would you be interested?"

"Here?"

"Yes."

"I'd have to tour the place first." Everyone laughed. With that, we continued our tour with Lisa. Lisa and Jessica walked together and Erick and I followed.

"So, now you want to be a gynecologist?"

"I don't know."

"Why didn't you want them to know you worked in Sampson's Family Center?"

"And embarrass myself?"

"So being an abortionist is now embarrassing?" I asked.

"No."

"But, you're ashamed to tell people—"

"Shut up."

"I think you should be a pediatrician," I said, changing the subject.

"Why?"

"Kids bring the good out in you. You're always nice to kids, like Jessica, and mean to your buddies."

"No," Erick said, grinning. "I'm always kind to young girls and ladies."

"Oh yeah, that's right, like the one from Quality Tissue, Inc."

"Well, I broke up with her in a very kind way."

We both laughed.

"This is the exercise room," Lisa said. We entered the room, where about a dozen pregnant women were sitting on the floor doing exercises. Some of the young women had their parents with them.

"Judy, over there, is with an adoptive mother," Lisa said to Jessica as we continued walking. "In the other section of the clinic, we have a counseling center. That's where we'll meet your parents when they come.

"This section is for tutoring," she explained as we entered another large room. "We try to help our young mothers with their schoolwork so they don't fall behind during their pregnancy. As a matter of fact," Lisa added proudly, "many of the young ladies started doing better in school after coming here."

We left the building from a back door and entered a courtyard. The yard had a swimming pool in the center and a small park on the left. To the right, there was a child's playground.

"You have kids here?" I asked.

"Yes, some of our mothers want to keep their babies but have limited resources, so we let them stay with us for some time until they can get on their feet. We offer child care to any woman using our services.

"Over there is the resident building," said Lisa, pointing to a newly constructed building across the grass. We went over to it and entered through a sliding glass door. The first floor consisted of several sitting rooms, as well as a library, kitchen, dining area, and exercise room. We took an elevator to the next floor to tour the bedrooms.

"This bedroom is for an adult woman," Lisa told us. "Each room comes with a mini-kitchen and a seating area." The room looked like a hotel suite.

We left it and went into another room where there was more than one bed. "For younger girls, we put them to sleep together for company," Lisa said. "We have different sleeping arrangements to accommodate everyone's needs."

"Who pays for all of this?"

"It's mainly paid for by donations from members of the pro-life movement. Most of our workers are volunteers. In addition, we teach our resident girls responsibilities. They help in cleaning their rooms and in cooking. They have chores to do each day, just like they would at home."

We met a few young girls and adoptive families on the tour, and, by the end, Jessica seemed happy.

"About my parents," she said when we arrived back at the café.

"Yes, we can ask them to come today, and if things work

out, you'll go back with them. If not, you'll stay here. But, Jessica, your parents should know, and know very soon."

"What if her parents want her to have an abortion?" Erick asked.

"We've had quite a few parents who wanted their daughters to have abortions. But, the majority, I would say, respect their daughter's wishes after we've sat down and discussed everything."

"Jessica, why don't you come with me so we can get your information and call your parents?"

Jessica left with Lisa, and I went outside to the courtyard. It looked so peaceful, so sheltered from the outside world. It looked like a loving community.

"Randy, I want to go and talk to Dr. Emanuel about volunteering here," Erick called to me. "I'll be back."

"I'm sure your dad will be pleased," I whispered.

***

"Randy," Erick said.

"That was quick—"

"I haven't seen her yet. I just came to give you this." Erick handed me a copy of that day's *Chicago Tribune*.

"Page twelve!" he shouted as he went into the building.

I opened the paper to page twelve, and, there in the middle, was a picture of Mr. Johnson and me pushing Victoria's empty chair out of the courtroom. As Dr. Emanuel had said, the whole closing speech was printed. I looked at the picture of Mr. Johnson. *Poor man, he never forgave himself for thinking of aborting Victoria.* He paid a high price for not accepting forgiveness. I closed my eyes, my heart aching because I'd lost Victoria. I opened my eyes and looked at the picture again. It was just like her dream—Mr. Johnson and I holding onto her chair. *She must be walking by now,* I thought, and the ache subsided a little.

"Randy!" Erick called out to me. He was walking toward me with a very happy-looking Jessica.

"Do you want to go out for lunch to celebrate Jessica's new baby, your victory at the court, and my new job here?"

"I'd love to."

***

Notes

General Note: Quotation marks for exact quotations or slightly edited quotations from other sources were omitted when used in dialogue. This was done to make it easier for the reader to follow the text. A reference number was put as close to the quotation as possible.

---

[1] John C. Wilke, MD and Barbara H. Wilke, *Why can't we love them both* (Cincinnati: Hayes Publishing Company, Inc., 1997).

[2] Ibid.

[3] Ibid.

[4] Ibid.

[5] Ibid.

[6] Ibid.

[7] Ibid.

[8] Ibid.

[9] Sidney Callahan,"Abortion and the Sexual Agenda: A Case for Prolife Feminism" in *Abortion*, ed. Lloyd Steffen (The Pilgrim Press, 1996), 342.

[10] Ibid.

[11] Lloyd Steffen, "Just Cause for Abortion" in *Abortion*, ed. Lloyd Steffen (The Pilgrim Press, 1996), 396.

[12] "Catholics for a Free Choice" in *Abortion*, ed. Lloyd Steffen (The Pilgrim Press, 1996), 120.

[13] John C. Willke, MD and Barbara H. Willke, *Why can't we love them both* (Cincinnati: Hayes Publishing Company, Inc., 1997).

[14] Sidney Callahan,"Abortion and the Sexual Agenda: A Case for Prolife Feminism" in *Abortion*, ed. Lloyd Steffen (The Pilgrim Press, 1996), 345.

[15] Marjorie Reiley Maguire, "Personhood, Covenant, and Abortion" in *Abortion*, ed. Lloyd Steffen (The Pilgrim Press, 1996), 263.

[16] Sidney Callahan,"Abortion and the Sexual Agenda: A Case for Prolife Feminism" in *Abortion*, ed. Lloyd Steffen (The Pilgrim Press, 1996), 343.

[17] Lisa Sowle Cahill, "Abortion, Autonomy, and Community" in *Abortion*, ed. Lloyd Steffen (The Pilgrim Press, 1996), 363.

[18] Mary C. Segers,"Political Discourse and Public Policy on Funding Abortion: An Analysis" in *Abortion*, ed. Lloyd Steffen (The Pilgrim Press, 1996), 422.

[19] Beverly Wildung Harrison with Shirley Cloyes, "Theology and Morality of Procreative Choice" in *Abortion*, ed. Lloyd Steffen (The Pilgrim Press, 1996), 336.

[20] "Feminists for Life of America: Official Statement" in *Abortion*, ed. Lloyd Steffen (The Pilgrim Press, 1996), 354-355.

[21] Sidney Callahan,"Abortion and the Sexual Agenda: A Case for Prolife Feminism" in *Abortion*, ed. Lloyd Steffen (The Pilgrim Press, 1996), 349.

[22] Ibid.

[23] "Feminists for Life of America: Official Statement" in *Abortion*, ed. Lloyd Steffen (The Pilgrim Press, 1996), 354.

[24] John C. Willke, MD and Barbara H. Willke, *Why can't we love them both* (Cincinnati: Hayes Publishing Company, Inc., 1997).

[25] Ibid.

[26] Ibid.

[27] Ibid.

[28] Ibid

[29] Ibid.

[30] Sidney Callahan,"Abortion and the Sexual Agenda: A Case for Prolife Feminism" in *Abortion*, ed. Lloyd Steffen (The Pilgrim Press, 1996), 352.

[31] Ibid., 353.

[32] David C. Reardon, "The Abortion Experience for Victims of Rape and Incest."

[33] Francis J. Beckwith, "Is abortion justifiable in cases of rape or incest?" (www.christiananswers.net/q-sum/q-life005.html)

[34] David C. Reardon, "Rape, Incest and Abortion: Searching Beyond the Myths" (1994, Elliot Institute).

[35] Frederica Matthewes-Green, "Rape and Incest are Tragic, But Abortion Doesn't Heal the Pain" (www.physiciansforlife.org/content/view/238/)

[36] "Post Traumatic Stress Disorder in Rape Survivors" (http://survive.org.uk/PTSD.html#symptoms)

[37] John Walker, "Abortion in the Case of Pregnancy Due to Rape" (Libertarians for Life, 1998).

[38] John C. Willke, MD and Barbara H. Willke, *Why can't we love them both* (Cincinnati: Hayes Publishing Company, Inc., 1997), chapter 24

[39] Charles Hartshorne, "Concerning Abortion: An Attempt at a Rational View" in *Abortion*, ed. Lloyd Steffen (The Pilgrim Press, 1996), 56.

[40] Ibid., 58.

[41] Richard A. McCormick, S.J., "Rules for Abortion Debate" in *Abortion*, ed. Lloyd Steffen (The Pilgrim Press, 1996), 40.

[42] Sidney Callahan,"Abortion and the Sexual Agenda: A Case for Prolife Feminism" in *Abortion*, ed. Lloyd Steffen (The Pilgrim Press, 1996), 346.

[43] Ibid.

[44] Lisa Sowle Cahill, "Abortion, Autonomy, and Community" in Abortion, ed. Lloyd Steffen (The Pilgrim Press, 1996), 361

[45] Ibid., 366.

[46] Ibid., 363.

[47] Ibid., 363 - 367.

[48] Stanley Hauerwas, "Abortion: Why the Arguments Fail" in Abortion, ed. Lloyd Steffen (The Pilgrim Press, 1996), 301.

[49] Ibid., 300 - 302.

[50] Lisa Sowle Cahill, "Abortion, Autonomy, and Community" in Abortion, ed. Lloyd Steffen (The Pilgrim Press, 1996), 369.

[51] Sidney Callahan,"Abortion and the Sexual Agenda: A Case for Prolife Feminism" in *Abortion*, ed. Lloyd Steffen (The Pilgrim Press, 1996), 344.

[52] Peter S. Wenz, "The Law and Fetal Personhood: Religious and Secular Determinations" in Abortion, ed. Lloyd Steffen (The Pilgrim Press, 1996), 401.

[53] Ibid.

[54] Ibid.

[55] Ibid.

[56] Charles Hartshorne, "Concerning Abortion: An Attempt at a Rational View" in Abortion, ed. Lloyd Steffen (The Pilgrim Press, 1996), 58.

[57] Ibid., 61.

[58] Peter S. Wenz, "The Law and Fetal Personhood: Religious and Secular Determinations" in Abortion, ed. Lloyd Steffen (The Pilgrim Press, 1996), 403.

[59] Charles Hartshorne, "Concerning Abortion: An Attempt at a Rational View" in Abortion, ed. Lloyd Steffen (The Pilgrim Press, 1996), 58.

[60] Sidney Callahan,"Abortion and the Sexual Agenda: A Case for Prolife Feminism" in *Abortion*, ed. Lloyd Steffen (The Pilgrim Press, 1996), 345.

[61] James B. Nelson, "Protestant Attitudes toward Abortion" in *Abortion*, ed. Lloyd Steffen (The Pilgrim Press, 1996), 142.

[62] Charles E. Curran, "Abortion: Its Moral Aspects" in *Abortion*, ed. Lloyd Steffen (The Pilgrim Press, 1996), 252.

[63] Charles Hartshorne, "Concerning Abortion: An Attempt at a Rational View" in Abortion, ed. Lloyd Steffen (The Pilgrim Press, 1996), 59.

[64] Marjorie Reiley Maguire, "Personhood, Covenant, and Abortion" in Abortion, ed. Lloyd Steffen (The Pilgrim Press, 1996), 266.

[65] Charles Hartshorne, "Concerning Abortion: An Attempt at a Rational View" in Abortion, ed. Lloyd Steffen (The Pilgrim Press, 1996), 58.

[66] Peter S. Wenz, "The Law and Fetal Personhood: Religious and Secular Determinations" in Abortion, ed. Lloyd Steffen (The Pilgrim Press, 1996), 402.

[67] Ibid.

[68] James B. Nelson, "Protestant Attitudes toward Abortion" in *Abortion*, ed. Lloyd Steffen (The Pilgrim Press, 1996), 142 - 144.

[69] Marjorie Reiley Maguire, "Personhood, Covenant, and Abortion" in Abortion, ed. Lloyd Steffen (The Pilgrim Press, 1996), 267.

[70] Peter S. Wenz, "The Law and Fetal Personhood: Religious and Secular Determinations" in Abortion, ed. Lloyd Steffen (The Pilgrim Press, 1996), 409.

[71] Charles E. Curran, "Abortion: Its Moral Aspects" in *Abortion*, ed. Lloyd Steffen (The Pilgrim Press, 1996), 252.

[72] Sidney Callahan,"Abortion and the Sexual Agenda: A Case for Prolife Feminism" in *Abortion*, ed. Lloyd Steffen (The Pilgrim Press, 1996), 344.

[73] Ibid., 347.

[74] Charles E. Curran, "Abortion: Its Moral Aspects" in *Abortion*, ed. Lloyd Steffen (The Pilgrim Press, 1996), 256.

[75] Peter S. Wenz, "The Law and Fetal Personhood: Religious and Secular Determinations" in Abortion, ed. Lloyd Steffen (The Pilgrim Press, 1996), 410.

[76] "Abortion: Medical Facts" on the webpage of National Right to Life organization.

[77] National Right to Life, "Abortion: Medical Facts" (www.nrlc.org/abortion).

[78] Ibid.
[79] Ibid.
[80] Ibid.
[81] Ibid.
[82] Ibid.
[83] Ibid.
[84] Ibid.
[85] Ibid.
[86] Ibid.
[87] Ibid.
[88] Ibid.
[89] Ibid.
[90] Ibid.
[91] Ibid.
[92] Ibid.
[93] Paul B. Fowler, *Abortion Toward an Evangelical Consensus, (a critical concern book)* (Oregon: Multnomah Press, 1987).
[94] Ibid.
[95] National Right to Life, "Abortion: Medical Facts" (www.nrlc.org/abortion).
[96] Ibid.
[97] Ibid.
[98] Ibid
[99] Ibid
[100] Ibid
[101] Ibid
[102] Ibid
[103] Ibid
[104] Ibid
[105] Ibid
[106] Gametogenesis (http://cats.med.uvm.edu/cats_teachingmod/embryology/1_3/week_1/gameto.html)
[107] Dianne N. Irving, "When Do Human Beings Begin? 'Scientific' Myths and Scientific Facts" (International Journal of Sociology and Social Policy 1999).
[108] Gametogenesis (http://cats.med.uvm.edu/cats_teachingmod/embryology/1_3/week_1/gameto.html)

[109] Dianne N. Irving, "When Do Human Beings Begin? 'Scientific' Myths and Scientific Facts" (International Journal of Sociology and Social Policy 1999).

[110] B.A. Robinson, "Stages Of Development, From Ovum And Sperm To A Newborn Baby" (Ontario Consultants on Religious Tolerance, 2000).

[111] Gametogenesis (http://cats.med.uvm.edu/cats_teachingmod/embryology/1_3/week_1/gameto.html)

[112] B.A. Robinson, "Stages Of Development, From Ovum And Sperm To A Newborn Baby" (Ontario Consultants on Religious Tolerance, 2000).

[113] B.A. Robinson, "ABORTION: FACTS AND OPINIONS" (Ontario Consultants on Religious Tolerance, 2001).

[114] B.A. Robinson, "Stages Of Development, From Ovum And Sperm To A Newborn Baby" (Ontario Consultants on Religious Tolerance, 2000).

[115] Ibid.

[116] Ibid.

[117] Ibid.

[118] Ibid.

[119] Ibid.

[120] Ibid.

[121] Ibid.

[122] John C. Willke, MD and Barbara H. Willke, *Why can't we love them both* (Cincinnati: Hayes Publishing Company, Inc., 1997).

[123] Ibid.

[124] Ibid.